The Legend of Hornigold's Treasure

C. JOSEPH ELDER

ALLEN B. GRAVES

DEDICATIONS

C. Joseph Elder

To my daughters, Kaitie and Jacy, for your love and for being true EcoExplorers, to my mother Mary Ann Elder for always believing in me and for supporting my efforts and to my lovely wife Alison, for always being there and sharing the everyday adventures with me. Love you bunches!

Allen B. Graves

To my parents, Ilar and Carter Graves, thank you for being wise and supporting.

CONTENTS

CONTENTS (CONTINUED)

ACKNOWLEDGMENTS

Editors:

Alison Elder for her ongoing editing of the novel throughout its creation.

Dr. Jean Haskell retired as director and professor from the Center for Appalachian Studies and Services at East Tennessee State University. She is co-editor of the award-winning Encyclopedia of Appalachia, as well as several other books and publications on regional development in Appalachia. As the Whisman Appalachian Scholar for the Appalachian Regional Commission in Washington, D.C., she has most recently researched and written about local food system development in the region, leading to her latest book project, Elegant Sufficiency: Stories of Food in Appalachia. She works as a writer, editor, oral historian, folklorist, and speaker (and runs a really cool movie theatre/restaurant, the Commodore Theatre, in Portsmouth, Virginia).

Cid Scallet for his final copy-edit of the novel to make sure that it is grammatically correct and consistent in language and tone. Cid is a freelance writer and editor who has spent the past thirty years working on projects ranging from long-form fiction to software manuals. He has written a novel of his own but specializes in helping other word-smiths make their writing as appealing as possible to their chosen audience.

Readers:

Kaitlin and Jessica Elder for their input from a young reader's perspective. Kathy Rabe, Steve Hutchinson, Alex Hausrath, Betsy Cartier, Ilar Graves and Jackie Shanck for input, ideas and suggestions.

Guidance and Support:

Dr. Ben Bohl, Executive Director of International Field Studies, and the exceptional Forfar Field Station staff whose interest, hospitality, facilitation and encouragement allowed us to live the story by exploring the various dive sites described throughout Hornigold.

We also wish to thank the teachers, parents and students whom we had the pleasure of sharing experiences with during our research trip to the island of Andros.

Gary Eisenhuth- A high school and college educator for over 30 years. Gary currently teaches chemistry at Western Albemarle High School and marine biology courses at Piedmont Virginia Community College. He has directed backpacking / ecology courses for high school students for 10 years before an overwhelming interest in marine biology caused him to change his emphasis to marine ecosystems.

Alex Hausrath who explored and dived with us on the island of Andros.

Art:

David Dees for his exceptional work creating the front cover art.

PROLOGUE

December 12, 1717
NASSAU, NEW PROVIDENCE, BAHAMAS

A loud clanking sound made by the rapping of the old metal knocker upon the front door echoed through the dilapidated, two story wood framed house. A young boy, a servant to the tenant of the house, walked down the long central hallway to open it. Standing outside the doorway was a tall, weather-beaten, seafaring man. He removed his tattered straw hat, revealing a sunburned scalp with just a few patches of graying hair remaining on the back and sides. He was dirty, unshaven and wore soiled brown trousers with a simple leather jerkin and a strapped-on wooden peg leg below the knee on his right side. The boy stood quietly behind the half open door without saying a word and stared at the stranger.

"Is Captain Hornigold about?" asked the man.

"He's lying down and asked not to be disturbed," answered the young boy who turned his nose away from the foul smelling seaman, whose stench, mixed with the ocean breeze, wafted through the door opening.

"What be your name, lad?" he asked.

"Billy, sir," answered the boy. "Billy Simms."

The stranger pulled a folded paper out of the waist of his pants and handed it to the boy.

"Well, Billy Simms, can I trust you to give this letter to the Captain as soon as he be about? Don't fret about here boy. It be your hide if it's missed!"

The servant boy grabbed the paper from the seaman and held it in his hand. He noticed that it was neatly folded, unopened and sealed tight with a circle of red wax bearing an impressive family crest that gave the letter an air of great importance. He looked up wanting to ask the stranger his name, but the mysterious deliverer of the letter had already gone. The boy quickly shut the door and raced down the hallway and up the rickety wooden steps of the narrow stairwell. He turned the corner and ran to the door at the far end of the hallway. The boy took a deep breath, regained his composure and timidly knocked on the bedroom door.

"Captain Hornigold," the boy said in a low voice. He waited for a reply.

"Captain Hornigold" the boy repeated a little louder. A rustling was heard from the other side of the door—and then footsteps. The door swung open and the Captain grabbed the boy by the front of his shirt with one hand, plucking him straight up off the floor.

"Didn't I tell you not to disturb me," growled the giant of a man while shaking the boy back and forth.

The boy was stunned. In tears from fright, he raised the letter up to his face. The Captain grabbed it with his free hand.

"What's this," asked the Captain, still holding the boy by his shirt.

"A letter," the boy sobbed.

He dropped him to the floor and the boy fell to his knees. "Where did it come from?" demanded the

Captain, staring at the servant boy through cold, black eyes.

"A man j-just d-delivered it to the front door," said the frightened boy. "He said it was important."

Captain Hornigold stared at the letter, stepped back into his room and slammed the door behind him. Grabbing a knife from his desk, he sliced open the letter and began to read:

November 6, 1717
Benjamin Hornigold
I hope this letter reaches you in fair time. I'm writing to advise you of plans by King George to seize Nassau and the Bahamas by appointing Mr. Woodes Rogers as the Royal Governor of the Bahamas. Rogers will arrive sometime during the summer months commanding two of his majesty's ships, the 350-ton "Duke" (36 guns), and the 260-ton "Duchess" (36 guns), with 333 men. He will convene with his majesty's man of war, the "Rose," to end all pirating and restore commerce. I hear rumors of a proclamation offering clemency will be granted to all those willing to swear an oath against future pirating offences. Be advised and take suitable measures to protect what you value the most.
Your friend,
Henry Moore

Hornigold sat down at his desk and read the letter for a second time. The letter verified what he already knew of King George's plans to seize New Providence Island after he discovered a document on a recently captured ship that stated the British government's plan to eradicate piracy in the Bahamas. He pondered for a moment about his options, knowing that the time would come when his days of piracy would end.

A gathering of the pirate society in the Bahamas had already been held and the pirates were divided, one wishing to swear against pirating and accept the conditions stated as part of a proposed amnesty described in the document, the other intending to continue pirating until the devil himself is paid. Hornigold, one of the most feared pirates of the day—a man who had led more than two hundred men on numerous captured ships--once again emerged as the leader of the camp planning to seek pardon. He and his closest followers (with the exception of his two most revered colleagues, Mr. James Bellamy and Mr. Edward Teach, who could not be persuaded to give up their occupation as pirates), had already planned to sail to Jamaica in January to take the pardon. But prior to Woodes Rodgers arrival, steps would need to be taken to put his personal affairs in order and protect his treasure.

Hornigold yelled out for the servant boy from his room. "Billy, where are you, boy!"

The boy quickly scurried up the stairs but kept his distance from the captain.

"Go find Mr. Thomas Maynard aboard me ship Adventure. Tell him to prepare the ship and crew for a short voyage. We'll sail first thing in the morning. Hurry boy, we've got no time to lose!"

It was nearly sunrise. A warm sea breeze blew gently across the Nassau harbor, carrying blends of pungent smells from the anchored vessels that loomed like ghosts against a starless sky. Captain Benjamin Hornigold, elegantly dressed with a sword in scabbard at his side, walked briskly along the overgrown shore trail that headed away from the ramshackle of a town, remnants of a once vibrant growing seaport. Its decline was due in part at the hands of the Spanish when they leveled Charles Town in retaliation for their pirating of their ships. By 1700, the pirates dominated Nassau with, as the citizens stated, "lawless riot and drunken revelry," and chased off the remaining law-abiding citizenry to exile in Great Exuma. After years of neglect, Nassau lay in a state of ruin with the town filled with dilapidated structures and an island population consisting of approximately two hundred former pirates and several hundred fugitives who had escaped from nearby Spanish colonies.

Hornigold headed towards the far side of the harbor located next to a busy tavern near the edge of the ramshackle seaport. Despite the early morning hour, the tavern was still stirring with abundant activity. Barmaids were serving a roomful of drunken pirates with flagons full of bumboo. The sounds of song and laughter poured out of the busy tavern. The inharmonious singing from drunken pirates blended well with the stench of stale ale that spilled onto the wooden floor from pewter mugs swaying in agreement with the rhythm of the sailor's songs.

A horse-drawn wagon arrived at the designated meeting point as the sun began to break above the horizon. The two-wheeled wagon had hauled necessary food and supplies for the voyage, with wooden rope-strapped barrels filled with fresh water and rum. Stashed in the front of the wagon and slightly hidden was a heavy wooden sea chest.

Two long boats with crew were landing at the planned rendezvous as Hornigold arrived by foot. The 15-foot long wooden rowboats slid gracefully on to the sandy beach and listed over to one side as the crew of four climbed out and walked ashore. All of the crew were selected by Hornigold, were his most trusted members of the pirate's society and had served under Hornigold with years of loyal service. They quickly loaded the provisions from the wagon into one of the boats with the exception of the large wooden sea chest that was still to be unloaded.

Under the watchful eye of Captain Benjamin Hornigold, two crew members, each grabbing a rope handle on each end of the heavy chest, slid it out from the back of the wagon. The wooden chest was fastened together with forged iron strapping, wrapped in chains and latched with three pad locks. The two crewmen followed by Hornigold carried the heavy chest to the second long boat, lifted it up over the gunwale and placed it safely inside. The crew with Captain Benjamin Hornigold on board pushed off the beach back into the clear, warm Bahamian water and quietly oared the long boats out past the numerous anchored vessels, out past his flag ship, a Spanish sloop named Ranger, to his vessel in waiting, a Bermuda sloop called the *Adventure*.

The *Adventure*, a much smaller two-masted gaff-rigged sloop designed for speed, could easily be sailed close to the wind, making her a very maneuverable boat. Under full sail she carried a jib, staysail, gaff foresail, gaff mainsail, and, above that, a main gaff topsail. The hull of the vessel drafted less than eight feet of water, a perfect design for the shallow waters close to shore and the hidden reefs that surrounded the islands. The *Adventure* was fitted with twelve cannons, six on each side, and two swivel guns, fore and aft. It was a favored vessel by pirates for hunting down larger, heavier, and slower ships carrying cargo through the Florida straits. She could easily be sailed and handled with a crew of thirty.

The ship was loaded with the provisions and the chest was carefully hauled aboard. Without delay, the crew quickly pulled anchor and got underway, unnoticed by other ships as she sailed out of the harbor with the two long boats in tow. Hornigold charted the course on his map for the short voyage to his planned destination. They hoisted the gaff-rigged fore and main sails and put the *Adventure* on a heading due west of New Providence Island.

With a cool island breeze blowing off the stern and the warm heat of the rising sun at their backs, Hornigold sailed his ship towards an island discovered in the late 15th century by the first Spanish explorers—an island the Spanish named La Isla del Espiritu Santo, the Island of the Holy Spirit. And then to a place called Lucifer's Lair!

1

THE ARRIVAL

A twin-engine airplane lifted off from Fort Lauderdale, Florida, and climbed into an overcast sky. Heading to Andros Island in the Bahamas, the plane soon climbed through the thick cloud cover and emerged into a bright blue sunlit sky. The pilot set a south-easterly course and once cruising altitude had been reached he throttled the turbocharged engines back that droned in rhythmic unison.

Molly McNeil peered through the small plane window and scanned the tops of the thick, white cumulus clouds that blocked the view of the Atlantic Ocean below. With nothing interesting to see, Molly pulled out a folder from her carry-on bag and settled back into her seat for the hour long flight in the small airplane. Mike, her husband sitting directly across from her, twisted and squirmed in his seat, trying to find a comfortable position for his 6 foot 4 inch frame and size 14 shoes. Molly watched with great amusement while her husband finally unraveled himself out of his cramped place and stretched his long legs and big feet out into the narrow center aisle.

"You know, it seems to me that each year these seats

get smaller and smaller," Mike McNeil said to his wife.

"Maybe it's not the seats that are getting smaller," she replied with a grin.

Mike smirked at Molly and returned to his incessant fidgeting while she returned to her folder. This was their eighth summer of bringing teenage students to Andros for a one-week field school to study marine biology, reef ecology, snorkel and SCUBA dive. They were all members of a student organization called the EcoExplorers. Mike and Molly, both science teachers from Albemarle County, Virginia, founded and led the organization created to offer interested students an opportunity to expand their knowledge and skills in a field study program. On this trip, eight rising juniors and seniors from different central Virginia high schools were traveling with the McNeil's to their final destination, Rockwood Field Station, a privately run field station for students located at Bollard Creek on the east coast of the Island.

A crackling sound came from the small ceiling speakers followed by the voice of the pilot.

"Good morning and welcome to Island Charters!" the pilot announced. "You may feel a few bumps as we begin our descent through some turbulence. We should be landing at the San Andros Airport in approximately twenty minutes. The temperature on land is a balmy eighty-two degrees with overcast skies, but the weather forecast predicts clear skies by noon. We are currently flying above the Great Bahama Bank that stretches from the Florida Coast to the west end of Grand Bahama Island and the northern end of Andros. You will get a glimpse of the ocean and Andros in the distance when we descend through the clouds."

Soon the view from the plane was of a vast expanse of subtropical water surrounding the Bahamian island of Andros. Like a rainbow hugging the shore, the water was segregated into various hues of blue between the barrier reefs, inner sandbars, tidal flats and tidal pools. The dark blue of the deeper ocean turned into light tones of subtle blues as the Atlantic Ocean became shallower closer to the island. Bubbly waves crashed over coral reefs and white sandy beaches snaked around a crooked shoreline. Logging roads crisscrossed the island, creating large checkerboard patterns through the swampy creeks, marshes and pinelands. Pines, palms, and numerous other trees grew in thick tight patches around the marshes where snowy white egrets clustered in high treetops.

Soon the plane met the tarmac with a gentle thump and slowly taxied over to the north side of the small San Andros Airport terminal. The pilot opened the door in the fuselage, a mix of humid Bahamian air blended with the acrid aroma of aviation fuel and wafted into the plane when the passengers began to exit. A man appeared from the side of the terminal with a clipboard in hand and walked briskly to the new arrivals.

"Hello," he began with a friendly smile. "I'm Dr. Lounsbury, Director of Rockwood Field Station, welcome…welcome to Andros." He stood tall and sure under the blue Bahamian sky. Dressed in khaki shorts, he wore a white long-sleeved shirt with the Rockwood logo patch sewn on the front and tattered leather sandals on his feet. "Mike and Molly McNeil…it's so wonderful to see you again! I was so excited when I checked the roster this morning and saw the EcoExplorers on the list. Welcome back, or should I say welcome home?" He embraced Molly and shook Mike's hand.

"It does feel like home to us," Molly said.

"And it's never quite the same when you folks leave. Now then," Dr. Lounsbury continued, turning to address the eight members of the EcoExplorers, "it's customary at Rockwood for everyone to pitch in and help during their stay. That's one way we're able to keep your trip affordable. So, if everyone will lend a hand, we'll get our truck Big Blue loaded with supplies and be on our way. Please place your personal luggage over there, out of the way," he explained, pointing to a place on the tarmac where close-cropped vegetation grew from jagged cracks. "You'll need to carry your luggage with you through customs before departing the airport."

Big Blue, a large flatbed Ford truck with a deeply rumbling engine, backed toward the plane and squeaked to a halt. Three sides of the stake body were fitted with stout wooden benches fastened to the planked floor. Big Blue, the workhorse of the field station, carried everything from passengers to perishables. A slender man stepped down from the truck and approached the group.

"Ah, Newby, just in time," Dr. Lounsbury said.

"Hello, how ya'll doing," Newby Marshall said in a southern drawl and opened the back gate of the truck.

Newby directed them to form a line of people from plane to truck in bucket-brigade fashion. The numerous hands, including Dr. Lounsbury, soon had the truck piled high with various boxes of vegetables, fruits, canned goods, sacks of flour, and other sundry items that kept the field station running on the remote island. Newby then started the truck; it coughed to life and a few wisps of smoke billowed out of the rusted muffler. Then it crept off the tarmac and headed to the front of the terminal for clearance from Bahamian customs.

"Mike and Molly know the routine in the terminal. So please take your bags through that door," Dr. Lounsbury said. "I'll meet you in front of the terminal when you clear customs."

A low rock wall constructed of local limestone separated the tarmac from the white terminal and surrounding area. The sweeping canopy of a massive tree shaded a grassy courtyard. Cab drivers sat on small stools with checkerboards perched on top of rickety crate tables. They eyed the group, sizing up the arrivals for potential business. A few lazy dogs lay scattered under the tree like ripened fruit that had dropped to the ground. One got up, arched his back as he stretched, yawned with tongue lolling out, and then plopped back into a small scrape in the loamy soil. Bored, he propped his snout on his dusty front paw.

A gathering of people stood near the shade tree as a photographer directed the group photo shoot from behind a tripod-mounted camera. They were departing high school students leaving Rockwood and stood in stark contrast to the incoming members of the EcoExplorers. The girls wore local batik dresses and skirts made of cotton printed in bright blues, greens, and yellows with handmade jewelry of shells around their necks, wrists, and ankles. Their hair was fashioned in elaborate braids woven with colorful wooden beads. The guys wore various types of shorts and sandals; some had Rockwood T-shirts and others had floral printed island shirts. All stood with radiant smiles as the camera clicked, capturing the digital image. It was obvious, judging by the keyed up conversation, that the group was departing with memories of an incredible Androsian adventure.

"Check out the outfits those girls are wearing," Laura said, glancing at the departing group. "I wonder where they're from."

"Beats me," Beth said, shifting the strap of the heavy bag to her opposite shoulder. "Who knows, maybe you'll be dressed like that when you leave."

"I don't think so," Laura said, flipping her long blond hair out of her face and peering again at the departing students. "But I do plan to leave next week with a terrific tan."

Inside the dim open-air terminal, people were milling about checking tickets and preparing for departure. A bored female customs official sat behind a counter waving the next traveler past while an armed Bahamian military guard stood sentinel. Soon, with passports stamped, the McNeil's and their anxious students headed toward the entrance to look for Dr. Lounsbury. Outside, under the wide portico, the group stacked their luggage and waited for their transportation to the field station to arrive.

"Look, there's a gift shop," Beth said, pointing to the doorway of the small store recessed into the exterior wall of the terminal.

"Let's check it out. I want to get some post cards to send home," Laura said, heading for the door with Beth. She looked at her brother, Justin. "You coming?"

"Nah, I'm about to bust after that flight...I'm going to find the restroom." He re-entered the crowded terminal. Moments later, a speeding taxi turned into the entrance of the San Andros Airport and pulled up under the shaded portico in front of the departure doors. A man wearing a frantic look on his face jumped out of the back seat, crossed the sidewalk and entered the terminal. A few quick steps in, he collided with Justin. "Sorry," the stranger said, shoving his way through the growing crowds of incoming and departing passengers. His upper lip was carpeted with a black mustache that accentuated a small mouth and a long, slender nose. His wrinkled seersucker suit clung to his body, damp from the heat and humidity. He held a black leather briefcase against his chest and walked through the disorganized mob of people.

Justin spotted the sign for the restroom to his left and headed in its direction.

The black-mustached stranger worked his way in the opposite direction and made his way to the check-in counter. After a brief discussion with the busy airline check-in attendant, the man was informed that he had just missed his flight. He checked the flight departure screen for other available flights off the island, discovering the next flight out of Andros for the United

States was not for hours. He left the counter and dashed towards the doors leading to the tarmac but found them locked. Turning away, he revealed a face that was streaked with rivulets of sweat. The man headed towards the entryway, but as he grew closer, he noticed something outside that startled him and made him change direction. He scanned the small terminal for another exit, but realized that the remaining exits were either locked or guarded. Spotting the sign for the restrooms, he headed for the door.

Justin stood out of view inside an enclosed bathroom stall. He heard the door open and footsteps upon the tiled floor. Hidden from view was the man with the black mustache who inspected the interior for an alternate way out, but the bathroom was enclosed except for a pair of small windows, high off the ground and too small for escape. In desperation, he placed his briefcase on the narrow counter top, put his thumbs on either side of the locks, and flipped the two hasps up in unlocking unison. He pulled a legal-sized envelope out of the briefcase and closed the lid. Then, noticing someone's open backpack hanging from the edge of the partially closed stall door, he slipped the envelope inside.

Moments later, Justin opened the stall door and walked over to the sink. He washed his hands and glanced into the mirror, noticing the stranger that had bumped into him earlier.

Outside, a shiny black Jeep Cherokee pulled up under the portico. Three burly men exited the vehicle and one who was older appeared to be in charge. The men pushed through the double doors that led into the terminal. The leader wore a sport coat covering a dirty white polo shirt tucked carelessly into his khakis. A stout leather belt encircled his bulging belly like the equator on a globe. Sporting a weathered wide-brimmed felt hat with a brown felt band, he wore aviator glasses with dark green lenses, hiding constantly roving eyes. He scanned the interior of the terminal. Not finding his party, he dismissed the two men at his side and turned back towards the entryway. Suddenly the sign for the restrooms captured his attention. His hand signaled the others to stay and he headed towards the bathroom door.

The door flew open and the stout man entered. "Well well well, Dr. Stein, what an unexpected pleasure," the man said in a snide, mocking tone. "Did you miss your flight?"

"I'm catching the next one off the island," the man answered, mopping his sweat-beaded face with a paper towel.

"I don't think you're going anywhere except back to the boat with me," the man bellowed and then opened his sport coat to display a holstered pistol hanging below his left arm. "Now, I don't think you want to make any fuss, do you?"

Justin was still at the sink. He stared into the mirror, trying to mind his own business. But the room was too small and he could not help overhearing the conversation between the two men that was becoming more heated with each exchange. He dried his hands, walked over to the stall door, recovered his backpack and turned toward the exit. He didn't like the looks of either of the two men, especially the one with the pistol. All Justin wanted was to get out of there--now!

"Going somewhere?" the large man mocked. He put his arm up against the wall in front of Justin, blocking the exit.

"I was…was just leaving," Justin stammered. He noticed a hideous scar on the man's forearm, exposed by the hiked-up sleeve of his sport coat.

"Leave him alone, Winfrey! This is between you and me," Stein said.

"Shut up!" Winfrey barked as a wave of anger washed over his face, his brow knitted into a deep frown.

"Now," he said turning to Justin, lowering his voice, "this is a private matter and no concern of yours. Understand?"

"Yeah, I understand. Now would you please let me by? The rest of my group is waiting for me outside," Justin pleaded. For a moment that seemed an eternity, Justin looked into the man's eyes and felt only evil and darkness staring back at him.

"Leave!" Winfrey barked, with a wave of his hand, and moved his scarred arm for Justin to pass.

Justin ran from the bathroom while his thoughts beat louder than his adrenaline-charged heart. Outside the terminal a caravan had formed of a passenger van and two taxis with Big Blue in the rear. From one taxi, already loaded with luggage, Jeff was impatiently waving for Justin. Justin rushed over, climbed in through the rear taxi door, and sat next to Beth and his sister Laura. He plopped his backpack on the floor in front of him and closed the door. Looking back over his shoulder, he saw the two men from the bathroom leave the terminal with two other men and walk toward a black Jeep. Once the men were all inside, the Jeep pulled away from the curb and then stopped opposite Justin's taxi while a dog crossed the road, blocking the Jeep's progress. Justin peered at the Jeep, seeing his own reflection in the passenger window. Then, shifting his focus slightly, he noticed the shadowy shape of the man named Winfrey staring back at him from behind dark tinted glass; superimposed over his reflected image, the two images morphed into one. A horn blared, the dog quickened his pace and the Jeep sped away from the terminal.

"Justin, you okay?" Jeff asked. "You look pale!"

2

ROCKWOOD FIELD STATION

"See that black Jeep Cherokee?" Justin asked, pointing at the vehicle while it sped away.

"Yeah, so what?" asked Jeff, who was seated in the front of the taxi.

"The man in the back seat was taken out of the restroom at gunpoint!"

"What?" They all swiveled their heads toward the Jeep, then back to Justin.

"When I was in the bathroom, there was this man hanging around acting kind of weird. I was about to leave when the door flew open and this big guy barged in," Justin explained. "Well, the two men knew each other and in no time at all, the conversation got pretty loud. That's when the big guy opened his sport coat and showed his pistol!"

"No way... I bet that scared the piss out of you! Good thing you were already in the bathroom," Jeff said with a smirk.

"You're so funny Jeff," Justin countered. "That's when I decided to get out of there."

"I bet the one man was a criminal and the other with the pistol was a policeman," Laura suggested.

"No, I don't think so!" Justin continued. "The guy with the pistol told me when I was trying to get out that it was of no concern of mine and he was real serious about it. Does that sound like something a cop would say? Oh, yeah! I almost forgot," Justin said, pausing.

"Forgot what?"

"He had this gross looking scar on his arm!"

"Did you say the man had a scar on his arm?" the taxi driver asked while he started the vintage Cadillac's engine and pulled away from the curb. In front was the field station van with Mike, Molly and Dr. Lounsbury. Just behind was another taxi with more of the group, and further back Big Blue brought up the rear of the four-vehicle caravan.

"I overheard your story and I'm sure I've seen this man before," the old man said, in a strong and melodious Bahamian accent.

Justin leaned forward, closer to the driver.

"I was in White's Pub, a few weeks ago. My buddies and me, we were having a drink and playing dominoes when a man like the one you just mentioned came in. He sat at the bar with some other shady-lookin' folk, talking all loud, saying this and that. He was bragging 'bout how he got in a tangle with a shark and how that shark nearly bit his arm off. Sounded like a big ol' fish story to me. The more he drank the bigger it got!" The cabbie was grinning from ear to ear. "If I remember right, I believe the man's name was Brimley or somethin' like that."

"Winfrey! That was his name," Justin said. "He was called Winfrey and the other guy's name was Dr. Stein. Have you seen Winfrey around?" Justin asked.

"No sir! He and his buddies are not from round here, but I know they've been on the island for a while. One of the other taxi drivers told me he'd picked up these folks some weeks ago at Benny's Marina and that they had come in on some big yacht, but they're not fishermen. They've recently been seen driving all over this island in that black Jeep. Haven't got a clue what they're up to, but I got a feeling they're up to no good."

"Why do you think that?"

"Just a hunch. Usually if there's a problem here, it's from outsiders. Everybody knows every one's business here on this island. We have something called the coconut telegraph and it's how gossip moves from person-to-person faster than a dolphin can swim in the sea. Keeps folks honest! So problem is, since we don't know what they're up to, they're probably up to no good. I'll put a word out about him; the local folk will keep an eye out for you, not to worry, man!"

"Thanks," Justin said.

"I wouldn't go snooping around looking for him either. It's best to leave that man and his shady business alone," the taxi driver said.

"I'll agree with that," Laura suggested.

The aged driver reached into the left pocket of his light-blue shirt and then felt the front pockets of his trousers. Appearing confused, he rubbed a day's worth of gray whiskers that hugged his face like powdered sugar. He removed the fisherman's cap from his head and wiped the sweat off his brow with the back of his hand.

"There they be," the taxi driver said, replacing his worn cap, he reached to the sun-bleached and cracked dashboard. "Here's my card. Just give me a call if you need me while you're on the island. Day or night." He passed a card over his shoulder to Justin.

"Grover Baskerfield," Justin said, reading the card.

"That's me but my friends call me Basky. And students at Rockwood are friends of mine."

"Well it's nice to meet you, Basky," Beth said. She introduced herself and then proceeded to introduce Laura, Jeff and Justin. Beth explained that they were part of the EcoExplorers from Charlottesville, Virginia.

"Hey Basky, have you ever seen a Lusca Monster?" Jeff asked, dying to change the subject. He had read the island lore in a tourist pamphlet regarding Andros and the Bahamas and was curious about the legendary creature.

"Let me see, Lusca," Basky said, rubbing his forehead. "Well now. That's one of the great island tales. From what I'd been told, it's a sea monster, sort of a mix between a shark and an octopus. They live here in the sink holes or what the scientist folk call blue holes found all over this island. Never saw one myself, but a number of local folk swear by it! I knew a man once years ago that had his new fishing boat swallowed whole by the Lusca. Had the boat out in one of them sink holes letting the wooden boards swell so he could use it in the ocean. Said it somehow came untied and floated into the middle of the hole. And the next thing, there was a whirling pool of water and the boat was sucked down and never seen again. Now, you wouldn't catch ol' Basky in one of those holes. No sir! That Lusca might just have a taste for me." Basky cackled while slapping his thigh. "Although one bite and he'd probably spit me out, thinking I'm too gristly like a cheap ol' piece a' meat."

Leaving the airport behind the van, Basky pulled onto the left side of the two-lane Queen's Highway--paved sandy white with local limestone. Dense vegetation grew close and thick on both sides, and iguanas and geckos, startled by the passing vehicle, scurried for cover in the shady underbrush. Birds, numerous in bushes and overhead, flew in all directions under the partly cloudy Bahamian sky. With the windows down, fresh air blew freely through the car, blending scents of dried vegetation and salty sea air with the stale musty aroma of the aged car. Basky, wasting little time, drove fast and sure on the familiar Androsian road.

"Look out," Laura yelled, as a large truck carrying

freshly cut logs lumbered down the road on the adjacent side. Screaming, she ducked down and buried her face in her lap. The noisy eighteen-wheeler passed with a loud whoosh of wind, leaving the stench of diesel fuel in its wake.

"Chill out Laura!" Jeff said. "They drive on the left-hand side of the road down here."

"I forgot. I thought we were dead for sure—"

"How far to Rockwood Field Station?" Jeff asked, interrupting Laura.

"We'll be there in about twenty minutes, old Cadillac willing," Basky replied, patting the aged dashboard. "Is this your first trip to the Bahamas?"

"No," replied Beth, her brunette hair whipping in the breeze. "I visited New Providence Island with my parents for Christmas one year. We even watched the Junkanoo."

"Oh, yes indeed, the Junkanoo is a very festive time in the Bahamas. Sometimes the local folk go over and join in the parade at Nassau. We have a small Junkanoo here, but nothing like the one in Nassau."

"What's a Junkanoo?" Jeff inquired, pushing his bottle-thick glasses up his nose.

"Junkanoo is a Bahamian celebration held each year on Boxing Day and New Year's Day," Basky answered. "The parade starts about two in the morning with colorful floats made of crepe paper and cardboard in a rainbow of colors. Music from instruments carries all around the island, and if you get a clear night under the stars . . . you would think the Junkanoo is the center of the entire world. Quite a happening to behold!"

"Hey Basky, do you know anything about pirates or treasure on the island?" Jeff asked.

"Treasure? Hmmm now, that's one of my favorite subjects," Basky replied flashing a wide smile of pearly white teeth. "Andros is rich with tales of pirates and buried treasure. Pirates sailed through these islands all the time. Legend says they stashed chests full of treasure in caves at Morgan's Bluff. Ole Captain Morgan was a Bahamian privateer."

"What's a privateer?" Laura asked.

"Privateer or pirate, they're all the same; only difference was a pirate worked for himself and a privateer was hired by the King of England. Or, you might say one worked for the king and the other was leading a gang of swashbucklin' cutthroats."

"I read that Morgan's Bluff is the highest point on the island," stated Jeff. "That it was named after him because he used to hook a lantern to a goat's neck. The goat walked along the cliff's edge, luring passing ships onto the nearby reef. Morgan's men would raid the wreck. The book also said that Morgan hid treasure inside the caves below the cliffs."

"That's what they say," said Basky. "But as far as I know, Morgan's treasure has never been found. Maybe Morgan's bluff is…just that…a bluff! Andros is a big island with remote parts still unexplored. Many tourists have wasted their time and money treasure hunting here. The closest most folks get to finding treasure is a sand dollar on the beach," Basky joked.

"Yeah! You'll get rich finding a bunch of sand dollars," Laura jested.

"Not," said Jeff.

"Once, I found a gold coin in the shallow waters along the shore," Basky paused. "I made the grave mistake of showing and telling a friend about it and the next thing I know, half the island of people was there, hunting and digging in the sand. Good thing I told that snitch the wrong location. When it comes to gold you'll find out quickly who your friends be!"

"Any other treasure tales you know about?" Jeff asked.

Basky thought for a moment while rubbing his whiskers. "I heard that a pirate named Blackbeard hid a treasure here long ago at a place called Small Hope Bay. The story goes that he buried a treasure in a sand dune and then killed all of the crew that had come ashore with him. They say Blackbeard told the rest of his gang that it would be a small hope that anyone would ever find his treasure. That's where the name Small Hope Bay came from."

"Are those stories for real?" Justin asked, sitting back in his seat.

"Don't rightly know," Basky reckoned with a smile. "Wasn't there myself; it was long before my time. But you know that's the problem with old stories. Never really know if they're true or not. And, you know stories are always changing. I bet you a dollar that if I asked you to repeat the story about ole Captain Morgan right now, I'd get a different version out of each one of you. Now you can imagine how much these stories have changed over hundreds of years. Most weren't written down until present time; years ago they just passed the stories along from person to person, one generation to the next. Some stories I imagine are like the Winfrey man's shark story… just got bigger and bigger over time!"

"Are there any books with these stories in them?" Beth asked. "I'd like to read and learn more about the legends of the island."

"I think there may be a book but I can't remember the title. You should ask Dr. Lounsbury at the field station. That man has more books than the island has cars, so if anyone would have it, he would. If not, the library in Coakley Town should."

"Thanks Basky! I'll check it out."

After a few more miles, they came to a small sign marking Bollard Creek and rumbled over a short bridge with a steel-grate deck. Then the taxi slowed and turned left onto Andros Drive, a sandy lane covered with water-filled potholes. A sign, 'Rockwood Field Station,' marked the entrance to their much-anticipated destination. Palm trees grew on both sides of the road and created a tunnel of vegetation framing the deep blue ocean at the far end. On the right, scuba tanks stacked outside a low-slung building made from weathered boards marked the location of the scuba shop. Basky drove into a clearing with at least two-dozen log stools arranged around a fire pit on the left and a rustic lodge on the right. Dogs came from all directions, barking with excitement at the new arrivals. Beyond the beach, the ocean was glistening in the afternoon sun, and waves crashed over distant reefs.

"Here's home for the next week," Basky said, pulling to a stop behind the van while another taxi stopped beside them. "I'll be around, stopping in from time to time, so if there's anything I can do to help, please give ol' Basky a call."

The EcoExplorers thanked him, stepped out, and began to unload luggage from the trunk of the taxi while a thin woman approached. She was dressed similarly to Dr. Lounsbury in a white, long sleeve cotton shirt and khaki colored shorts. Her pitch black hair was cropped short and framed her narrow face and large, dark brown eyes.

"Welcome to Rockwood," she said with a smile. "My name is Carmen Foster. I'm the assistant director of the field station. Mike and Molly, it's so nice to see you again. Like clockwork, here you are just like every year," Carmen said, embracing them both.

"It's so nice to see you too Carmen. Allow me to introduce this year's EcoExplorers," Mike said. "Our seniors are Justin Dulaney, his sister Laura Dulaney, Jeff Loundon and Beth Britton. Then, Debbie Mead, Jane Hubbard, Mitch Martin and Steve Barlow, our rising juniors."

"You're going to have an awesome week and I look forward to getting to know each of you." Carmen said with a smile. "Now, the first course of business is to carry your luggage over to the lodge. Inside you'll find some refreshments. Our cook Stilly will be available to help you. Our staff is very busy on Saturdays with groups coming and going, so you'll meet them later this evening at the beach fire. Mike, Molly, could you do us a big favor and help get everyone settled in? One of our staff members has the day off; he's away scuba diving and won't be back until this evening. So, we're a little short-handed at the moment."

"We'll be happy to do whatever we can to help," Molly offered.

"I'll go and get the list of cabin assignments and meet you in the dining room," Carmen instructed while a large vehicle rumbled across the Bollard Creek Bridge. "Ah! There's Newby with the slow moving Big Blue. And you thought you left work at home."

The loaded truck rumbled up to the dive shop behind the lodge, and squealed to a stop. Newby got out and walked over to the students.

"Well folks, I could use y'all's help unloading Big Blue," Newby said.

In bucket-brigade-fashion, like at the airport, the supplies were soon stacked into a store room behind the lodge. With the task at hand completed, the EcoExplorers walked back to the mounds of luggage scattered about at the end of the dirt drive and hauled it to the front of the lodge. The building was constructed from sandy limestone rocks gathered from the island and set in concrete. They created both the exterior and the interior walls.

They entered through the creaky screen door. Inside the main lounge were sofas covered with blue Androsian batik fabric arranged around a handmade pine coffee table scrapped together from driftwood boards and covered with stacks of outdated magazines. The ceiling was supported with wood trusses of rough-hewn Bahamian Pine that gave the lodge a rustic, somewhat Adirondack appearance.

Along the back wall were doors for bathrooms and one marked 'Computer Room Keep Closed.' On the right side of the room, a massive bar covered the wall next to a doorway that led into a large, open classroom. To the left stood a large limestone fireplace open to the lounge on one side and the dining room on the other. A thick, wooden oak mantle axed out from the keel of an ancient shipwreck displayed a vintage three-masted ship's model along with numerous wooden bird decoys suspended from the ceiling high above the opening like birds in flight. Past the fireplace and into the dining room, numerous pine tables with chairs tightly packed the room. On the wall close to the food table hung a large wooden board cut in the shape of an octopus, with cups hanging from numerous hooks screwed into its eight wooden arms. An aged, gray-haired man could be heard humming out loud with an old sailor's song while he placed silverware, food and beverages on a long stainless steel buffet table in the dining room. The dark-skinned islander was wearing a white apron and fisherman's cap.

"Hello everyone, I'm Stilly." He looked at Mike and Molly. "Dr. Lounsbury told me at breakfast this morning you would be here today. It's so good to see you," Stilly said, hugging Molly and shaking Mike's hand.

"It's good to be back," Molly said.

"I know it will be a fun week with you here." When Stilly smiled two front teeth sparkled with gold fillings. He was a heavy man and his hands were the size of dinner plates. His deep voice sounded Jamaican mixed with British, which was common among the islanders. "The octopus board has cups swinging from numbered hooks and there is a sign-up sheet on the table below. Place your name by a cup number and use the same cup throughout your stay. That way we only wash them once a day and conserve water. Plates are on the table, so please come in and help yourselves to the snacks. Don't eat too much because dinner's at six followed by a beach fire at sunset. You'll be introduced to the staff and I'll tell you some of my stories about the field station and its ghost." Stilly smiled, showing his shiny bright gold-capped teeth.

"Ghost?" Mitch said, brushing his disheveled brown hair out of his face.

"Oh yes. We have the ghost of ole' Ross Rockwood here," Stilly said.

"Who's he?"

"Humph," Stilly grunted in a dismissing tone. "Now you have a bite to eat and then get settled in. Stories are best told around a campfire after dark." He departed through swinging double doors with Mike McNeil to talk in the kitchen.

"Ah, I see you've found the food," Carmen said, rejoining the group. "I have your cabin assignments here, so listen up. The boys will lodge in cabin number two, and the girls in number three. Molly, you and Mike will have your usual room in the staff cabin. When you're done eating, just head down the beach along the path past the director's cabin. There's a key already in the door of cabin three since that cabin is unoccupied. We already have another guest, Eric Cramer, staying with you guys in cabin two for the week, so that cabin is locked. However, you'll find an extra key to your cabin on the rack by the bar in the lounge."

Justin collected the key and soon left the lodge with the others in search of their designated cabins. Outside, the pack of resident dogs sniffed the new arrivals. Molly knew all of their names from previous trips: Dingo, Lester, Willie, Loona, and Earl. Loona was a small dog with a black coat and dark brown spots; the others were small sandy brown dogs and looked as though they were all born in the same litter.

The shore was lined with tall, swaying Australian Pines and palm trees that cast shadows on the narrow sandy beach and framed the view of the lagoon. Shallow blue-green water rippled and swirled in a constant easterly breeze that carried the sounds of waves crashing on distant reefs. A few boats, anchored just off shore, sat lifeless on sandy flats, marking low tide.

The first cabin was designated as the 'Director's Cabin' with a painted sign by the front door and they could see Dr. Lounsbury talking on the phone through a large picture window. His cabin like the others was built from rustic wood with the addition of a ramp leading up to the front door. Further down the winding path, they found a row of five matching cabins. One corner of each square-shaped cabin faced the lagoon like the prow of a ship and the five cabins together reminded Justin of a fleet anchored at port. The odd positioning was designed to reduce stress on the structures during the rare occasions when hurricanes blew with destructive winds and high storm surge.

Justin placed the key into the door of cabin two and opened it. The interior walls and furnishings of the cabin were built entirely of Bahamian pine. Each side had two pairs of bunk beds positioned against the wall with a partial partition in the center. In the back corner was the bathroom with an open shower stall next to it. Justin walked through the door and carried his bag to his choice of a bunk with Steve and Mitch following. Justin claimed the bunks next to him. One bunk on the opposite side of the room was already occupied and had a pile of wrinkled clothes thrown on the top bunk and a pile of books and other personal belongings on the bunk below. In total contrast, dive regulators, BC's and wetsuits were neatly hung on wooden pegs in the corner with other dive gear stowed neatly below in plastic bins. Justin thought to himself that their new roommate seemed to have his priorities straight. He knew that scuba gear is something that needs to be in good working order and neglectful divers tend to leave their equipment thrown about and left unkempt. You could tell a lot about a scuba diver just by the way they cared for their gear.

"Man, I'm ready to do some exploring. Let's go look around," Mitch said anxiously.

"Yeah, we've got plenty of time before dinner. We can unpack later," Steve replied, pitching his luggage on his bunk, racing for the door.

"You coming Justin," Mitch asked?

Justin shook his head. "Not right now. I think I'll get settled in and hang around for Jeff," he said, really wanting time to himself to get organized.

"Okay, catch you later."

Justin grabbed his bags and opened them up. He unpacked his clothes from one bag and stored them in the small slide-out drawers beneath his bunk. From another bag, he removed his scuba gear, checking off his equipment list. Finally, he opened his backpack and took out the field study book and class schedule that Mike had given out before leaving for the trip. Then the door swung open and Jeff walked in toting his luggage.

"Hey, what's up?" Jeff asked, as he heaved his heavy bags onto the bunk above Justin.

"I'm just finishing unpacking. Mitch and Steve are out exploring the grounds," Justin said, emptying the items from his backpack "and there's the other guy's stuff over there on that bunk...looks like he's a scuba diver too."

Jeff cast an eye over at the stranger's bunk and gear hung tidily in the corner.

Justin continued to organize and put away his belongings when he discovered a large manila envelope mixed in with his stuff in his backpack. "What's this?"

"What's what," replied Jeff.

"This envelope, I don't remember packing it."

"It's your field station packet the McNeil's gave to you." Jeff said, unzipping his bag and removing his clothes.

"No, I've already unpacked that."

Justin stared at the envelope, trying to remember the contents, then squeezed the metal clasp together, pushed the flap out of the way and let the contents slide out onto the bunk. Inside was an old worn and tattered leather bound book wrapped tight in plastic. Justin picked it up, pulled off the wrapping and carefully started to flip through the tattered pages. "Wow, look at this! It looks like a really old handwritten book or diary of some type," Justin said, inspecting the first written page of thick yellowed paper with faded ink penmanship.

Jeff stopped unpacking and sat down next to Justin to check out his discovery.

"Can you read it?" asked Jeff. "What's it say?"

Justin pondered for a moment, attempting to decipher the old English handwriting. "The ink is so faded and the calligraphy style is really hard to read, but I'll give it a try. Okay, it looks like Captain Benjamin Hornigold and it's dated the twelfth of December, seventeen seventeen. It says here that he left Charles Town on a ship named the Adventure, a sloop that he captured near the island of Martinique. It says that he sailed with his crew on a west by southwest course to an island called La Isla del Espiritu Santo."

"La Isla del Espiritu Santo! Hey, I read about that on the plane in the history section of the field station manual. Hang on a second and let me grab my manual." Jeff dug through his backpack and pulled out his copy and searched for the section titled history of Andros and the Bahamas Islands. "Here it is…it's Spanish and means the island of the Holy Spirit. It was the first name given by the Spaniards when they discovered this island. So it appears that they were coming here to Andros!"

Justin continued to read the page. "It says here that he sailed south by southwest and anchored inside a reef close to a place where they found fresh drinking water.

They loaded a chest onto a long boat with a trusted crew of eight, waited for the tide to run high and rowed to shore."

Justin flipped forward to the next page. "Reached known devil hole before dusk and lowered the chest into the depths of Lucifer's Lair, where it would be safe until he returned. It goes on to say something about losing a crewmate named Maynard, Thomas Maynard, then something more about the devil hole, but it's too faded and I can't read it."

Jeff then took a turn examining the faded script. "Look," said Jeff pointing to the binding of the book. There are pages missing here between the last page and this one."

"You're right," said Justin. "Someone has torn a section out." Justin flipped forward, examining more pages of what appeared to be a Captain's log. "He's written here about returning to his ship and then something about sailing to the Exumas." Justin said, quickly inspecting the rest of the handwritten pages. Then he found two folded stained heavy cloth-like papers stuffed in the back of the book and carefully removed them. They appeared to be thicker and more brittle than the paper used inside the book, possibly made from an animal skin of some type, and the pages contained numerous pen drawings of sailing ships, mermaids, sketches of the island and a fancy compass drawn in the upper right corner with a big arrow pointing north. Justin read out loud from the page.

Manifest
Captain Benj. Hornigold

Loaded into the 'Margaret' on this 12th day of December in the year 1717 a wooden chest measuring three cubits by two cubits by two and one half cubits in height, fastened together with forged iron strapping, wrapped in chains and latched with three padlocks.

Eight cloth bags of gold doubloons
Twelve cloth bags of silver pieces of eight
Three bags filled with gold and silver necklaces, pendants and
jewelry of sorts
Me swept hilt silver rapier with ruby and gemstone guard
Diamond studded cross made for the King of Portugal
A ruby the size of a hen's egg
A solid gold swan shaped necklace with big ruby eyes on gold
chain
A jewelry box filled with diamonds and gemstones.
A silver lock box filled with pearls the size of filberts

"Treasure, this is the list of treasure that's in the chest," said Jeff. Both boys sat for a moment speechless and mesmerized.

"I think it's a hoax," Justin finally said. "Someone could have created this logbook, made it look really old, like the real thing, and then planted it in my backpack to make me believe that there's treasure on Andros. How else could it have gotten into my backpack? I bet you anything it's a gag that they play here on all their incoming guests. Pick out an unsuspecting visitor, slip the package into their belongings when they're not looking and then see what they do with it! Remember, the cook said that they tell ghost stories around the campfire tonight! Ten to one Mike and Molly are mixed up in it too. Mike is always playing jokes on us back home. He picked me out because I'm this year's president of the EcoExplorers and he wanted me to look like a fool. This even smells like something that you would cook up and I bet you're a part of it too!"

"Me? Justin, I swear to you that I have nothing to do with this!" Jeff said, emphatically.

"Well how else would the envelope get into my backpack? It's been with me all day long. The only time that it was out of my sight was when we were unloading the boxes from the truck which puts us here at the field station."

"What about around the plane. Where was your backpack then?" Jeff asked.

"It was my carry-on luggage and next to me the whole flight. There's no time that I can think of that my backpack was not with me."

"Well it certainly got into your backpack somehow," Jeff said.

"I think I'll call their bluff and give this to Mike and Molly or Dr. Lounsbury. That way, if it's a hoax, and I'll bet you anything that it is, then that will be the end of it. I have zero interest in being this week's gullible student visiting Andros!"

"What, are you kidding?" Jeff answered. "What if this stuff's for real? Remember what Basky said in the taxi on the way here? He told one person that he found one gold coin and the word spread across the island through the coconut telegraph. Then half the population showed up the next day hunting for gold coins. I can only imagine what would happen if word of this got out. The island would be crawling with treasure hunters."

"Jeff! We're here to study marine ecology...not to wander around the island on a ridiculous treasure hunt! Even if this old book is for real, which I don't believe for one second that it is, what would we do with it? There's no time in our schedule to go hunting for a treasure on this island whether we wanted to or not."

"I don't know. Maybe we could ask around this evening and see if anyone might know something. It can't hurt. And if it's a hoax, then we'll probably hear about it at the campfire. Let's just play it cool for now, act like nothing's happened and see if we can find out anything about Hornigold. But we better tell Beth and your sister about this. If they knew we were hiding a discovery like this from them, we'd never hear the end of it."

"Okay, but no one else. I still think this is a hoax,

probably the field station's idea of a snipe hunt."

Jeff shook his head in agreement. "OK, I'll go along with that. But if it's the real deal…."

3

ANDROSIAN MYTHS

Whoot...whoot...whoot!

"What in the world's that awful sound?" Jane asked, as the distant and throaty sound washed over the Rockwood grounds.

The girls had nearly completed unpacking, settling into their home for the week. With only four in the cabin, they spread out, sleeping on the bottom bunks and storing their clothing, books, and snorkeling gear on the top bunks.

"Let's go see where it's coming from," Laura suggested. They left their cabin and followed the direction of the strange sound. Finding Jeff and Justin in front of their cabin, they walked together towards the lodge.

Whoot...whoot...whoot!

"It's Mitch! What does he have pressed against his face?" Jane asked.

Mitch blew as hard as he could into a large conch shell; his face turned bright red, his cheeks puffed out and the throaty sound came bellowing out.

"Stilly asked me to call you to dinner by sounding the conch shell. Apparently, the conch is used instead of a dinner bell as a signal that meals and events are about to begin. I was wondering how long it would take for you to figure it out," Mitch said with a laugh.

"Are you folks going to eat, or should I feed dinner to the dogs?" said Stilly. His shadowy frame appeared behind the tight mesh of the lodge's screen door, a white apron was tied around his waist, and he kneaded a ball of bread dough in his stout hands.

"I guess we'd better get inside," Mitch suggested. "I don't want my dinner pitched to the hounds. Coming?"

Mitch entered with the others and was first in line for the buffet-style dinner. Soon Dr. Lounsbury arrived in the dining room together with other staff members and the McNeils. They were seated when Newby entered the dining room, followed by a tall young man, and they both walked to the buffet table beside the kitchen door.

"Evening. I'd like you to meet Eric Cramer. He'll be rooming with you in your cabin, guys." Newby said and began to fill a plate.

"Hi, I'm Jeff," Jeff said, then introduced Justin, Laura, and Beth seated together at the same table.

"Nice to meet you!" Eric said, filled a plate and joined them at their table.

"I think we've kind of intruded on your privacy," Jeff continued.

"Not at all," replied Eric. "I've already been here for a couple of weeks. You're the third group I'll room with. Last week the field station was at maximum capacity and the cabin was pretty cramped. So, as long as you don't snore too loud I think we'll get along fine," he said with a grin.

"It must be nice to be staying here for so long. A week just doesn't seem long enough," Jeff said with a tone of envy.

"Well, it's not exactly all fun and games. I'm headed

to college in the fall, and my grandfather wanted me to have an idea of what I'm getting myself into. I'm majoring in marine biology and this is a great place to get some first-hand experience. So, I, or we actually, decided that I'd spend the summer here at Rockwood. He said I couldn't just vacation, so I'm treated just like the staff," Eric said.

"Wow! I'd love to spend the summer here," Laura exclaimed.

"You're all going to have a great week. The diving is fantastic, the snorkeling is awesome, and the food is incredible. It might take you a day or so to learn the ropes, but by the end of the week you'll feel at home."

"Have you seen any sharks?" Laura asked, trying to make conversation.

"I saw a sand shark the other day and a few reef sharks. They seem to be pretty skittish, definitely not the fierce man-eaters you see in the movies. The coolest thing so far was the other day out near the Tongue of the Ocean; we saw five spotted eagle rays swimming by us. They reminded me of jets flying in formation."

"Where are you from?" Justin inquired, sizing up their new acquaintance.

"I'm from Texas."

"Texas! But your accent doesn't sound Texan. I can't place it," Justin stated.

"Well, you see, my parents traveled around a lot while I was growing up. I never really lived anywhere long enough to establish an accent. Then, after they died in a plane crash, I moved to Texas to live with my grandfather. So I say Texas, but I guess I never really had just one home." Eric took a few bites of food then asked, "So what about you folks? Travel far to get here?"

"We're from Charlottesville, Virginia, and the four of us will be seniors in high school this fall," Justin explained.

"Have you been diving long?" Jeff inquired, breaking

a momentary lull in the conversation.

"Since I was twelve. My grandfather owns a yacht, and I used to spend some of my summers traveling and scuba diving with him. We would cruise throughout the Caribbean. One summer, we crossed the Panama Canal and traveled up the West Coast and through the Inside Passage to Alaska.

"Wow, that sounds like a great trip," Laura suggested, fascinated. She admired his dark hair and hazel-green eyes.

"Well, it's fun," Eric said unpretentiously.

"Eric!" Newby said, walking by the table with an empty plate.

"Yeah?"

"All of the scuba tanks need filling this evening, and I'm going to be at the beach fire. Think you can handle it?" Newby asked.

"Sure, no problem," Eric said while he stood to leave. "Well, it was nice meeting you folks. Work calls, so, I'll catch you later tonight, or in the morning."

"He seems pretty cool . . . doesn't he?" Jeff asked after Eric left.

"Um, yeah . . . we'll see!" Justin stated. He rose, scraped his plate into the trash can, placed it in the dish pan, hung his cup on the designated hook on the octopus and left the dining room.

"What's eating him?" Beth asked.

"Not sure . . . it's been a busy day. And, do I have news for you," Jeff said excitedly. "Let's go out to the beach where we can talk in private."

Outside Jeff described in detail the discovery of the mysterious envelope found in Justin's backpack. The girls, wanting to read the documents for themselves, followed Jeff to the boys' cabin. Inside, Justin was reading the documents. The girls, skeptical, quickly scanned the pages. They agreed that the possibility of a hoax was high, but swore not to say anything about the discovery. Then the conch shell whooted and they walked to the beach fire.

The sun reflected a warm golden glow on the distant clouds. Shades of reds, oranges, and pinks painted the sky with a palette of delicate tones and hues. Birds, high up in the canopy of palms, chirped as if announcing the end of the day. A slight ocean breeze blew, but not strong enough to retard the unrelenting doctor flies that fed on unprotected skin. Seated on the stout wooden stools in a circle around the fire, young faces glowed orange from the flames that lapped and danced over charred logs. The resident dogs followed and curled up in the sand near the fire, or in front of whoever would pet them or scratch their backs.

Dr. Lounsbury stood to speak and cleared his throat. "May I have your attention please? I would like to welcome the EcoExplorers to Rockwood Field Station!" Everyone cheered. "Soon I'll introduce our staff, but first, I want to orient you to the field station and the week's activities. Each morning the conch shell will sound, announcing breakfast at eight a.m. You snooze you lose! At eight forty-five we will load either a boat or Big Blue, depending on whether you're taking a land-based or sea-based tour for the day. At nine a.m. you'll depart for your day's activities. Lunch is at noon. If you're at Rockwood, you'll eat in the dining room. You'll return here to the field station around four o'clock every day. Dinner will be served at six p.m. sharp. Then, at seven-thirty p.m. you'll have a daily presentation by a staff member in the classroom. Finally, and this is very important, the lodge closes at ten p.m. and quiet time commences at the field station until seven a.m. Please respect your fellow roommates, and keep your voices and activities as quiet as possible. After a strenuous day's activities, I don't expect you'll be making much of a fuss anyway!" added Lounsbury.

"Water conservation is very important here because

of our shallow wells. You're already familiar with our method of using the same cup all day and washing once. For the showers, please keep your usage to a minimum. We have low-flow shower heads, but please turn the water off while you lather with soap for extra conservation. And regarding the toilets, we have a self-explanatory saying, 'if it's yellow let it mellow, if it's brown flush it down,'" he explained and they laughed.

"Finally, Stilly has Wednesday night off and we'll all go down to Obediah's fish bake and dance, which is always a fun time," Dr. Lounsbury paused briefly. "Now, we'll go around the circle and give our staff a chance to introduce themselves."

A young man with a muscular build and wavy brown hair stood and squared his eyeglasses on his nose. "I think I've met most of you loading and unloading Big Blue today, but for those I haven't met, I'm Newby Marshall. I'm from North Carolina and graduated from East Carolina University last year with a degree in biology. I've worked here at Rockwood for a little more than a year now. I do everything from supervising scuba divers as a dive master to fixing boats and making repairs around the facilities. Constant repairs!" He rolled his eyes skyward. "This week I'll be leading you on some of your outings, and I'll lecture in the classroom later in the week about the Androsian terrestrial wildlife. You've definitely picked one of the best places in the world to come and study marine biology." He sat back down.

In the silence the beach fire became more noticeable.

"Evenin' everyone," announced the next staff member; standing, she scanned the faces around the beach fire, and buried her toes into the cooling sand. Long, feathery brown hair flowed over her shoulders and swirled around her face with each breath of the ocean breeze. "I'm Nicole Gunter and I have a degree in geology from Florida State University. Later in the week, I'll lecture on how the island of Andros was formed from a geological perspective. I'll be with you this week on most boat trips and land tours. I've been here at Rockwood for three months now and hope to stay on for at least two years. I came here years ago as a student on a trip just like you. It was then that I decided to come back after college and stay for a year or two before I get settled into a job in the geology field. So far, it's been the best decision of my life," Nicole finished and sat down.

"Hello. I'm Carmen Foster, the assistant director here at the field station. I'm from California and have a degree in botany from UCLA. The field station has been my home now for about five years. I'm a dive master, like Newby, and will be with you on some of your snorkeling trips this week." She spoke in a relaxed and sure voice. A beautiful woman with Asian features; she wore short-cropped dark black hair and had developed an athletic build from the chores of living at the field station. "I look forward to working with all of you this week. We always have a fun time with Mike and Molly here, and I know you will this week as well." Dr. Lounsbury stood up again for the final introductions of the evening. "Grant Campbell, our head dive master, has the day off, so you won't meet him until tomorrow morning. Now last, but not least is Nathaniel Stillabower, or Stilly as everyone knows him. Most of you have already met him, and if not, you've enjoyed his incredible cooking," Dr. Lounsbury said. "Stilly is famous here for a number of reasons. One, of course, is his cooking skill; the second, and perhaps the one that'll leave you with the most memorable impression, is his story- telling ability. The field station has quite a colorful history, and Stilly will be happy to share it with you."

Stilly pet his dog slowly and appeared to be gathering his thoughts. His face reflected the vibrant colors cast by the raging fire, making him appear possessed, while the dancing flames cast eerie shadows that seemed to prowl over him. A log shifted in the fire and long streams of sputtering sparks rose into the sky.

"I was 'bout your age," he began, looking around the circle into each of the EcoExplorers eyes, "when I first met a man named Ross Rockwood. He had come to Andros back in the sixties on his sailboat. Not much of a sailor, he cracked the boat up on the reef and swam ashore. My family gave him a place to stay for a time. He bought this property and started the first scuba diving business on Andros. That was when the lodge was built and the building you had dinner in this evening. I helped him with the work, my family helped him, and many of the locals around here helped as well. We built that lodge, all the furniture, and mixed every shovel of concrete here on site. It was back-breaking work, but we got it done, and I know it'll outlast me, maybe you too," Stilly paused sipping from his steaming cup of coffee.

"It wasn't long after construction that Ross got interested in exploring the blue holes on the island and then started exploring the deep walls out there." Stilly clenched his fingers together with his thumb up and pointed over his shoulder. "He had a girlfriend at the time, named Ann. She was a pretty woman, and he hired her as a dive instructor for the business. She trained hard with Ross to set a deep diving record. They went out to the Tongue of the Ocean; you know that wall drops off into the bowels of the earth. Some say it be bottomless but doesn't matter much to me. Might as well be on the surface of the moon for that's as close as I'm ever going to get to it." He sipped coffee again.

"Well, the day he was attempting to break the world record for deep air diving, they were down about five hundred feet when his safety diver saw Ross trying to help Ann. He had what they call nitrogen narcosis and it was affecting his thinking at that depth. Of course, I think someone's mind is already affected if they choose to dive that deep in the first place. Anyway, the safety diver had to come to the surface to save his own life.

The boat crew waited and waited until they knew that the divers' air supply had to have been used up and still no signs of Ross and no Ann." Stilly removed his hat and held it close to his heart. He continued:

"Now the strange thing is…a few days after Ross and Ann drowned, money disappeared from his account in Miami. Also, here at the Field Station in the director's cabin is a safe that only he, Ann, and I had the combination to. When I opened his safe, two of his prized slit shells were missing. Some people think that Ross and Ann never died that day, other folks say they've seen his ghost around here for years." He paused, then peered into each set of eyes. "Often in cabin number three." He paused again, did the circuit of eyes again. Then he continued. "Some eerie things have happened around here. One time many years ago a little girl was staying here with her father. She was sick and during the night a strange man came and comforted her by rocking her in a chair while her father slept. In the morning her father didn't believe the girl's story since the door was locked all night and they had been the only two in the cabin. Well, they go into the lodge for breakfast that morning and that little girl looks up on the wall and sees a picture of Ross Rockwood that hangs by the fireplace. She goes to it and points and tells her father that it was a picture of the man that had rocked her to sleep!"

No one made a sound. They were all riveted to his every word, especially the girls who were bunking in cabin number three.

"Do you think Ross Rockwood died that day with his girlfriend?" Mitch asked. The fire crackled and sounds of the distant surf washed in on the salty breeze.

"Well, I don't know for sure. Some of the things that happened seem strange to me. Other people say he took out a large insurance policy before the accident. I just don't know for sure! Now, I did have an encounter with his ghost once. The staff cabin was being painted, so I stayed in cabin three. I was alone here on a Wednesday night when everyone was down at Obediah's. I turned in early, enjoying the peace and quiet and a night off from cooking. About ten o'clock, I heard this whistling, like the wind had picked up and was singing through the rafters. That was very strange to me, because when I turned in, the ocean was flat calm and the night air was dead still. Opening my eyes I could see a dark outline of a man standing near my bed. I called out to him, 'What do you want? Who are you?' But, I didn't get an answer. I stood, slowly, with my legs shaking so bad you would think I was going to topple over onto the floor. Walking closer to the light switch, I could feel the presence of someone or something behind me. And as I stepped, he stepped too. I could hear the floorboards creaking behind me. Then my teeth started to chatter like they do when you're cold. I thought I would bust all the teeth out of my mouth…that's how hard they were a clacking together. As I got close to the light switch I could almost feel the breath of this man, this shape, this thing, close behind me. I reached for the lights and flipped the switch. I was frozen in place. I started to turn around, not wanting to see, but needing to know what was following me. All the hair on the back of my neck was standing straight up. So, when I could get my body to turn around to look, I couldn't believe my eyes," Stilly said, pausing to sip his coffee. A hushed silence hovered over the campfire with heavy anticipation for the rest of his story.

"When I turned around, whatever it was, was gone! The odd thing was that as soon as I turned on the lights, that sound, like the wind blowing through the rafters, stopped. Then, I thought that I was going to lose it when I opened the cabin door and looked outside." Stilly looked around the campfire again. "Does anyone have any idea what I saw?" He waited, dramatically. No one even dared to try and guess as they were all absorbed by his vivid story. He continued, a sharp gleam in his eyes:

"There down the few steps on the sand were the five dogs from the field station. There's nothing unusual about that, but what was different was all five dogs were lined up almost shoulder-to-shoulder. Had their heads cocked to the side as if they were possessed or something. But my yell seemed to break whatever spell they were under. They all stood up and began to act like they always do, like dogs. I spent that night in the kitchen under the counter. Had a big soup spoon for a weapon, but didn't sleep much with all the lights on. Since that night I've never, and will never, set foot back in cabin three!"

"Is it too late for us to change cabins?" Jane asked while they broke into laughter, except the four girls staying in cabin three.

"What about the Chickcharnies?" Debbie asked. "I read that a Chickcharnie can put a spell on you. Is that true, Stilly?"

The group's attention turned back to Stilly as he began to speak again. "The Chickcharnies are bird-like elfin creatures that live deep in the forest here on Andros. I've never seen one myself. They live in the most remote parts of the island, coming out only at night when they drink in the blue holes and hunt around the marshes. I don't go into the forest at night, and I'm not planning to anytime soon either, so I'll probably never see one. They say they can put a spell on you and you would be dizzy for the rest of your life! My mother once told me that her neighbor, who likes to go out into the forest at night, saw a Chickcharnie once. She said he was never the same after that. Seemed to have memory losses and would sometimes just stare off into the distance like he was looking at something that no one else could see. I'm not sure if it was the Chickcharnie that put some kind of curse or spell on him, or the high mound of empty whiskey bottles behind his house that he had drunk that pickled his brain!" Stilly let out a hearty guffaw, and the others laughed with him.

As the laughter died down, Dr. Lounsbury stood to speak. "Stilly, thank you for your stories tonight; as usual they were most entertaining. It's getting late so I think we should end the meeting here. Morning will come early and you're going to have a full day. For those of you who are certified divers, remember you have a checkout dive in the morning. You need to be up and on the beach at six a.m. with all of your dive gear. The rest of you can sleep in until breakfast at eight. Any questions?" Lounsbury paused. "Well, in that case, good night and I'll see you in the morning."

Jeff, Justin, Beth and Laura lingered behind to talk with Stilly; he poked at the dying fire and the last of the glowing embers with a stick; Loona curled up at his feet.

"Stilly! Do you know anything about pirate treasure?" Justin asked.

"Humph," Stilly, putting a match to his pipe, grunted in a noncommittal tone.

"Have you ever heard of a pirate captain named Hornigold…Benjamin Hornigold?" Jeff asked, being more specific.

Stilly's head jerked around, his eyes widened, and he peered into Jeff's eyes. "Hornigold! Who told you about him, boy?" Stilly seemed surprised by the question. He looked down at the fire, poked at the glowing embers with his long stick and puffed his pipe.

"Well, we found some old papers that, well, we thought you might know something about him, like if his treasure was ever found?" Jeff asked.

"Never heard anything 'bout it. It's getting late. I think you should go and get some rest. You'll have an early start in the morning." Stilly continued to poke at the fire.

"But you've lived here all of your life, you must—"

"No son, I don't know anything 'bout no Hornigold," Stilly said in a firm, dismissing voice.

"W-well, good night Stilly, thanks for the great stories," Jeff said.

They walked a short distance, turned and looked back. Stilly was still poking at the fire. His eyes were fixed straight ahead and he did not look toward them again. A large stream of sparks rocketed into the night sky. The dogs gathered around him, enjoying the last of the fire's heat. Justin looked at Jeff.

"What do you make of that?"

4

FIRST DIVE

Dawn crept onto Andros with a gentle breeze, scented by the aroma of salty-Bahamian air. Sea gulls called out, greeting the day with melodious tones of joy, gliding effortlessly above the calm water of Bollard Creek. A cool misty fog, soon to lift with the first rays of the sub-tropical sun, hugged the island close like a soft fluffy blanket. Songbirds, high in the canopy of coconut palms, chirping, gathered insects and jockeyed for the best perches. Down in their cabins the EcoExplorers slumbered in peace, tucked under the covers in their bunks. In front of cabin number three a gentle but anxious knock broke the pervasive calm and roused Beth and Laura out of a deep and restful sleep.

"Who's there?" Beth muttered, just above a whisper, in a half-awake voice, her sleepy moss-green eyes fluttering open. No one answered as the knock rapped again, more frantic than the first. "I said who's there?" she said again in rising frustration at the early morning disturbance. Still, there was no answer as the knock sounded yet a third time. Frustrated, Beth got out of bed, wiped her eyes, crossed the room still half asleep, opened the creaky door, and peered outside. A loud scream erupted from deep within Beth's lungs when she peered into the eyes of a large gruesome face that looked like something out of an African Witch Doctor movie. A heinous looking mask covered the face of someone, something, with long strands of dried reeds covering the rest of its body. Laura, startled in the other bunk, rose and screamed along with Beth, shattering the lingering peace of the dawn. Debbie and Jane, who had been sleeping on the other side of the cabin, saw the freakish looking thing, screamed too and pulled bed covers up over their heads.

Beth grabbed the broom positioned by the door and swung with all her might at the intruder in the face. It ducked. The broom whooshed over its head. The mask flew off, twirled a few times like a kite out of control, and came to rest on the sandy ground next to the steps. She recognized the goofy face of Jeff. Jeff, enjoying his prank, said in a squeaky tone, "Chickcharney! Chickcharney!" and broke into laughter that infuriated her more. Beth swung at him again with the broom and missed as he stepped back, stumbled down the few steps and fell onto the sand below. He recovered, jumped to his feet, and began to run as Beth followed close behind, swatting at him with the broom.

"You're in for it, Jeffrey! Wait until I catch up with you," Beth yelled, swinging the broom, grazing Jeff's head and ruffling his hair. Jeff ran past the director's cabin and a sleepy Dr. Lounsbury, awakened by the commotion. Past the staff cabin and along the lodge, Beth caught up and batted Jeff in the head with the broom. Parts of his costume were falling off all along the path; some parts from his gyrations and other strands of the grass reeds fell off from Beth's well aimed and frequent broom hits. The resident dogs, excited about the commotion, and perplexed by the running pair, joined the fray, barking and yapping while adding decibels to the once quiet and windswept field station.

Jeff turned toward the beach and ran out onto the low tide sandy flats. With few options left to avoid Beth, he jumped up on one of the beached boats. Beth pursued him to the end of the skiff; Jeff turned to face his attacker, while she swung again with the broom. Jeff stepped back and ducked, trying to avoid the broom, but it grazed the top of his head with a whoosh of wind. Losing his balance, he tumbled out of the boat, over the side, and splashed into the shallow water below.

The small crowd, now gathered on shore laughed as they watched the finale of the morning's episode. Beth turned triumphant, stern in face with broom in hand, and marched out of the boat, across the sandy flats toward her cabin. Receiving a round of applause, whistles, and cheers, she bounced up the few steps to her cabin and slammed the creaky door.

Newby Marshall, working nearby on an outboard motor, witnessed the morning's event and scratched his head in disbelief. Never before had he seen such commotion at the field station. He offered his hand to Jeff, grasped tight, and helped to pull him to his feet.

"Seems she got the better of you," Newby said with a chuckle, removed his glasses and wiped them dry on his sleeve.

"That's okay! It was worth every minute of it," Jeff said in a voice of victory. He looked like a water fountain, droplets dripped from the end of each golden strand of straw.

"Is that straw covering your body a new form of sunscreen?" Newby chuckled. "Or, you know, if you could do a dance you just might get it to rain!"

"Very funny. It's some costume I found in the lodge. It was the perfect opportunity to scare the girls after last night's ghost stories. And, once I saw this, I couldn't resist," Jeff said.

"Dive briefing in fifteen minutes! Unless you folks want to chase each other with brooms all day," Newby said in an elevated voice, so all could hear. The group headed back to their cabins still laughing, talking about the morning's excitement and Jeff's ridiculous looking costume. Soon, Jeff reappeared with Justin and Eric.

"Morning," Mike said, standing on a wooden deck, just above the high tide line on the beach. The deck, about ten feet deep and twelve feet across the front, had a shower and hose for washing off sand and rinsing dive gear. Benches wrapped around three sides, and posts were set in each of the four corners. From the posts boards ran around the top at eye level with numerous wooden pegs set into the inside face for hanging items to dry. Two wide steps ran across the entire front where an indolent resident dog was curled up watching.

"Morning," Justin replied, and the others greeted Mike.

"We're going to need tanks for seven divers," Mike said. "Why don't you guys go and load a cart from the dive shop. Eric can show you where to go." Placing their gear on the rinse deck, they walked towards the dive shop in back of the lodge.

Beth and Laura soon appeared carrying their dive gear. "Good morning, Mike," said Laura." I hope you slept well last night." She yawned.

"Not bad!" Mike replied. "I like to sleep next to the ocean with the sound of the surf."

"Well, we didn't sleep at all." Laura frowned and glanced down at her feet. "I couldn't get Stilly's ghost stories out of my mind." Beth joined in: "It seemed like we'd just fallen asleep when Jeff knocked on the door wearing that ridiculous costume. I'm going to get back at him if it's the last thing I do!" Standing with a hand on each hip, she leaned forward and rose up on the balls of her feet for emphasis.

"Well, I'm sure you'll get your chance sometime this

week," said Mike. "Just don't let things get out of hand. We're here for a reason, and I don't want the teasing between you and Jeff to be at the expense of our objectives." He began searching through his dive bag for gear.

"I know, but after this morning's fiasco, he'd better watch out. I don't get mad, I get even!" Beth said, rising up again to make her point.

Beth and Laura placed their dive gear on the wooden deck and played with the dogs who had gathered around the activity. The sounds of a rumbling cart could be heard as the boys headed back with the dive tanks; Newby and Eric followed close behind.

"Oh, isn't this typical? The guys are out working and the girls are sitting around doing nothing," Jeff said; pulling the cart up to the rinse deck.

"Jeffrey, you better watch your step! You won't know when or where, but I am going to get even with you!" Beth exclaimed.

"Oh boy, I'm scared," Jeff mocked.

"Well at least you are well suited to the task this morning as cart mule," Beth jested.

"Cart mule? I'll have you know that—"

"Okay, knock it off," Mike said, his voice stern. "All of this foolishness needs to end here and now. We're about to go scuba diving, and I'll not tolerate any of this aboard the dive boat. Is that understood?" Mike didn't mind the kids teasing, but diving was serious business, and it was time they got focused. Both Jeff and Beth nodded their heads in response to Mike's strong words.

"Your dive master for the day is Grant Campbell," Newby said, breaking the sudden tension. "While we're waiting, go ahead and get your gear assembled for the dive. Set up your BC on a tank with your regulator and carry it out to the skiff. The boat will be full, so please line up your gear along the bottom to even out the weight. Any questions?"

47

Everyone followed Newby's instructions, gathering their gear and assembling it for their check-out dive. Eric and Jeff, both very experienced, had their dive gear assembled and on the skiff first. Mike soon followed with Justin and they stowed their dive gear.

"Why do I always have trouble with this thing?" Beth asked out loud to no one in particular, still on the rinse deck with Laura.

"Here, let me help. The first stage of your regulator is upside down," an unfamiliar voice suggested.

"That's okay, I can do it—" Beth's words trailed off when she turned around and peered into the eyes of a handsome stranger. Standing about 6'2", he had long blonde hair tied neatly into a ponytail. Wearing only red lifeguard shorts, he revealed his muscular and tanned body with defined abs. Beth, stunned by the sudden appearance of the stranger, stood with mouth agape while he adjusted her regulator.

"I'm Grant Campbell, the head dive master," he said to Beth. "Are you all right?" he asked. Beth seemed lost in a trance.

"I'm Beth, and this is my, my friend Laura. It's nice to meet you! I'm fine, I guess, I just, I mean, I didn't get a lot of sleep last night," she stammered.

"Nice to meet you both," Grant said, flashing a smile. "I understand. It's a common problem your first night. Stilly's ghost stories are directed at the arriving female population. Let me guess, I saw the roster, the cabin he'll never step foot back into is cabin number three. Right?" Beth nodded. "Well last week it was cabin two. Stilly is always right in the kitchen when cabin assignments are given out and plans his stories accordingly. But, trust me, after today's activities you'll be tired enough to sleep through a hurricane, or ghosting." Grant picked up Beth's assembled dive gear, carried it to the skiff, and introduced himself to the rest of the group.

"Oh my gawd! Did you see how handsome he is?"

Beth asked Laura.

"Well, I'm not sure who I noticed more…Grant, or you gawking at him," Laura said with a smile and giggle.

"He must think I'm an idiot. No one has ever affected me like that before!"

"I doubt that he noticed your gawking. You know how guys can be. Anyway a guy like that probably has a girl friend who keeps him on a tight leash," Laura suggested.

"We'll, I'm going to find out."

"If you two on the beach will join us, we'll go over buddy teams for this morning's scuba dive before we get going," Grant said.

Laura and Beth collected their remaining scuba gear and waded over to the skiff, which was named Kontiki. The tide had shifted and the skiff, the recent scene of the broom chase, was now floating in deeper water. They stowed their gear and took seats near the bow.

"Mike has assigned buddy teams and as I call out your names please raise your hands. Jeff and Justin," Grant read from a list on a clipboard. They both raised their hands. "Justin you're an advanced diver; Jeff you're listed as a rescue diver. Impressive at seventeen! Where did you get your certifications?"

Jeff looked at Grant and said, "I got my open water certification in Florida five years ago on summer vacation with my dad. I've worked in Key Largo every summer since then at a dive shop my dad owns with my uncle. Last year I got my advanced and rescue diver certifications. Once I'm eighteen, I plan to become a dive master and, after that, instructor."

"You're progressing well," responded Grant with a nod. "Many divers stop after their initial certification, but I have found the best divers continue with their training." He continued:

Next, Beth and Laura, you're listed as a buddy team." Both girls raised their hands and Beth smiled at Grant.

Returning her smile. "Beth you're an advanced diver and Laura, this is your first ocean dive. Is that correct?"

"Yes! I got certified just before the trip. Beth and Justin got me interested in scuba and I decided to get certified before coming to Andros. I didn't want to pass up the opportunity to dive here."

"Beth, have you had a chance to dive with Laura before? Perhaps we should buddy her up with Mike or me since it's her first ocean dive?" Grant asked.

"Well, I did dive with her in the quarry when she was certified. I'm sure we can work together as a buddy team, she'll be fine," Beth replied.

"Okay," Grant said. "We'll see how she does in the water; we can always make changes later. I'm not trying to single anyone out, but I take dive safety seriously and ask questions accordingly." He turned to Eric. "Hey, why don't you buddy up with the girls today?"

"Sure!" Eric said, looked at the girls sitting in the bow of the skiff and nodded.

"And finally, Mike, who I've had the pleasure of diving with before, why don't we buddy up this morning?" Grant said. Mike nodded, and Grant continued:

"Do you all have your gear set up? Check your air pressure gauge. You should have at least 3,000 PSI in the tank. Make sure your tank valve is fully open, and test it by placing your regulator in your mouth, take two breaths, and watch the gauge. If the needle stays steady then you should be good to go. Also be sure you have your mask, snorkel, fins, wet suit, and booties. You should have a weight belt setup and there's more weight here in the wooden box if you need it. Also make sure your buoyancy compensator, or BC as we usually call it, is strapped tight to your tank. This morning we're diving at Calabash Cay. Our boat ride will take about fifteen minutes. Let's see, Jeff?" Grant asked, looking at Jeff, hoping he had remembered his name. "Grab that pole there in the bottom of the boat please, and give us a good push."

Jeff did as requested and soon they were in water deep enough for the motor to be tilted down. Newby turned the ignition key and the outboard motor rumbled to life with the acrid scent of two-cycle engine oil. The unmarked channel out of Rockwood was precarious; impassable by vessels other than shallow draft boats, it snaked through mounds of sandbanks, many covered with dark patches of turtle grass. Newby expertly maneuvered Kontiki through the narrow channel, into the deeper water of Stafford Creek, and throttled the motor into high. The skiff thrust forward as the flat-bottomed boat planed and skimmed south across the tranquil water along the Bahamian coast. The sea air blew across their faces, whipping their hair in every direction, while the skiff sped along in the direction of Calabash Cay.

A short fifteen minutes, with the help of GPS, brought them to a sun-bleached orange buoy on the surface that marked their dive site. Grant stepped up onto the flat bow decking, grabbed the buoy with a hook attached to a long pole, and tied off the boat. The boat now firmly attached, Newby switched off the motor. The breeze swung the skiff taut on its mooring.

"May I have your attention, please?" Grant asked. "Who can tell me why we use a mooring and don't just drop anchor. Laura?"

"Um, the anchor could damage the coral reef?"

"Excellent! Well done! This is just one of dozens of mooring buoys we use to protect the reefs. Now, Calabash Cay is one of my favorite dive sites. You'll see a lot of marine life here. Angelfish, groupers, and various reef fish. Also, keep an eye out for eels and lobsters in the crevices amongst the coral heads. Our dive profile here will be thirty-five feet for forty minutes. Returning to the surface at the end of the dive, I want everyone to do a five-minute safety stop at fifteen feet. Make sure you're back on the boat with at least five-hundred PSI in your tanks. Finish gearing up. Go through your buddy checks, and familiarize yourselves with your buddy's dive gear. Secure any dangling gear such as gauges, cameras, or underwater lights to your BC's to protect the coral reef. Please be aware of your body position in the water when you approach the reef. Keep your fins elevated above the level of your head and always maintain proper buoyancy control. When you've completed your buddy checks, sit on the gunwale and we'll all do a backward roll into the water together. Any questions?"

"Wow! Look at the visibility. I can see the bottom!" Laura said with excitement, kneeling down and peering into the clear turquoise water.

"Actually, the visibility is not all that great," Jeff said. "We're not in very deep water."

"That's right," Grant confirmed. "We've had a number of storms with high winds blow through in the last week. The visibility is down to about sixty feet, and it's usually well over a hundred."

"Will we see any sharks here?" Laura asked. "I'm not thrilled to be in the water with them."

"Sometimes we'll spot an occasional reef shark, nurse shark, or maybe a sand shark. But remember these species of sharks are not interested in humans as long as you respect their space. Any other questions?" Grant asked, as he eyed all the divers. "Okay then, let's go diving!"

Soon they were all sitting in buddy teams along the gunwale with gear in place, waiting for further instructions.

"We'll enter the water in buddy teams; stay with your buddy and follow Mike and me. First one to reach 1750 PSI in your tank signals the turnaround, and we'll all head back to the boat together. Let me see an okay sign from each diver and we'll go." Grant looked around the boat one last time to make sure that they were ready. Satisfied, he nodded toward Newby, who was staying aboard as safety lookout, flipped backwards into the water with a big splash. Each diver followed.

Below the surface the aquamarine water glistened and undulated with penetrating rays from the early morning sun. The EcoExplorers descended close to the sandy bottom, adjusted their buoyancy for the depth and began to explore the reef. Laura, Beth and Eric followed Mike and Grant while Jeff and Justin brought up the rear. The reef was populated with various tube sponges, sea fans, and vibrant colored fish. A school of blue tangs passed by as they all stabilized at thirty-five feet, finning along, trailing bubbles from their regulators. They passed many types of hard coral: brain, elkhorn, staghorn, and star. On one of the soft corals there was a flamingo tongue from the mollusk family. Azure Vase sponges grew in abundance on the reef, along with numerous encrusting sponges. In amongst the hard corals, there were some feather dusters and numerous Christmas tree worms.

Up ahead, Grant and Mike stopped, hovering weightless in the water column and signaled for the group to come up and take a look. The girls arrived first and looked over to where they were pointing. There, above a blue hole, was a large barracuda. Its slender shiny silver body hovered over the opening that was only two feet across. However, its cavernous mouth, menacing rows of sharp teeth, and penetrating dark eyes gave it an ominous presence, while it protected the opening to the small blue hole like a vicious guard dog.

The boys caught up and took a look. Then they all turned to cross a sandy patch and a sand shark appeared in the distance, heading in their direction. Laura saw it first and began to turn around when Beth grabbed her arm to calm her. The shark approached and glided through the water underneath them. With a rhythmic twisting of its gray body, it slowly disappeared behind a coral head and was gone.

Beth checked Laura's air gauge and noticed that her air supply was at the 1750-psi turnaround point. She signaled to Grant, and they all turned and headed back in the direction of the moored Kontiki.

Down on the sandy bottom, a large cushion sea star plodded, at a snail's pace, across the sandy bottom, yellow tail snappers schooled above. At an outcropping of reef a stoplight parrotfish nibbled on the coral. Little colorful fish darted about in numerous directions around the reef and in amongst the sea fans. In a small open spot a peacock flounder blended in with the sandy color of the bottom, hid in the open, confident of its camouflage.

Nearing the boat, Mike, Grant and Eric reached the mooring line first with the rest of the group close behind. The girls finned along enjoying the weightless sensation of the dive. Below them studying each coral head Jeff found something interesting and signaled to the girls with a wave of his hand. Laura and Beth descended to each side of Jeff and moved in close to see what he had found. Nestled inside a crevice was a giant green moray eel. Laura watched with great excitement as its mouth opened and closed, revealing rows of sharp jagged teeth while pulling in water to breathe. The eel's two dark eyes seemed small to Laura in comparison to the enormous size of its silky body. The eel rocked back and forth in the current, patiently waiting for night fall when it would rule the reef with its highly developed sense of smell to ambush unsuspecting prey.

Laura backed away and gave Beth the opportunity to move in for a closer look. At the same time, Justin had dropped down and moved in to also see what the others were observing. In the course of exchanging positions, Justin tried to adjust his buoyancy, made a hard downward kick with his fin and caught Laura directly under her chin on the upward stroke. The fin blade continued up her face, dislodging the regulator from her mouth, and stripped the dive mask away, exposing her eyes to the sting of the salty Atlantic Ocean water.

The strong blow to the face left Laura feeling dazed and disoriented. She felt her heart pounding hard, like it was going to explode in her chest; adrenaline coursed through her veins and a wave of panic rocked her body. Unable to see clearly or breathe, her survival instincts kicked in gear and took charge. Laura remembered her training, cleared her mind and focused on the task at hand. In one quick movement, she dipped her right shoulder downward, and swept with her right arm in a circular motion to recover the second stage of the regulator dangling at the end of the hose to her side.

Beth saw Laura in trouble and came to her aid. She reached down and grabbed Laura's sinking dive mask before it became lost in a crevice of the massive coral head. She turned just as Laura swept up the air hose in her hand and stuck the mouthpiece back into her mouth, pushing the purge button to clear out the sea water. Laura drank in the air, filling her starved lungs in deep gulping breaths. Beth placed the mask back on Laura's face and pulled the strap behind her head. Laura turned her head up towards the surface, pulled the flooded mask away from her face and exhaled through her nose, clearing her mask until she could finally see again through salt-burned eyes. Laura, still unnerved by the mishap, was hyperventilating and blowing a cloud of bubbles out of her regulator.

Beth checked Laura's pressure gauge and saw that the needle was in the red danger zone. She unhooked her backup regulator that was clipped to her BC and dangled it in front of Laura's mask. Laura was confused at first, checked her own air pressure gauge, realizing her tank was empty; she switched to Beth's backup regulator. Then with both girls breathing from Beth's tank they swam arm in arm toward the anchor line and began their slow ascent to the fifteen foot safety stop. Five minutes later, they continued to the surface and climbed aboard the stern ladder of Kontiki.

"I thought I was going to die down there!" Laura gasped. She pulled off her fins and dropped them on the deck of the boat. She continued to remove her mask and then stripped off her remaining dive gear.

Beth stepped over and gave her a hug. "Any diver could have panicked in that situation," Beth said, reassuring Laura. "But you solved the issue while at depth like a seasoned diver."

"I don't think I'm cut out for diving!" Laura said, feeling drained and unnerved. "That really freaked me out!"

Grant carefully navigated his way through the growing piles of wet dive gear scattered about the deck in the small skiff. He placed a hand on her shoulder and looked into her bloodshot eyes. "I saw what happened. I'm very impressed how you and Beth worked together as a team. Mike and I were heading over to assist but you had things under control. Kudos to you, Laura! What happened today will just make you a better and more confident diver."

"Thanks!" Laura said and hugged Grant. "Maybe I'll give it another try."

"This is why we always dive together in buddy teams," Mike exclaimed. "As long as you stay close to your buddy, when you find yourself in a bad situation, you'll have someone there to help."

Justin climbed up the ladder and started to remove his gear. "Sorry about the fin kick, Laura. I should have waited until you all had cleared before dropping in like that. Are you okay?"

"I'm fine, just feeling a little shaken. Besides, it wasn't your fault. I guess I wasn't being very observant."

"Well, Beth sure was. I've never seen anyone move so fast!" Jeff added.

"I was just in the right place at the right time," Beth replied. "She would have done the same for me, right Laura?"

Laura nodded her head in agreement and then stared out over the crystal clear blue water of the Atlantic. Composure regained and confidence restored, Laura started to feel a sense of accomplishment.

Grant started the outboard motor and let it idle while Newby disconnected the mooring line from the buoy. Soon Kontiki was skipping across the surface toward the field station. Laura turned and looked at Justin with a wan smile and Justin smiled at her in return. She laid her head back on her dive bag and closed her burning eyes. The cool ocean breeze blew across her face and whipped her blond hair while the skiff raced back to the field station. She was ever so thankful to be a part of the EcoExplorers and surrounded by good friends.

5

PIGEON CAY

Molly McNeil, wide awake since the broom chase, walked barefoot onto the beach soon after the scuba divers had departed. The cool sand massaged her feet and sand fleas tickled her toes when darting out of her way. Thick mats of turtle grass mixed with colorful shells marked the last high tide. Invasive Australian Pines and palm trees towered above her head, their needles and fronds dancing in the breeze. Dried husks from coconuts dotted the white sand. Across Bollard Lagoon a misty fog was beginning to lift and the golden sun started to peek through the defiant clouds. Down the shore, a great blue heron, annoyed with Molly's intrusion, ran a short distance on stalky legs and took to the air with an indignant throaty croak. Doctor flies were out in abundance, but the gentle breeze pushed them inland and away from the beach.

Standing at the water's edge Molly reminisced about a trip years ago when she first met her husband, Mike McNeil, on Andros. Mike was leading a trip for the biology students in the high school class he taught in

Virginia. Molly was part of a group of science teachers with their students from South Carolina. They both found they had so much in common that within a year Mike proposed, they married, she moved to Virginia and they began teaching science in a private school. Not able to have kids of their own, their horses, two dogs, a cat and an endless stream of students became their family.

Molly lifted her arms skyward, arched her neck backwards and stretched. She twirled her dark-brown hair behind each ear, turned and walked to the south. Willie and Loona, always eager for a walk, fell in step behind her. In places, branches from the undergrowth hung over the shore and across the high tide mark. In others, the vegetation grew further back, nestled under the towering trees. Sandy flats were slowly disappearing, covered by the incoming tide. Mangroves with knees like old ribs from a shipwreck protruded in small islands of vegetation. A flock of seagulls landed nearby and began fighting, creating a great ruckus. Little mounds of sand like tiny castles marked the entrance to numerous crab burrows and when Molly's shadow passed over they scurried down and out of sight.

After about an hour Molly returned to the field station to excited voices. Down by the shoreline Jane and Debbie were pointing at something in the water. Mitch and Steve joined in when Molly caught up with them.

"What's going on?" Molly inquired.

"Look, there, right there," Jane said pointing at the dark figure of a ray gliding along in the shallows. Beating its wings in a gentle rhythm it swam along as easily as a shadow crosses the ground.

"That's a yellow stingray," Molly explained. "You can tell by the numerous spots and the rounded wing tips. They can actually change color from dark to light. Don't try to pick one up though; they have a venomous spine near the end of their tail."

"Look at the shell I found, Molly," Debbie said holding the dripping wet shell in the palm of her hand. It was a slender, elongated shell about two inches in length, and had a yellowish tint with pinkish rays. "I saw this one in my book before we left home. I'm pretty sure it's a sunrise tellin from the mollusk family."

"That's right Debbie. You're starting to sound like a marine biologist. That's one of the prettiest shells around. I keep one on my dresser at home and it always reminds me of the sunrises here on Andros."

"Look at the conch shell I found," Mitch said, holding up a large shell. "I tried to blow through it, but it doesn't sound like the one in the lodge."

"I believe you have to cut a slit into the shell in a specific place in order for it to sound," Molly suggested.

"Well, if Mitch doesn't have enough hot air to make one trumpet, I'm sure Jeff does," Jane joked.

"Oh, listen. That must be the boat returning with the divers," Molly suggested, as the distant whine of an outboard motor mixed with happy voices grew near. The sound amplified as the dive boat approached the field station. Heading straight toward shore, then cutting north in alignment with the channel, it maneuvered through the shallows. The sound was momentarily muted when the boat disappeared behind Pigeon Cay and then grew louder when it reappeared on the other side. Grant, at the helm, made the course change and headed straight toward the beach where Molly stood with the others.

"Is he trying to run us over?" Steve inquired as the boat bore down on them.

"No, he's keeping the speed up," Molly explained. "At the last moment, he'll cut the motor and pull the prop from the water. That way he can use the momentum to drift in as far as possible."

Grant, as if on cue, did exactly that and brought Kontiki to rest several yards away.

"How was the dive?" Steve asked.

"Incredible! We saw a reef shark, a massive green moray eel, and lots of blue tangs," Jeff explained, gathering his dive gear and carrying it toward the rinse deck.

"You guys are going to love snorkeling later," Justin said, splashing through the shallows carrying his dripping scuba gear.

"We spotted a yellow sting ray right over there," Jane said, walking out toward the boat. "I can't wait for our snorkeling trip this morning."

"You missed a great dive, Molly," said Mike. He gave his wife a peck on the cheek while standing in the shallow water.

"And you missed a great walk down the beach," Molly said. "So, how did our divers check out?"

"Well, everyone did fine until the end of the dive, responded Mike." Unfortunately, Laura got kicked in the face by Justin's fin. She lost her mask and regulator, but kept her composure and quickly got things under control. Beth recovered her mask and helped her put it back on. They also ended up sharing air from Beth's tank when Laura's ran out. I'm proud of the way they worked together as a buddy team, just like they were trained to."

"Wow! I'm impressed," Molly replied.

Mike turned back to the group in the boat. "Okay. We have about twenty minutes before breakfast. Rinse off your dive gear and leave it on the rinse deck to dry and separate your snorkeling gear out for later. Put the empty tanks in the cart and the ones who didn't bring them over this morning can return them to the dive shop."

"That would be the girls," Jeff noted without missing a beat.

"Ouch!" Beth said, slapping her thigh. "These pesky doctor flies really bite!"

"They're worse when your skin is wet with salty water," Grant explained. "It attracts them like magnets. You'll soon get used to them."

Justin, busy hosing off his scuba equipment, noticed Beth approaching and gave her a good drenching from head to toe.

"Stop it!" Beth yelled.

"Grant just said it's the salt water that attracts the flies. I'm just doing you a favor." Justin flashed her a devilish smirk.

Jeff was approaching and Justin knew he could count on him for support. Beth snatched the hose away from Justin and readied herself to take on the next one who opened his mouth. A deep voice came from behind; she swung around with the water hose at full blast and directed the stream into Grant's face! The smile Beth wore dropped away; a look of deep anguish washed across her face, and a cloud of crimson appeared. Embarrassed, she diverted the hose away from Grant, but the water hitting the rinse deck still splattered onto his sandals.

"Are you quite finished with that?" Grant asked, with a hint of displeasure in his deep voice.

"Sorry, I, I, um..." Beth said.

Grant took the hose away from her and turned it off, then walked in the direction of the dive shop, dripping from head to toe. A squishing sound came with each step of his soaked sandals.

Jeff and Justin doubled over in laughter. Jeff rolled off the rinse deck and onto the sand as Justin stood by, both tormenting her. Beth's crimson-colored face now turned to an outraged blood red.

"I've had enough," she screamed at the boys as she turned the hose onto them full blast. It didn't diminish their laughter. Then with tears in her eyes, she dropped the hose and much to Justin's astonishment, she turned and walked away. Justin was left standing; he scratched his head and wearing a confused look came over his face. Jeff, with eye glasses askance, regained his composure and sat on the sand looking to Justin.

"What gives?" Jeff asked. "That's not like Beth at all!"

"I don't know," Justin said with a shrug. "I guess she's embarrassed. We should knock it off for a while. It's pretty obvious she's been hurt."

"I guess so! We've both had fun teasing each other. But you know, today out on the reef, I was really proud of her. Don't tell Beth I said so, but she could be my dive buddy anytime."

Mike and Molly, who had observed the whole fiasco, walked by shaking their heads. Molly looked into Jeff's eyes, then Justin's. She gazed down at the scuba tanks and the empty cart, then back to the boys' eyes. Without saying a single word, she smiled, turned to Mike, held his hand, and they both walked away.

"You know what, Jeff? Molly can say more with a glance than you can with a hundred words," Justin said.

"Yeah! I almost heard her say tank duty."

Jeff and Justin took over the girl's task and headed to the dive shop, pulling the cart behind them with scuba tanks clanging together. Mitch trumpeted the conch announcing that breakfast was being served and soon everyone was seated in the dining room. Beth ate with Debbie and Jane and glared at Justin.

"May I have your attention please?" Carmen Foster announced from her table. "After breakfast we'll be leaving on our first snorkeling trip. The drink cooler and our lunch will need to be carried to the boat. Wear your bathing suits, and bring your snorkeling gear, sunscreen, hat, and anything else you might need during the day. Any questions?" she asked before sitting down.

After breakfast, with snorkeling gear in hand together with cameras, towels, and other sundry items, the EcoExplorers met Newby, Grant and Nicole by the shore. They loaded the boat named Day Tripper with two large red plastic jugs of gasoline, a blue jug for drinking water, and a huge white cooler filled with Stilly's famous fried chicken and all the fixings. Then they piled all of their gear onboard and took seats. The boat consisted of two large pontoons with a seventeen-foot metal deck attached to the top. Powerful twin outboard motors, mounted on the stern, provided ample propulsion. Wooden seats, with stout metal frames bolted along both sides, allowed extensive seating space. The helm was positioned aft with a small wheel, console, GPS, radio, flare gun, gauges, and a tall white antenna that swung as the boat rocked.

"Okay, I want to cover a few things before we get started," Nicole began in her quiet and gentle voice; the excited conversations died down. "We're headed to Pigeon Cay, which is approximately twenty-minutes away. Please remain seated while the boat is moving. We have dry bags," she mentioned, holding up an example of a rubber-coated bag, faded from years in the sun, "if you don't want your personal items to get wet, store them in here."

Grant started the port motor; a few wisps of blue smoke billowed out and floated away in the southerly breeze. Next he started the starboard motor while Newby pulled the anchor and stored it neatly on the bow. Nicole jumped down into the shallows, pushed the boat into deeper water and then climbed back onboard.

Grant engaged the engines and piloted the boat into the channel close to the mouth of Bollard Creek. As soon as they were in deep water, he eased the twin throttles forward and soon had the boat skimming across the clear water with twin white bubbly trails in their wake. The early morning fog had burned off, and now there were only a few distant puffy white clouds hovering on the horizon pasted on a Maya blue sky.

They arrived on the eastern side of Pigeon Cay: a low, windswept, little rocky island with a few shrub bushes and thick undergrowth. Grant let the pontoon boat drift in close to the shore, near a sandy beach, and switched off the twin outboard motors. Newby picked up the anchor, splashed into the shallows, walked it up onto the beach, and pulled the twin tines into the soft sand.

In the undergrowth hundreds of hermit crabs moved in profusion under the shady canopy. Sage bushes grew in tight patches near conch shells scattered in a line deposited by an unusually high tide. Bits of flotsam jettisoned by unknown passing ships and fishing boats mingled in with mats of turtle grass, small pieces of driftwood, and a few colorful cork buoys. On each side of the shallow lagoon where the boat was moored, large sandbars snaked into the water and disappeared beneath the waves. The beach was sandy-white and covered with a variety of colorful shells. The bright sun baked their surroundings, but the cool Bahamian trade winds made the heat less oppressive.

"May I have your attention please?" Nicole asked once they were all standing in the shallows with snorkels, masks and fins in place. "This is a perfect day to snorkel around Pigeon Cay. The waves are small, and we'll be able to snorkel around the entire island before lunch. I have a vest here for anyone without a wet suit. It will give you the extra floatation you need. Let's try to stay together as a group. That way I can show you some of the more exotic creatures like octopi and starfish."

"Wow! I've never seen an octopus before," Beth said, putting her mask down in the water for a quick peek.

"We'll see them around the cay today," Carmen stated. "Once you know what to look for, you'll be able to spot them easily on your own. The eastern side of Andros is the third largest barrier reef in the world. So, you'll get an opportunity to see a tremendous variety of shallow coral gardens, with the bulk of the shallow formations consisting of elkhorn coral and sea fans."

"I have some fish identification cards here if anyone

would like one," Nicole offered, waving the plastic cards that had pictures of colorful fish with their common names printed by each one.

"That way you can identify any man-eating sharks coming after you, Debbie," Mitch joked.

"Funny, Mitch, but we know better than that. Besides, they only like short boys like you anyway," Debbie retorted; Mitch glared.

"Now, you'll experience a light current here today," said Nicole. "But it'll only help to push us along the eastern side of Pigeon Cay."

"What about fire coral?" Jane inquired. "I understand that a sting from it really hurts."

"We'll see some around on the far side of the cay. I'll show you what fire coral looks like, so you can easily avoid it," Nicole indicated. "But yes, it should be avoided and it does feel like being burned, hence the name."

"My dive instructor in Florida told me that a bearded fire worm is the cure for fire coral," Jeff said in a serious tone.

"How's that?" Jane asked.

"Because the fire worm hurts so much it'll make you forget all about the fire coral," Jeff said smiling.

"Very funny!" Jane replied, not amused.

"Are there any stinging jelly fish around Andros?" Debbie asked.

"We do have a small variety of jelly fish called sea wasps. They mostly come out at night and are attracted to lights. We rarely experience them during the day, and since we won't be diving or snorkeling at night, you'll probably never see them," Grant explained. "You also want to look out for sea urchins around the island, so be careful where you place your feet. Now, let's get geared up and if we all stay close together, I'll show you some of the amazing varieties of sea creatures we have here around Andros."

The bottom was sandy in places, and in others, turtle grass grew in thick patches on the bottom. A gentle current pushed them along the eastern side of Pigeon Cay. The sun shined onto the sandy bottom, and the water, acting like a multi-faceted prism, cast rippled shadows across the white sand. Swimming along the cay with fins, Grant stopped and stood up in the chest-deep water.

"I've spotted an octopus and I'm going to dive under and point him out. I'd like for you to watch and then, taking turns, you can see him under the ledge of the coral," Grant explained.

He dove down to the bottom and swam close to a large coral formation. As he started to point out the octopus, it suddenly swam out of its hiding place and floated right in front of him. They watched the octopus with wide-eyed amazement, riveted by this beautiful and strange creature. Hovering for a moment in front of Grant with tentacles undulating in the current, the octopus changed color from light gray to dark brown, and then slipped down onto the white sand. Scurrying across the bottom, the cephalopod continuously changed colors to match its immediate surroundings. It swam right past Debbie, submerged on the bottom, and when she reached out to see if she could touch it, the octopus inked the water with a large black cloud, shot off at a rapid rate, and was gone.

"Whoa! That was incredible," Mitch said from where he stood in the shallow water. "I've never seen anything like that before. I can't believe how many times the octopus changed colors."

When they had all surfaced Grant said, "I just want to remind you that we're only here to observe the wildlife and not touch. Debbie I know you didn't actually touch the octopus, but please keep this in mind in the future."

"I'm sorry! I guess I just got carried-away." Debbie explained.

"It's okay, we're all out here to learn and we also got to see that common octopus ink the water in a defensive behavior," Grant explained. "They love the turtle grass beds around the island, and are generally the only type of octopus you'll see during the day. Can anyone guess how I found him?"

"It seemed to me like you just happened to look in a hole and there he was," Mitch suggested. "Then you called him out. You must be an octopus whisperer!"

"Well, not exactly," Grant chuckled. "If you'll take a closer look at the hole the octopus came out of, you'll notice a carapace. Octopi love to eat shrimp and crabs, and their holes are generally littered with the remnants of their meal."

Upon closer inspection, they noticed the hole was covered with carapace and parts of shrimp just as Grant mentioned. Further down the side of Pigeon Cay, Laura spotted a small hole filled with shells. She swam down and peered in. Hidden deep inside was another octopus. Excited, she shared her discovery with her friends.

The current pushed the snorkelers along at a gentle pace past small coral formations, colorful sponges of red, green and yellow, and occasionally a black and white crinoid. Many cushion sea stars dotted the bottom with long-spined urchins and a donkey dung sea cucumber. Beth found numerous flamingo tongue snails attached to sea fans and reef; Nicole pointed out a lettuce sea slug. Along the western side of the island there was little current, so they worked harder, kicking with their fins. Soon they circled back to the beach and climbed out for lunch, resting in the sparse shade cast by patches of thick brush growing on the cay.

Following lunch and some time spent exploring the island; they returned to the field station, unloaded the boat and carried their gear to the rinse deck. Jane and Debbie headed back to their cabin for showers. The others stayed behind, rinsing gear and chatting with

Grant and Nicole about the amazing discoveries of the day.

Jane and Debbie yelled from their cabin. Justin, Jeff, Mike and Grant took off running in their direction with the remainder of the group following close behind. Reaching cabin number three, Jane met them at the door with a dismayed look on her face.

"Look," Jane said pointing to the mess scattered on the floor. "Someone broke into our cabin. My purse was emptied onto the floor. My money and passport are gone."

"Anything else missing?" asked Mike.

"I'll have to look through the rest of my stuff to see."

Laura and Beth entered and looked around the cabin amazed at the mess. Their clothes were on the floor, the mattresses were pulled from their beds, and the cabin looked like it had been rampaged by a band of thieves.

"Look at this," Beth said, picking her purse up off the floor. "All of my money is here, every last cent. Maybe we startled the thieves when we arrived."

"Maybe," Grant said, glancing at Beth. "It looks like they came in through the bathroom window where they would have been hidden from sight. We've never had anything like this happen at the field station before. I can't believe anyone on the island would do something like this."

"What's all the commotion?" Dr. Lounsbury asked, ducking to enter cabin three, then seeing the mess.

"Hey Mike! Come look!" Justin yelled from next door and Mike walked over to the boy's cabin. "We got hit as well!" Justin continued when Mike entered, observing all of their belongings spilled onto the floor. "I'm not sure what they could have taken; all of my money's here."

"They took the gold necklace that my grandmother gave me for Christmas," Jeff said. "I hung it on the bed frame before we left so I wouldn't lose it snorkeling. That was the only thing of any real value that I left in here."

"I'm very sorry this happened. I don't know who could have done this, but I'm going to go and call the authorities right now," Dr. Lounsbury said when he walked by the open door, heading back to his office.

"Guess what?" Molly said, peeking into the boy's cabin. "Our cabin has been hit, too."

The rest of the afternoon, they inventoried their belongings and developed a list for Dr. Lounsbury to present to the Andros police. Jeff's necklace and Jane's money and passport were all that seemed to be missing. A local policeman came by and took a great deal of time writing up the report. Before dinner, while Jeff and Justin showered in their cabin and changed clothes in preparation for the evening, they talked about the incident.

"I still can't believe that someone broke into our cabins and took stuff like that," Justin said. "Why would they take your gold necklace and leave Beth's money? I looked at the list of missing items with Mike and there's very little's actually missing. Why would a thief go to the trouble of breaking into all of our cabins, randomly take stuff and leave money behind?"

"Beats me," Jeff replied.

"Unless!"

"Unless what?"

"Maybe the robbers were looking for something else," Justin suggested.

"What else would they be looking for?"

"Look," Justin said, pulling his mattress back to reveal only bare springs below. "The folder with the Hornigold documents is gone!"

6

AN INVITATION

Jeff and Justin walked over and knocked on the door to Dr. Lounsbury's office. Through the screen door they noticed a stranger sitting next to Mike and Molly on a couch.

"Come in," Dr. Lounsbury called, sitting at his desk.

"Hey guys," Mike said when they entered.

The boys stood in the doorway, troubled and without saying a word.

"Come in, come in," Dr. Lounsbury said. "Allow me to introduce Nelson Horton. He's one of our local game wardens.

"Nice to meet you boys," Nelson stood and shook their hands. He was a dark-skinned islander with a muscular build and wore olive-green shorts, sandals, and a light tan shirt with two bulging breast pockets. Dressed more like a local bone fisherman than a game warden, he had a leathery complexion that was centered by a friendly smile.

"Nice to meet you," Justin said, his hand squeezed in Nelson's firm grip.

"We were just reviewing the details of the burglary,"

Nelson began. "I read the police report and I must say, I'm a little perplexed."

"I agree," Dr. Lounsbury added. "We've never had an incident like this before. In fact, the island is virtually crime free. And the items that were taken don't add up. They took money from one cabin and none from another. A gold necklace and a passport. Why would they just choose these items?"

"I think I, I mean we, might have an answer to this," Justin stammered.

Everyone looked at him.

"Do you have something to share?" Mike asked.

"Well, yes. There was another item taken that I think you should know about. I found an envelope with an old hand-written document. It was a manifest describing a treasure and somehow it was hidden in my backpack. Jeff and I decided that it was a prank that gets played here at Rockwood. I hid it under my mattress for safe keeping and now it's gone. We were planning on turning the documents over to Dr. Lounsbury, but first we decided that if we acted like we hadn't found the documents, eventually the prank would fall apart and the truth about who planted the documents in my backpack would come out."

Mike and Dr. Lounsbury shook their heads.

"Well, I guess whoever broke into the cabins found what they came for," Dr. Lounsbury surmised. "I believe that explains the reason for the odd burglary and hopefully that'll be the end of it."

"Well, I guess I'd have to agree with the boys," Nelson said. "If I'd discovered the documents the way Justin had, I would've thought it was a prank, too. How could they have known that the papers were real, or at least real important to someone? Their explanation for the burglary is very plausible. Now the question is, how and why did Justin get the envelope in the first place and who came here to recover it?"

"Did anyone approach you yesterday…or, did you leave your backpack where somebody could have gotten to it?" asked Mike.

"No, I had my backpack with me the whole day. It was with me at the airport and under my seat on the plane. The only time that I can remember it being out of my sight was when we arrived here at the field station. We helped unload Big Blue and got some snacks in the dining room while our luggage and my backpack were stacked outside the lodge. So there was plenty of time then for someone to put it into my backpack."

"Well, since it's not a prank anyone played here at the field station, there must be something you've overlooked. Maybe you sat your backpack down at the airport. Did you go to the bathroom?"

"Bathroom, that's got to be it!" Justin's face reeled with astonishment when the possibility dawned on him. He explained that he had hung his backpack on the door to the toilet stall and had his back to it. Then he described the verbal incident in the airport bathroom between the man with the black mustache named Dr. Stein and the other man, Winfrey. He continued to tell them about the discussion with the taxi driver and how Basky had heard that Winfrey and other strange men had arrived by yacht and had been seen all around the island. "Maybe that man Stein must have slipped the envelope into my backpack when I wasn't looking."

"And I guess you thought that incident didn't need mentioning either," Mike stated, his eyes narrowing.

"No, things got really busy when we arrived here and I kind of forgot about it. I didn't make the connection until just now because I was so blinded by the thought of it being a joke and why would a stranger put such a thing in my backpack in the first place?"

"Maybe he was trying to hide it and thought that he could retrieve it from you later, like he just did," said Nelson.

"Nelson, would you give Basky a call and see what he knows about these characters?" asked Lounsbury. "Maybe you can find out what yacht they're on and where they're staying. See what the islanders might know." "No problem. I'll check into it," Nelson said. Dr. Lounsbury turned to Mike, frowned, and then offered him a tight smile. "A treasure map hidden in a student's backpack does sound like a prank you would pull." He paused. "Right?" Mike smiled, while Molly rolled her eyes and then stared at her husband.

"Well, let's head over and see what Stilly has cooked up for dinner." Lounsbury nodded toward Nelson. "You're welcome to join us."

"Stilly's cooking always sounds good to me," Nelson said.

They all walked to the lodge, where Carmen and Nicole were in the dining room discussing the day's events with Grant and Newby. A line had already formed at the buffet table and generous portions were piled high.

The hot topic for the evening was the mysterious theft in the cabins and Justin finding the old treasure documents. He retold the story again and the conversations turned to speculation about pirates and treasure.

After dinner Jeff lingered behind in the dining room and poured a fresh glass of iced tea from the cooler on the buffet table. He grabbed the last of the dessert cookies when Ooma, Stilly's daughter, walked through the pair of swinging doors.

"Could you bring those dishes into the kitchen please?" Ooma asked, peering at Jeff.

"Sure!" Jeff replied. Inside, Stilly was busy baking breakfast pastries and the warm air had a sweet scent.

"Evenin', Jeff. It's Jeff, isn't it?" Stilly asked.

"Yes sir, you're correct. Your dinner was great. You're quite the chef, Stilly, and your stories around the beach fire last night were awesome. You really scared the girls. Were those ghost stories for real?"

"All those stories are true. If you live on an island like Andros, you don't need to make things up. In fact sometimes we have to tone the stories down." Stilly wiped his hands on his apron and adjusted his fisherman's cap.

"Thanks for dinner," Jeff said, turned to leave the kitchen, and put his hand on the door. He nodded toward Ooma and looked back at Stilly "I'll see you both in the morning,"

"Still interested in learning 'bout Hornigold?"

Jeff stopped dead in his tracks and turned back, the doors flapping behind him. Looking into Stilly's eyes, he saw the usual twinkle replaced with a look of seriousness.

7

JOHN DETTOR

"Hey, what's up?" Justin asked when Jeff entered their cabin after dinner. He was lying on the top bunk reading a novel. "Where've you been?"

"You'll never guess what happened after dinner," Jeff said, closing the door behind him.

"What?" Justin asked more interested in his novel than small talk with Jeff.

"Stilly wants to meet with us in the kitchen after the lecture tonight."

"Why? Does he need help with the dishes?"

"No! We've been invited to meet a man who's an authority on Hornigold!"

Justin slapped his book shut and hopped off the bunk, his feet hitting the floor with a dull thud. "A Hornigold expert? Why does he want us to meet with him?"

"He didn't go into any detail. He just said that it had to do with the documents that you found. This confirms our suspicion that Stilly knew something; remember the way he acted when we asked him about Hornigold after the beach fire last night?"

"I wonder why he wants to talk about it now. He must have heard about the break-in."

"Beats me. All he said was that he wanted all the scuba divers to join him in the kitchen after tonight's lecture."

"The scuba divers, you mean the two of us?"

"Yes, plus Beth, your sister—and Eric, too."

"Eric!"

"Yes, he said all the divers, including Eric," Jeff explained. "And he also asked that we not discuss it with anyone else."

"Hmmm, that's odd! I wonder why the big secret?"

"I don't know, but I guess we'll find out soon enough."

"Well, we better get with it. Tonight's lecture starts in half an hour and we need to find the others."

The boys found Beth first, sitting on the beach deck talking with Grant. Nestled between two large Australian Pines, the deck had numerous benches allowing sweeping views of the lagoon and the boats moored just offshore. The full moon had just risen and the calm water shimmered with silvery-light.

"Beth," Justin said, interrupting.

"What?" Beth asked, displeased at the sudden intrusion.

"We need to talk with you for a moment," Jeff said.

"Can't it wait? I'm busy."

"Actually, I need to prepare for tonight's lecture," Grant said, standing to leave. "I'll see you all in the classroom."

Beth turned to Justin as soon as Grant walked out of earshot. "Your timing stinks, Justin. Couldn't it have waited until I was finished talking with Grant?"

"You mean flirting with Grant," Justin said, and added: "You know he has a girlfriend."

"How do you know?"

"He told me at dinner. She also works here at the field station but is off the island this week visiting her parents."

"So what!" Beth stood and glared. "I was apologizing to him for this morning's drenching with the water hose that was your fault!"

"My fault!"

"You started the whole thing and—"

"Will you both stop it!" Jeff interrupted.

Beth sat back down and said, "So you wanted to talk to me? What is it?"

"Well, you'll never guess what happened after dinner," Jeff said, then sat down next to Beth and filled her in on the planned meeting in the kitchen. "So, you and Laura are also invited along with Eric since we all scuba dive."

Beth's expression changed from disgust to disbelief. "I'm not interested," Beth said.

"Why's that?" asked Justin.

"Why a meeting in the kitchen with only the scuba divers and not in the lodge with everyone?"

"I don't know but it should be pretty interesting meeting an expert on pirates. Maybe he can tell us about Hornigold's treasure," said Jeff.

"Well, what did Laura say about it?" Beth said.

"We're headed to talk with Laura," Jeff replied. "Stilly also asked us to keep this meeting to ourselves."

"Doesn't that seem a little odd to you? Why the secrecy?" Beth asked.

"I don't have an answer for that. Why don't you just go and find out for yourself. If you think the meeting is stupid, then leave."

"Okay. If Laura goes, then I'll go."

They left the beach deck together and walked the short distance to the lodge. In the dining room Mitch, Steve, Debbie and Jane were playing dominoes with Stilly and Ooma. Laura and Eric were sitting on the sofa in the great room, talking and waiting for the lecture to begin. Jeff was telling them about the meeting when Mike and Molly entered the lodge.

"How's everyone doing this evening?" Molly asked.

"Great!" Laura said.

"It's about time for Grant's lecture," Mike said looking at his wrist watch. "Let's all move into the classroom."

On the opposite side of the lodge from the dining room, Grant stood at the lectern in a spacious classroom filled with numerous desks; he shuffled through a stack of papers, organizing himself for the upcoming lecture. Directly behind him was a blackboard, and on the opposite side of the wall was a massive hand-painted map of Andros, dominating from floor to ceiling. Between the map and blackboard a doorway led to a laboratory with a screen door on the opposite side that opened to the back of the lodge and the dive shop. Suspended from rafters, in the classroom, were skeleton remains of an Atlantic bottle-nosed dolphin and a pygmy sperm whale. A large turtle shell hung on the wall next to three windows that faced the beach. Shelves on the walls held sponges, a large vertebra, coral, and various shells. Multiple ceiling fans cast a gentle breeze while the EcoExplorers gathered and took seats for the lecture.

"Evening," Grant said, and the various conversations died down. "Did you enjoy your day?"

"I think the coolest thing was seeing that octopus ink the water!" Mitch said and they all briefly discussed the fun they had snorkeling. Grant began:

"Well, now that you've experienced the ocean along Andros, the topic of tonight's lecture is Coral Reefs: what is a coral reef, what's happening to them around the world and what you can do to be better stewards of the ecosystem." He continued:

"Coral reefs occur around the world in very limited regions, ranging from thirty degrees north to thirty degrees south of the equator. They occupy about six-hundred thousand square kilometers, which is only point two percent of the entire ocean. About one hundred nine countries have coral reefs in their waters, including the Bahamas. In fact, Andros has the third largest barrier reef in the world at one hundred forty miles in length. Over thousands of years the tiny coral polyps, aided by dinoflagellate algae, calcifying algae, and some other organisms that secrete calcium carbonate, slowly build up massive reefs. This production of calcium carbonate, or limestone, is called calcification. Photosynthesis plays a crucial role in the reef-building process."

"Many of the coral reefs are being destroyed, primarily because of human activities. These activities include the dumping of raw sewage, over-fishing, deforestation, air pollution, global warming, ozone depletion, and international trade in coral reef organisms. Also, one of our biggest problems here on Andros is the fertilization of developing crops planted around the island. Unfortunately, efforts to alleviate these environmental threats lack necessary funding for enforcement."

"So, getting back to the decline of the reefs," continued Grant. "With phytoplankton blooms, sediment from farming and sewage entering the water, the amount of available light to the corals is reduced and reef growth is stunted."

Grant continued the lecture for about an hour, discussing the many issues concerning the decline of the Bahamian reefs. After the lecture and discussion were over, Jeff, Justin, Laura, Beth and Eric waited in the classroom for the rest of the students and staff to leave.

"Finally! Let's go," Jeff said, standing in the doorway leading to the lab beside the huge map of Andros.

They quietly walked through the lab, slipped out the backdoor and plunged into the darkness of the tree-covered moonlit night. Behind the lodge the shadows seemed to prowl over them as they worked their way along the wide alley between the dive shop and lodge to the door at the back of the kitchen. Above the screen door a single dim bulb offered little light surrounded by a swarm of insects. In the distance a repetitive clickity-click sound echoed through the night from an automobile speeding across the steel-grate decking on the Bollard Creek Bridge. An occasional bark from a resident dog added to the chorus of croaking frogs and chirping insects.

Justin opened the screen door and entered the kitchen with the others. The interior was dimly lit and the surroundings appeared cold and sterile without the hustle and bustle of Stilly and Ooma preparing a meal. A lingering aroma of baking filled the air with the aid of a small fan perched on a table that oscillated apathetically.

"Stilly? Is anyone here?" Jeff inquired in a hushed voice.

The backdoor of the kitchen opened and a stranger appeared through the doorway. He was a man in his late 60's, with the physique of a man half his age. His shoulder length hair, dark and graying, was pulled back into a ponytail that fell over his collar and down his back. His face was covered with a trimmed beard, and he wore a white T-shirt under an unbuttoned tropical print shirt tucked into dirty shorts.

"Good evening?" the stranger said in a Scottish accent.

"We're looking for Stilly. He's expecting us," Laura replied. "Who're you?"

"I'm Dettor, John Dettor."

Grant then entered the kitchen to the surprise of all. They could hear Stilly behind a closed office door talking on the phone, ordering supplies.

"Stilly will be out in a minute," Grant explained. He introduced everyone, and then Stilly entered the kitchen and invited them back to his office.

Inside the small office two shelves filled with cookbooks lined the back wall above a messy wooden desk and telephone. On the left three chairs lined the wall just below numerous faded photographs and on the right a couch covered with Androsian batik sat just below a window that framed the staff cabin outside across a small alley. Stilly sat in a creaky swivel chair at his desk and the girls took the couch with Eric. The boys claimed the chairs along the wall with Grant. John moved to the right corner of Stilly's desk and avoided stepping on Loona, curled-up on the wooden floor. Stilly began:

"You've all had the opportunity to meet my old friend, John Dettor. I've known John for most of my adult life. We first met here on Andros back in the sixties." Stilly sat back in his squeaky chair. "John asked me if I could gather you here tonight. He has some questions that he'd like to ask, and then he'll be happy to answer all of your questions." Stilly paused, then turned to John and nodded. John took over:

"I appreciate your coming tonight, especially on such short notice. But the events that have taken place today are the reason for the meeting," He sat down on the corner of Stilly's desk. "Grant told me that some documents you had in your possession were stolen today. Is that true?"

"Yes," answered Justin. "They're gone."

"That's very troubling news." said John.

"Why's that?" Jeff inquired.

"The people involved in the theft have caused us a lot of trouble!" John stated.

"Trouble...who are they?" Beth asked.

"Why don't we hold that question for the moment and I think your question will soon be answered," John stated. "First, can you explain to me how you came to be in possession of the documents?"

"I'm pretty sure that they were stashed in my

backpack in the airport bathroom," said Justin. He recounted the lengthy story again, and the argument between Stein and Winfrey, leaving out no details.

"Interesting," John remarked, scratching his beard. "So Dr. Stein missed his flight and then Winfrey showed up and they both left the airport together?" John seemed to be asking the question of himself.

Jeff joined in: "So, you know who these guys are?"

"Unfortunately, yes," replied John. "The large, older man is David Winfrey. He's employed by TSL. The other man is Dr. Shubert Stein. He must've been trying to smuggle those documents that you had in your possession off the island. Dr. Stein is a maritime archaeologist by trade, but unlike his colleagues, treasure hunting is his passion. He's written books on the early pirating activities throughout the Bahamas and is considered one of the top authorities on the subject. TSL hired him to help find the treasure. Both men have big egos and I expect they were butting heads with each other. Dr. Stein, I would imagine, had decided to take the documents for himself."

"What's TSL?" Beth asked, puzzled.

"TSL stands for Treasure Seekers Limited. They're relatively new players in the treasure hunting business. I don't know much about them, but I do know they have considerable financial backing to support their ventures and have been very successful finding treasure in the past. They're here on Andros for only one reason." He paused and looked at the faces riveted on him. "To find Hornigold's treasure!"

"So the documents Justin had are for real and there really is a treasure?" Jeff moved to the edge of his seat and said with excitement in his tone.

John's voice remained calm as he responded. "It's still to be proven about the treasure, but yes, we believe it exists because those documents were penned by none other than Benjamin Hornigold himself."

"Wait a minute. I'm a bit confused," Justin said. "You're telling us that the documents that we had are for real. How's it that you know all of this and why are you telling us about it now?"

"Good question," John said. He turned to Stilly and they looked at each other for a second or two. Something seemed to pass between them. John nodded and turned back to the rest of the group. "Let me tell you a bit of history. As Stilly said, I originally moved to the Bahamas in the early sixties. I started here on Andros years ago working with a handful of pioneering divers, exploring the wall along the Tongue of the Ocean and many of the blue holes here on the island. After the initial discoveries, I moved on to explore other islands in the Bahamas. I've researched the history of these islands and have also written a number of books and articles for various publications on many historical subjects. That's how I know Shubert Stein."

"Wow, that sounds like an exciting career," Laura said. "You must be famous."

"Actually, I've chosen a more secluded lifestyle, unlike my more flashy and arrogant colleague. I do not care for publicity," John explained. "I prefer my privacy."

"You said you were here in the early sixties? Did you know Ross Rockwood? "Jeff inquired.

"Yes, I knew Ross. I probably knew him better than anyone. But enough about the past." He paused for several seconds, as if trying to decide whether to continue, and then said, "let me tell you what I know about the Hornigold documents. I met an antique dealer years ago in Nassau that deals in early historical documents, maps, nautical charts, that sort of stuff. He calls on me from time to time when he's acquired something of historical significance. I've bought a number of items from him through the years that have assisted me in my research and explorations. Recently, he called and offered to sell a very rare and valuable document. He had just attended a private sale held at one of the oldest residences in Nassau. The family that owned the property had lived there for generations and could trace the house and their history back to the early eighteenth century and Benjamin Hornigold. The dealer acquired a number of pieces of furniture and other unusual items. Included was an ornately carved mahogany domed-top sea chest of Jamaican origin. When he examined the interior, he noticed an outline of an edge in the old wallpaper lining in the lid. He took a knife and cut along the edges, and peeled back the paper, revealing a hinged flap. He pried it open. Hidden inside the domed lid was a box fitted tightly into a secret compartment. The dealer slid the box out, opened it, and removed the cloth covering. On top were several letters addressed to Captain Hornigold from England along with one penned by Hornigold but never sent. The handwriting on the letter and his signature matches the writing in the logbook and treasure manifest. Below the letters were ten gold coins, an exquisite thirty-inch pearl necklace, other jewels and personal effects including the captain's log and the treasure manifest. So we had our provenance."

"Provenance?" Laura asked.

"Yes, provenance, or historical proof. It's the source and ownership history that proves the origins of items, or in our case, a logbook and treasure manifest. We have a chest in a house that was Hornigold's, we have letters addressed to him, and we have a sample of his writing that matches the documents in the chest and those on display in museums. So it would be very difficult for anyone to claim that the documents were penned by someone other than the late Captain Hornigold." John paused again, took a deep breath, continued:

"Anyway, the items discovered inside the hidden box far exceeded what he paid for the chest. The dealer sold off all of the other items including the chest to a museum in Nassau but elected to hold on to the log and manifest sheet. Later he sold them to TSL for an exorbitant price. But before he did, he made a copy and, without TSL knowing it, sold the copy to me. He's truly a very good friend."

"So you own a copy of the original?" Justin asked.

"That's correct," John replied. "And that's why I'm here on Andros, to beat TSL to the treasure. They must not, and will not, get to it first!"

"Wow, I can't believe that all of this is happening. There's an actual treasure hunt going on right here on Andros," Jeff said.

"Maybe you should tell us why you asked us here and why you're so determined to beat them to the treasure? "Justin asked.

"Very good," John responded. "You certainly deserve to hear the rest. I want you to understand something very important; I'm not after the treasure for myself. If TSL finds it, they'll just sell it off piece by piece to the highest bidder. I don't want the people of the Bahamas to be cheated out of this treasure, because pirating here in the Bahamas is a part of their heritage. If it's here, then they deserve to keep it here. I want to find it and build a museum to house it so everyone, Bahamians, Americans, whoever, can come and see it. Do you understand?"

"Yes!"

"So, the reason that I called you here…the only two parties that were supposed to have knowledge of the Hornigold documents were the TSL folks and me. Then last night you show up asking questions about Hornigold. Stilly is one of the few that I've entrusted with this information. Naturally, he was quite surprised and contacted me immediately. We needed to find out what you knew about Hornigold."

"So why did you want all the scuba divers here?"

Justin asked.

"Well, that's the other reason for asking you here tonight. Stilly introduced me to Grant when I first started to hunt for the treasure, and he's assisted me ever since on his days off and in his free time. But it's only the two of us and Andros is a big island. TSL has a staff of trained divers, researchers and historians, the most advanced equipment, and unlimited funds. I have no idea what they've discovered so far, but I'm pretty sure they haven't found the treasure. Time's running out and we need help. Grant informed me that some of you have advanced dive experience," John said.

"Jeff does," Justin stated. "And Eric. But the rest of us are pretty new divers."

"Any help would be better than none," John replied, "if we're going to have any chance of finding this treasure."

"Humph." Stilly grunted. "John, I don't like the idea of you involving the students in your treasure hunt. I thought you were only going to discuss the documents... not solicit their help."

"I thought you might object, old friend, but it'll be a grand adventure for them and a great help to us! They look mature enough to make up their own minds." John swirled his eyes around everyone present.

"Humph!"

"Can I ask a question?" Eric said.

"Fire away, son," John suggested.

"Don't the documents describe where the treasure is located?"

"Not exactly. We're pretty sure that Hornigold stashed his treasure in one of the inland blue holes. In fact, that's the crux of our problem. We still have a number of blue holes to search since the location mentioned in Hornigold's logbook doesn't jive with any modern names and the description in Hornigold's papers is pretty vague. If anything, the documents have only helped to narrow our search to the inland blue holes." John stood up and leaned against the wall. "I've tried to take all of these factors into account. I did a lot of research before setting out in search of the treasure. I'll be more than happy to share any of my research with you once you've decided to join in the hunt."

"I don't know," Beth said tentatively. "How're we going to help? We can't just go off and wander around the island on our own."

"That's where I can help," Grant explained. "You can go on outings as long as you're supervised by a staff member from the field station."

"But even with your help," Laura said, "we still have our scheduled programs, and that takes all of our time. We're only here for a week. Besides, Mike and Molly would definitely object to us getting involved."

"Grant and I have a plan that I think might work," John replied. "Let us worry about that."

"What chance do we have of finding the treasure in such a short time?" Laura asked.

"Grant and I have already searched most of the known blue holes and eliminated them from the hunt. With your help and a little luck, anything's possible!"

"Humph," Stilly grunted through a cloud of cherry pipe smoke.

"I think it's going to take a lot more than luck," Eric said. "But it'll be fun to help. I'm not here with a group, so the decision is mine to make. You can count me in."

"Anyone else?" John asked and looked around the room at contemplative faces.

Jeff, Justin, Laura and Beth looked at each other. They didn't know what to do or say. Becoming part of an actual treasure hunt was an once-in-a-lifetime opportunity. But the reason for coming to Andros was to participate in the field school, studying and observing the flora and fauna of the island.

"Why don't you sleep on it tonight and you can tell

me what you've decided in the morning," John said and glanced at his gold watch. "There's no time to waste—"

Suddenly, outside Stilly's office, a loud metallic sound rang out when an empty trashcan in the alley, between the kitchen and the staff cabin, was knocked over. Dogs began to bark outside that roused Loona out of her slumber on the floor.

"Grant, go check and see what's going on."

Grant walked through the kitchen, over to the screen door, and looked out. A man dressed in dark clothes arose from behind the fallen can and ran away.

"Stop!" Grant yelled, pushed the screen door open and ran after him.

Jeff and Justin ran through the kitchen and followed Grant out the door, disappearing into the darkness".

"Grant, where are you?" Jeff yelled.

"Over here."

The sound of splashing water caught their attention. The boys followed the commotion to the water's edge where they found Grant. An outboard motor rumbled to life, and a small inflatable zodiac sped away before anyone could reach the intruder. They stood there and watched the shadowy figure vanish into the darkness across the lagoon.

"Did you see who it was?" Beth inquired breathlessly, catching up with the others.

"No! I couldn't see him in the dark," Grant said.

"I think we were being spied on," John explained in a serious tone when he reached the beach.

"Why would they be spying on us? They've already recovered the documents." said Justin.

"TSL probably wants to find out what we're going to do with the Hornigold information. Although I doubt they heard much of anything tonight." He paused and seemed to be taking time to catch his breath. He paused again, and then said: "I'll be here at breakfast in the morning and if you want to join in just follow my lead and agree to what I offer. In the meantime, I'll expect you to keep our conversations private." John turned, and within a few steps, disappeared into the inky Androsian night.

8

KING KONG

Early the next morning to the south, a cacophony of barking dogs echoed around the grounds as if the fabled Chickcharney had been treed. The barking grew louder as the dog pack approached the cabins. Imperceptible at first, then distinct, was the squeal of a wild boar mixed into the fray of high-pitched yapping and yelping dogs. The boisterous commotion spilled onto the grounds of the field station, zigzagged between cabins, and for a moment, paused outside the thin walls of the boy's cabin. The desperate squeals of a wild boar became more frantic while fighting its pursuers. Then, the rabblement moved on past the lodge and the boisterous commotion slowly diminished in volume while the chase continued northward toward Bollard Creek.

"Someone ought to muzzle those dogs!" Justin moaned, lifting his head from the pillow. He looked at the alarm clock. "Oh well, we need to get up soon anyway. Is anyone else awake?"

"I think the whole island must be awake," Mitch replied from the other side of the cabin. His feet hit the floor, and he shuffled into the bathroom, closing the door.

"Who needs an alarm clock with those mutts around?" Jeff complained, slipping down to the floor from the top bunk.

Justin, Jeff, and Eric quietly packed their backpacks for the upcoming dive and ambled over to the rinse deck. Off in the distance to the east, beyond the line of breakers, small puffy clouds reflected on the surface of the sea. The mirror image was divided in the middle by the deep reddish-orange glow of the soon-to-rise sun. A slight breeze was blowing from the northwest and the sky looked dark and ominous in that direction. The boys looked to the sea and then walked towards the lodge for an early snack. Inside, both Beth and Laura were seated, nibbling sticky buns and sipping orange juice.

"Good morning!" Justin said, entering the dining room and walking to the buffet table.

"Morning," both girls replied.

"Sounded like a fox hunt back home in Charlottesville when the dogs passed our cabin," Laura said.

"Yeah, I know," Jeff said. "They ought to pen them up so we can get some sleep. Although I didn't get much sleep last night anyway." Jeff sat down with the girls, along with Justin and Eric. "Can anyone guess how John Dettor will get permission from the McNeils and Dr. Lounsbury for us to participate in the treasure hunt?"

"Not a clue," answered Justin. "But I've given it some thought and if he gets permission, then you can count me in."

"Me too," Jeff said in an excited voice. "I had to pinch myself a number of times last night to make sure I wasn't dreaming."

"Well, I just don't know," Beth said, wiping her mouth with a napkin and scowling at Justin. "What're we getting ourselves into? I mean we worked hard to get here for this trip, right? Now, you guys want to throw all that away for some treasure hunt that'll most likely turn out to be for nothing. I think this treasure stuff has gone to your head and you have gold fever. You're forgetting why we're here."

"I'm not forgetting why I'm here!" Justin replied in an emphatic voice, looking at Beth, then Laura. "I'm here for the adventure, scuba diving and the fun of exploring the island. This treasure hunt could be the opportunity of a lifetime. I don't know about you, but if I say no, I'll wonder for the rest of my life what I might've missed."

"Yeah, I agree," said Jeff. "My dad once had the chance to dive with Mel Fisher when he was hunting for the Nuestra Señora de Atocha and Santa Margarita shipwrecks when he was my age and living in the Keys. Unfortunately, he decided against it for a higher paying job working as a bait boy on a charter boat. Said it paid bigger tips! He's kicked himself every day since because he did miss out on what turned out to be the adventure of a lifetime."

"Well, you guys do whatever you want," Beth said. "I'm going to wait and see what happens this morning when Mr. Dettor comes by after our dive." She turned to Laura." What about you?"

"I'll join the treasure hunt if the rest of you do." Laura said.

Justin, sitting at the end of the table, noticed the exchange of glances between his sister and Eric. They had talked often since they met, and he didn't like the idea of his sister getting involved with him.

"Morning everyone," Mike said when he walked into the dining room with Grant.

"Let's be ready to go in fifteen minutes," Grant said with sleepy eyes and a head of disheveled hair. "We'll need tanks from the dive shop and cans of gas for the boat. I've chosen a special site for you today—King Kong."

"King Kong?" Beth replied, looking at Grant with a smile.

"Yes, it's the largest of the ocean blue holes around Andros. You could probably get at least nine football fields into it; three wide by three long. It's located farther to the south than the usual dive sites. So we need to get moving soon." Grant turned to Mike and began talking to him while filling a cup with steaming coffee.

Beth lingered for a moment, hoping she would get to talk to Grant, while the others hung their cups on the octopus board and left. However, he was absorbed in conversation, informing Mike about John Dettor. Disappointed, she left and headed to the dive shop with the others. Soon they had their tanks on the rinse deck and cans of gasoline stored on Kontiki, making preparations for the dive.

"Darn this stupid thing," Laura said, while Jeff and Justin carried their gear out to the skiff, splashing through the shallows. "Beth had trouble with her regulator yesterday. Now I'm having problems with mine."

"I used to have trouble setting up my dive gear until an instructor told me to do it like this," Eric said, all too happy to help Laura. "Stand behind your tank with the BC attached, then take your regulator and place it over the valve the way you dive it, with the second stage coming over your right shoulder. Then putting it on the tank is easy because it's in the right position."

"Awesome, that'll be easy to remember," Laura said. "Thanks!"

"No problem. Hey, maybe we can buddy up today!"

"That'd be great."

"I'll suggest it to Grant," Eric said, carrying Laura's gear. She followed and they continued talking.

Jeff filled a square tub with fresh water and put his underwater camera with strobe in the bottom. Then he carried it out to the dive boat, set it down inside and climbed aboard.

"What's that for?" Laura asked. "Won't your camera get wet enough on the dive?"

"The fresh water pads the camera in the boat and after the dive I put it back in to soak. That way the salt water won't be able to crystallize on the o-rings. If that happens my camera could get flooded," Jeff explained.

"Oh!"

Justin was already seated and patiently waiting for the others. Beth was finishing with her gear when Grant and Mike walked over. Mike collected his dive gear while Grant lingered behind to speak with Beth.

"You'll love diving King Kong this morning," Grant began.

"It sounds like a great site," Beth said.

"My girlfriend Mary-Beth loves to dive there. Sometimes we go out together and dive that site with double-tanks. That way we can extend our bottom time."

"Does Mary-Beth work here at the field station?"

"Yes! She's back in the states for two weeks visiting her parents in Nebraska."

"Hey, aren't you guys coming?" Justin yelled from the skiff. "I thought we had to get going?"

Beth turned, grabbed her gear, and waded through the shallows to the skiff. Justin helped her lift the gear over the gunwale and laid it flat on the deck.

"Everything okay?" Justin asked quietly. Beth turned her head, trying to ignore him.

"I don't need to hear you say 'I told you so'!" Beth said and climbed aboard.

"What are you talking about?" Justin tried to ask while Grant walked to the boat. She ignored him. 'Girls!' He thought to himself.

"Okay. Everyone knows the routine," Grant said. Climbing aboard, he took his position at the helm.

Jeff and Justin had already connected the fuel line to

the gas tank, and with a quick push off from shore, they were soon motoring to the dive site. The sun, peeking above the distant horizon, cast a long shimmering shaft of red light across the breeze-rippled water. Back to the west clouds contrasted with the dark sky. The ever-present sea gulls, with their throaty whistles, flew above the boat, hunting for their morning meal. Motoring out of the channel into deeper water, the divers were rewarded with a rare treat: two bottle-nosed dolphins surfaced in front of the skiff and began to surf in the bow wave. Their dorsal fins, with a slippery sheen, would emerge from the water and then disappear again while they rode the bow wave, surfing forward in azure water. The dolphins swam along, their sleek and slender bodies matching the speed of the boat. Soon they moved off, spouted a mist of air into the sky, and disappeared beneath the water.

Navigating to an orange mooring buoy by GPS, Grant brought Kontiki to an idle. Jeff reached out, caught the line, and tied it onto a cleat. The increasing breeze pushed the skiff and it swung around on its mooring until it tugged against the line. Facing northwest into the breeze, Grant switched off the outboard motor and the boat rocked in the growing and choppy waves.

"Okay, if it's all right with everyone, we'll use the same buddy teams as yesterday and—"

"I'd like to buddy with Laura today," Eric interjected, interrupting Grant.

Grant darted his eyes at first Eric and then Laura. "Good idea!" He looked at his clipboard, a half-smile on his face. "Jeff, why don't you buddy with Mike, and Beth, why don't you and Justin buddy up together? If these buddy teams suit," Grant asked, eyeing the divers, "then I'll stay onboard the boat this morning as safety lookout. Mike has dived this site a number of times and will point out some of the unique features of King Kong."

"Wow! Look at the difference in the color of the water," said Laura as she looked out over the boat and into the water below.

"Blue holes are so named for the dramatic contrast between the dark blue, deep waters of their depths and the lighter blue of the shallows around them." said Grant. "They are basically an underwater sink hole and this is one of the largest around Andros and in the Bahamas."

With the three buddy teams ready, sitting along the gunwale of the skiff, they did a backward roll and splashed into the water. Descending to forty-five feet, they finned along the coral outcroppings, past the mooring line firmly secured to its metal pin in the ocean floor, and over to the rim of King Kong. Just as Grant had explained, the oceanic blue hole was immense, but even with the great clarity of water at over one hundred feet, they could not see across something that could swallow nine football fields.

Mike pointed his thumb downward and they followed while he finned over the rim and descended into the depths of the blue hole. Down the wall, small outcroppings of sponges clung to the sides. Fish were abundant, schooling just below the rim. Down to seventy-five feet, Mike hovered and switched on a dive light. Back in a small cavern dozens of tiny red eyes, from shrimps and lobsters, reflected the light and scurried farther back into the darker recesses of the overhang. Several sponges that had appeared dark-colored, due to the filtering effect water has on light, came alive in vibrant reds and oranges when illuminated with the dive light.

Descending further, Mike brought them down a large v-shaped formation. The walls narrowed on either side so that the buddy teams now had to swim single-file. Under a small overhang they passed through the arch, and then the walls began to open wider on the other side. Side by side again, they slowly ascended the inside wall of the blue hole and to the rim. South, away from the boat, they passed large brain corals and immense barrel sponges. More schools of blue tang, yellow tails, and a variety of small colorful reef fish darted about as they swam past.

The dive was interrupted with the metallic sound of a knife tapping a tank. They looked around and saw Eric pointing off in the distance, across the blue hole. There in the gloomy distance were the unmistakable fins of a green sea turtle. Gliding along, it swam near the group of divers. A few small fish followed, dwarfed by the immensity of the turtle. It slowed when it saw the divers, then curious, moved closer and swam right in front of Laura. The dark brown shell had a mottled pattern with wavelike accents. It glanced at Laura through big brown eyes and blinked at her. She reached out to touch its shell while it swam past, but reeled back remembering not to disturb the marine life. Jeff took numerous pictures while the massive sea turtle turned away and slowly crossed the breadth of the blue hole.

Eric noticed an encouraging smile from Laura's regulator-filled mouth while she watched the logy turtle swim deeper into the blue hole. Eric gave her an okay signal to see how she was doing and Laura returned an enthusiastic two thumbs up. He could tell that her apprehension towards diving was slipping away with each kick of her fins. She was now relaxed and breathing easy, enjoying the dive, fascinated by all of the sights and creatures she encountered.

Below, Mike had moved to the bottom and was pointing to a sharp-tail eel illuminated by his dive light. It was approximately two-feet long with a slender gray body covered with white spots and small yellow spots on its head. Unconcerned by the divers, the eel moved along the reef and then slipped into a hole and out of sight.

Mike glanced at his dive watch and realized that they had reached the halfway point of the dive. He signaled upwards using his index finger, circling his hand twice, indicating that it was time to turn around. They headed back north, parallel to the rim of King Kong blue hole.

The unmistakable sound of a revving motor carried through the water. Mike looked up and spotted the bottom of Kontiki in the distance. Grant was signaling him and calling off the dive. Mike unclipped a small orange-colored lift bag and attached it to a reel of line that he had stowed in the pocket of his BC. He removed the second stage regulator from his mouth and placed it below the opening of the bag, pushed the purge button and inflated it with air. He then put the regulator back in his mouth and let go of the small lift bag that rocketed to the surface to signal Grant that they understood and were returning to the boat.

They finned over as a group to the mooring line and ascended to 15 feet for a five-minute safety stop. Mike noticed as they waited that the surface, calm and clear 30 minutes earlier, was now dark and littered with a shower of piercing rain. The stern and boarding ladder of Kontiki rose and fell with each roll of the rising seas.

Laura and Eric were the first to attempt to re-board the boat. Eric removed his fins and handed them up to Grant, then grabbed hold of the ladder and placed his foot on the bottom rung, climbing up and over. Laura lingered for a moment, trying to get her footing on the ladder as the boat bobbed up and down in the peaks and valleys of the growing waves. Eric grabbed her hand and helped her maneuver on board.

Overhead, the sky was darkening and the winds began to shriek. The surface was now covered with rolling, white-capped waves. Jagged streaks of lightning flashed across the sky and boomed with roaring thunder. A dark line of heavy rain loomed ominously in the distance.

Justin struggled but made his way on board and turned to assist Jeff, who handed him his camera and fins and then lumbered aboard. Next, Beth stepped on to a ladder rung and grabbed the side rails with both hands while it plunged her down deep into the water. She held on with all of her might as the bucking boat pitched upwards, lifting her out of the water, then plunged her back down into the water while the boat rolled in the growing surf. Nearly losing her grip, Beth managed to remove her fins and tossed them on board. Then Justin grabbed her by the back of her BC and helped steady her up the ladder. Without hesitation Mike yanked off his fins and handed them up to Justin, then timing the rolls, climbed up as the boat lifted with a following wave.

"Storm's getting worse by the minute," Grant said to Mike. "Weather report is now predicting heavy seas and winds up to sixty miles per hour as the front moves through the area… could be even worse out here in the open."

Grant started up the engine and drove Kontiki up next to the mooring float. "Jeff, I need you to move up to the bow and unhook us." Jeff grabbed the snap hook and detached it from the float and the skiff pulled away, now on its own fighting against the raging seas.

"I need each of you to secure your gear on the floor of the boat and then put on a life vest. Find a safe place to sit and stay down as low in the boat as you can. It's going to be a rough ride back." Grant was shouting in the fierce wind.

He turned the boat heading north with the storm on them. He removed a small handheld VHF radio clipped to his belt and called the field station.

"Rockwood, this is Kontiki, over," Grant said into the radio.

"Rockwood, what's your position, over," said the voice of Newby.

"Just left King Kong and trying to make our way back, over."

"Weather update with small craft advisory with high winds and heavy rains, over."

"Got it," replied Grant. "The storm front is passing over us and we're really taking a beating. We're going to try and make a run for—" Grant's voice was suddenly cut off. A large rogue wave slammed into the side of the skiff, throwing Grant up against the wheel. The VHF radio was dislodged from his hand and bounced on a scuba tank, heading for the water. Mike lunged for the radio but was a split second too slow as he watched it topple over the side and disappear into the stormy seas.

The dark wall of torrential rain had moved quickly in their direction and was now on top of them. Grant struggled to steer the skiff, motoring between the troughs of waves, while lightning cracked and flashed in all directions. The heavy winds from the fast-moving front had whipped up the waves into a fury, making a safe passage back to the field station impossible.

"Mike, I think we need to head for Pigeon Cay. I know the approach is treacherous, even in the best of conditions, but it's the closest landing from this position," said Grant, his eye tracking 360 degrees, looking to spot Pigeon Cay. The view of land was lost behind high waves and blinding rain.

"I don't see that we have any other choice," responded Mike. "We'll never make it back to the field station. It would be suicide to try."

The motor revved wildly when the prop sprang out of the water at the top of a wave and then rumbled again with a spray behind as it drove back into the waves at the bottom of the trough. Then the unthinkable happened: the outboard engine began to sputter, and then died, and the small skiff turned broadside to the waves. Grant tried to restart the motor, but the engine just cranked and failed to turn over. The waves now broke over the gunwale, hammering the side of the helpless skiff. Water pooled in the bottom and the dive gear sloshed back and forth with every motion of the boat. Buckets of cold rain poured down and thumped the heads of the divers.

"I can't believe it," yelled Grant. "I forgot to switch gas tanks. Quick! Grab those paddles beneath the seats and try to keep the bow turned into the waves. We can't take many more hits like that." He opened the door of the console, disconnected the empty tank and reconnected the spare.

Jeff and Justin grabbed the paddles and struggled to maneuver the skiff into the wind. Mike grabbed two gallon-sized plastic bailers, tossed one to Eric, and together began to bail the pooling water from the boat. Their efforts appeared futile with the fierce waves lashing at the skiff, throwing as much water back in as they bailed out. The heavy rains added to the volume and the boat sat low in the ocean.

Finally, the engine coughed back to life and they shot forward into the rolling waves. Pigeon Cay loomed dangerously ahead.

Grant turned to Jeff and said, "I need you to go up and position yourself at the bow. We're going into Pigeon Cay and I'm going to try and drive us in on the leeward side. I need for you to keep an eye out and point to any reefs in the shallows. Got it?"

"No problem," answered Jeff.

No sooner had Jeff taken position when a wave broke over the bow, nearly washing him overboard. Jeff grabbed the bowline and wrapped it around his right hand, holding tight and steadying himself against the waves.

Grant piloted the skiff entering the treacherous shallows from the south. The tide was low and jagged patches of coral knifed through the surface, visible only after each passing wave. Jeff pointed to his right and Grant slipped pass the first outcropping of coral. They passed by a second and third patch when Jeff pointed to the visible reef on their port side, but it was too late. The incoming wave lifted up the boat and slammed it hard down on top of the reef. The bottom of the boat scraped over the coral, ending with a crack as the prop of the motor hit the coral, pulling the propeller off its shaft. The engine whined as it spun without accord until Grant switched off the useless motor. Seconds later, the next incoming wave picked up the skiff and drove it off the reef and forward for the last 50 yards to the beach. All hands held tight and shifted their weight from port to starboard, trying to keep the racing skiff from turning broadside and flipping over in the crashing surf. The skiff came to a shuddering halt as the wave thrust the small boat up onto the sandy beach.

They all huddled low in the middle of the boat while the storm continued to gust with angry ferocity. Close by, lightning struck and shattered the top of an Australian pine that showered splinters down upon them, blending in with the heavy rain. The fierce wind whistled through the trees of Pigeon Cay, and palm fronds blew through the air covering the beach and piled up against the outer hull of the skiff. Waves continued to hammer the transom with a misty salt spray blowing off the water's surface.

Laura huddled close to Eric while Beth held on to Justin, ducking with fright as each lightning flash popped and cracked overhead followed closely by the roar of loud thunder. Hypothermia threatened and total fear took over. They were now held captive by the fury of the raging storm.

9

HUNTING PARTY

As swift as the storm arrived, it spent its grumbling fury and passed to the north, across Rockwood and Andros. The driving rain and gusting winds began to subside and the sky brightened when the sun peeked through the remnants of the passing clouds.

"Is everyone okay?" Mike asked. They were huddled tight together inside the beached skiff.

"Y-yeah, I think so," Jeff said shivering. He stepped out of the flooded skiff and onto the palm-frond-strewn beach.

Grant was already out and studying the condition of the outboard motor.

"The prop is gone," he said, staring at the propeller shaft.

"Looks like we'll be using the paddles," Mike said, appraising the situation.

"Unfortunately! Well, let's unload the skiff and bail out the water. That'll lighten the load and we can drag it to the water," Grant explained. "Dr. Lounsbury will send Newby and other staff to look for us, but we're hidden here in the lagoon. We've got to get the skiff out beyond the cay so they can find us. We'll need to move fast; the tide's shifting and will soon be coming in. Strong currents pour into this lagoon and that will make for tough paddling."

"Let's get with it. Time's a wasting!" Eric said, beginning to bail water while the others removed the heavy scuba gear and piled it on the beach. Then Justin grabbed the other bailer and helped. Beth found a gallon-sized milk jug on the beach, and with a few quick cuts from a dive knife, she put a third bailer to the task.

"Resourceful, aren't we?" Jeff said.

"I'm a Girl Scout, what did you expect!" Beth harrumphed, and they soon had the skiff completely empty of water.

"If I can get three of you on each side, we'll try pushing Kontiki back into the water," Grant said, and took his position at the bow.

With gritted teeth, grunts and groans, they slowly pushed the heavy boat off the sand and back into the shallows, where it bobbed gently in the water. They reloaded the gear and the rinse pan with Jeff's underwater camera, then boarded the skiff. With the paddles, they pushed themselves through the shallows and then paddled, carefully maneuvering their way from the shallow lagoon around a small outcropping of rocks and reef. Half an hour passed before they reached the deeper water beyond the treacherous reefs of Pigeon Cay. The small craft bobbed in the settling but still choppy seas, and drifted with the tide and wind. Grant found a sandy spot and dropped anchor to avoid drifting out to sea.

"Look, over there, there's a boat," Jeff said, pointing, "but it's heading to the south."

Grant collected the binoculars from beneath the console and focused on the distant boat. "It's Newby and Carmen on Flat Foot!" Grant said.

"But they're going the wrong way! Why don't they see us over here?" Laura said.

"They're following Rockwood emergency procedure, heading back to our last known GPS coordinates to begin a search. That would be King Kong and for all they know we may still be at the mooring." Grant removed an orange colored plastic cylinder, about the size of a loaf of bread, from the boats tool box. Inside was a flare gun that he pointed skyward and fired. The flare rocketed into the sky with a jagged smoky-white trail and exploded into a ball of light, then dangled bright beneath a small parachute. Soon the skiff, with Newby and Carmen, turned and headed directly for them. Coming along side Newby tossed a line to Grant and he pulled Flat Foot close to Kontiki while the scent of two-cycle engine wafted in the breeze.

"What happened?" Newby asked. "Your last transmission was cut short." He was wrapped in a yellow raincoat and wore eye glasses that were sea-spray wet.

"A large rogue wave hit us and the radio got knocked overboard mid-conversation," Grant said, and then explained their ordeal on Pigeon Cay and the broken prop.

"Wow! You've had a rough time," Carmen said. "I've got hot chocolate here and Stilly put sweatshirts and towels in the clothes drier. We've got them stowed here in the insulated bags to keep them warm." She handed each person the needed supplies.

"Thank you," said Beth, and slipped the warm sweatshirt over her head. "I thought I was going to freeze to death." She sipped on her hot chocolate and began to dry her wet hair with a warm towel.

"Thanks," said Justin when Carmen handed a warm sweatshirt to him. Smiling faces began to replace the looks of distress.

"Rockwood, this is Flat Foot, over," Newby spoke into a handheld VHF radio.

"Rockwood, over!" came back the voice of a concerned Dr. Lounsbury.

"Divers are safe and adrift on Kontiki south of Pigeon Cay. Prop has been lost, initiating a tow, over."

"Acknowledged, initiating a tow, Rockwood out."

Back at the field station the remaining EcoExplorers and field station staff waited on the beach for their safe return. The sky had cleared and the Bahamian heat and humidity returned, beating down again in full force.

"Here they come," Steve yelled from the beach deck. Navigating the channel was slower towing another boat, but they soon arrived to cheers on the beach.

"Thanks, Newby," Grant said, patting him on the back, as he splashed towards the beach.

"No worries, man," Newby said.

"Listen up," Mike said to the weary divers. "We'll take care of the dive gear after breakfast. Go and get cleaned up and we'll meet in the dining room in twenty minutes. I'll inform Stilly. That should give him enough time to prepare breakfast for us."

"It may take me a little longer than that," Laura said. "I've got to scrub all of the sand and seaweed out of my hair."

Mike shook his head and walked away, holding hands with Molly.

Later, inside the dining room they finished breakfast and told tales of the morning's dive and disaster on Pigeon Cay. Mike sat with his wife and Dr. Lounsbury, recounting the event. Jeff was showing Steve and Mitch the excellent photograph of the green sea turtle he had taken earlier with his digital camera. Grant arrived with John Dettor and approached the McNeil's table.

"Please allow me to introduce John Dettor," Grant said.

"It's nice to meet you. Grant has told me all about your blue hole research," Mike said. Standing, he shook John's hand.

"I've read some of your novels," Molly said.

"Please join us, John," Dr. Lounsbury offered, "and help yourself to breakfast."

"Thanks, I've eaten, but I'll just get a cup of coffee and be right over," John replied.

Sitting at the adjacent table Justin, Jeff, Beth, Laura, and Eric anxiously listened to what transpired while Jeff showed pictures on the display of his digital camera. They were eager to find out how John Dettor was going to convince the McNeils and Dr. Lounsbury to let them join the treasure hunt. John winked at the EcoExplorers when he collected a cup of coffee; he walked back over and sat down.

"John, how's your research coming along?" Dr. Lounsbury inquired.

"Well, it's been tough. I took on this project when the Bahamian Department of Marine Parks accepted a grant proposal of mine to study the inland blue holes here on Andros, measuring the size and depth for the preliminary report. I'm counting the marine life in the blue holes for the more in-depth part of the study. I outlined a budget and a timeline; now I'm facing the deadline, and I have too many blue holes left to explore. In fact, if it hadn't been for Grant's help up to this point, I'd be very far behind, very far indeed!" John sipped his coffee.

"That sounds interesting," Molly said.

"Recently, in a deep cave on Grand Bahama Island, a rare species of fish was found. It was thought to be extinct just like the coelacanth, but Mother Nature fooled us again, and there it was, surviving in the caves. So it might be living in the blue holes on Andros as well. Who knows? I thought I was going to spend some time searching, but just the main thrust of my study is taking up all my time."

"Have you found any fossils or examples of that fish in any of the Androsian blue holes?" Mike asked, interested.

"I haven't found any live samples yet, but I did find some fossils in one of the blue holes; that was encouraging."

"Which one of the blue holes did you find them in?" Mike asked.

"It was far down to the south. It doesn't have a name; I called it Fossil Pool on my report because of my discovery," John explained. "In addition to the fossils, I have chronicled over fifty species of fish and other marine life living and thriving in the various blue holes.

"How many blue holes do you still need to visit to complete your report?" Dr. Lounsbury asked.

"Around ten. Five are small and close to accessible creeks. Three are deep inland and will require extended travel and maybe even require some bushwhacking to gain access. And two are visible on the satellite imaging survey map but don't seem to have any accessible roads nearby. They are the last on my list because of the logistical challenges involved." John paused and sipped his coffee. "I really need additional assistance from local divers if I'm going to complete this project. If not, I will simply run out of time and money."

"The McNeil's dive!" Grant boldly suggested. "And they're here with four certified student divers. Along with Eric, that makes seven that could possibly help you out this week."

"Hold on there," said Mike, his voice stern. "We're here for a marine biology course. We can't just change our schedule and drag our students into a blue hole survey." He raised his eyebrows and glanced at Molly. Molly responded to his look with a half-smile, and then said:

"Well, I think it would be an interesting opportunity for the EcoExplorers to help John with the survey, even if it was just for a day. They would gain some real fieldwork experience. We could spare a morning, or one afternoon, couldn't we dear?"

"What about the four students who aren't certified scuba divers?" Mike asked. "That means half of the group would be left out."

"Any of your staff and students are welcome to join us," John suggested. "However, the majority of the work is underwater and would be difficult to accomplish without scuba."

"Mike, if your divers would like to join in for a day, I'd be happy to allow Grant to go along and supervise, if it would make you feel any better," Dr. Lounsbury graciously offered. "In fact, I'll even make a Rockwood van available. We can't pay for the fuel, but we can allow the usage."

"That would be wonderful!" John said

"I've dived a number of these inland blue holes through the years," Mike said, skeptically. "They're not the safest places on Andros to dive, and I'm not sure I want our students submitting themselves to unwarranted dangers. I also have their parents to consider as well. I expressly outlined their daily activities. I'm not sure their guardians would approve of the change."

"Listen to yourself!" Molly said to her husband. "Whatever happened to the spirit of the EcoExplorers? I think the kids could gain some real hands-on experience, especially with someone with the knowledge and experience of a marine biologist like John, and it'd be beneficial to their education. I say you explain things to the EcoExplorers. They're smart; let them make up their own minds."

"I'd make sure that they limit their depth to recreational scuba diving limits and stay above the halocline," John said, hoping to further ease Mike's concerns.

"Okay! I'll explain the situation to them, and if they say yes, I'll do what I can to support you," Mike said.

Mike then stood to address the students and

explained John Dettor's proposal. Finally, he introduced John, and then John carefully outlined the project and sat back down.

"What's on our agenda today?" Steve asked, interested in the blue hole project.

"We're planning to drive to Fresh Creek and visit the Androsian Batik Factory," Molly said. "And then drive north to explore the caves at Morgan's Bluff."

"Morgan's Bluff! Count me in," Steve said, and his buddy Mitch agreed.

"What's there to see in the blue holes?" Debbie asked.

John explained the work in detail and the travel on the old logging roads. The more he talked, the less the others liked the idea. Soon the non-divers had decided not to get involved in the blue hole survey. But the scuba divers were all in.

Jeff, Beth, Laura, and Justin looked at each other in amazement as the reality of the moment set in. They had received the required approval to become part of John Dettor's dive team with no mention of treasure.

"I can't thank you enough," John said to the McNeil's. "This'll certainly help to expedite our search, I mean my survey."

"Well, by the look of those faces, I should probably be thanking you. I've never seen them so excited about a science project before," Molly said.

"We'll be leaving right after breakfast. So we'll need you to gather up your gear from the boat and meet us at the dive shop in about fifteen minutes," Grant explained.

Dr. Lounsbury walked into the kitchen to ask Stilly to prepare separate lunches for the divided groups today. Stilly had overheard the discussion and was already far ahead of him. Before him on the counter were several boxes of food.

Grant and John were making preparations in the dive shop when Justin, Jeff, and Beth arrived, hauling their dive gear. Eric and Laura arrived soon after and helped load the van with scuba tanks. The rest of the EcoExplorers headed towards Big Blue parked behind the dive shop. They climbed on board, sat on the wooden benches, and headed off for their day's activities.

"Now that we're alone I want to brief you on where we've been so far," John said as Big Blue rumbled down the highway with excited voices trailing behind. "Come on back in the shop and let's take a look at the map."

They followed John, walking past rows of tanks stacked high on a concrete floor. On the opposite side, a large air compressor sat idle in front of tall tanks that would bank the high-pressure air before being cascaded into the smaller tanks that divers would use. They turned to the left and entered a workshop filled with tools: a drill press, table saw, and various shovels, rakes, and hand tools. The gaps in the rustic boards, and translucent roof, allowed enough light to seep in to see clearly in the back, as they gathered around a wooden work bench made from native woods. Grant cleared the bench of tools and placed them on the floor. John unrolled multiple maps on the table, shuffled through a few, and then found what he wanted. He placed hand tools as weights on the ends to keep them from rolling up on their own.

"Okay, let's take a few minutes to familiarize you with the island and the blue holes that we've searched to date," John began, taking off his hat and wiping the sweat from his brow. "As you can see, I have with me various maps of the island. On top is a map from the 1920's. I had it reprinted on clear Mylar, so we can overlay it on a copy of an earlier map of Andros from the 1700's. Then, this map here." He pulled out another from the bottom of the stack. "It was printed when the island was being logged in the 1950's and 60's. They were not meant to be permanent roads and were abandoned after the trees were harvested. It's these old logging roads that give us access to the inland blue holes. Without these roads you could imagine how difficult it would be to try and cut a path through miles of swampy forest while hauling dive equipment to each and every site. I took the maps to a drafting store on the mainland and had them enlarged in size, or reduced to equalize the various scales. That way, the outline of each map overlaps with only minor geographical variations.

"What's this map on top?" Jeff asked.

"That's a satellite image of the island," John said, shuffling the maps. "It shows every blue hole on the island, big and small. We printed a clear overlay of it and now you can see, when placed over the map of the logging roads, how we'll access the remaining sites. The ones marked in red are the locations we've already explored."

"That's so clever," Beth said, looking at the maps. "It appears that you've already been to most of the blue holes."

"We have," John said, pointing to the maps. "We started with the blue holes that most closely met Hornigold's description and then moved out, a process of elimination."

"How did Hornigold and his men find access to the blue hole?" Justin asked.

"The native Lucayans had cut paths through the jungle that led to a number of the blue holes for fresh water. The Spanish, who first explored the island in the 16th century, discovered the great abundance of fresh water in these blue holes and limestone pools. Sailing ships from that time on would stop at Andros to fill their water barrels with this precious commodity. It was described in Hornigold's logbook." John paused and looked hard at Justin. "Didn't you read it?

"I read every word and I guarantee you there was nothing written about his journey into the jungle," Justin replied, looking perplexed. He turned to Jeff, who said:

"That's right. I'm sure of it. The logbook only described his arrival and hiding the treasure in the blue hole. There was nothing describing how he got there."

"You're sure of this?" John asked, amazed.

"Absolutely! But we did notice that there were a few pages that looked as if they had been torn out of the logbook."

"That doesn't make any sense," Eric suggested. "How can the pages describing Hornigold's journey be missing from the original but not in your copied version. Didn't you say last night that the documents you obtained were copied from the originals?"

"That's right," John replied.

"Maybe Dr. Stein or someone else from TSL tore the pages out for their own use or to keep anyone else from knowing how to get to the treasure," said Jeff. "I mean, if Stein was willing to hide the documents in Justin's backpack then wouldn't it be just as likely that he might tear the pages out and stash them somewhere else to keep them from Winfrey?"

"Or maybe Winfrey tore them out himself and has them locked away in a safe place," added Laura.

"It certainly seems plausible. Any of these possibilities could very well be true," said John. "Except for one thing. I can still remember the last conversation that I had with my old friend when he handed me the copy of the Hornigold documents. He told me while driving me to the airport in Nassau that he was returning a favor for helping him out in the past. Apparently, I had bailed him out from financial disaster by buying things when he really needed money. He reassured me that the documents that he had given me were complete. Refusing to elaborate on it, I was puzzled, but now I think I know what that favor was. He removed the pages of the Hornigold documents before selling the originals to the owner of TSL. Do you know what this means?"

John was gleaming with delight; the crow's feet in the corners of his eyes wrinkled. "I believe we're the only ones who have a copy of the complete documents and the only ones with directions to the treasure." A new wave of excitement washed over the group. "Now this certainly levels the playing field," said John.

"Maybe you've already eliminated the right location," Eric added. "I've dived a few of the inland blue holes with Carmen. Once you drop below the halocline, the visibility is so bad that you can't even see your hand in front of your face. The sediment on the bottom is thick. How could you see in the muck? It's like diving in a cup of Stilly's coffee?"

"We used an underwater metal detector," John answered. "And we probed into key areas and came up with nothing. I've been an underwater archaeologist for years and even though my techniques may not be text book, under the circumstances, we've been as thorough as we can with our limited equipment and the help we've had to date." He paused, seemed momentarily lost in thought, then smiled and continued:

"Okay, now, let's talk about today's hunt. We're going to this blue hole here." John thumped a finger down on the map. "It's called Lignum Vitae, named after the trees that once thickly inhabited that part of the jungle. It's a large blue hole and within our general parameters for searching. I also have a digital camera, so you can document any marine life you see during our dives for the Bahamian Department of Marine Parks and to share with the McNeil's and Dr. Lounsbury. Here is our field report showing what we've discovered so far and photographed in the other blue holes. Please familiarize yourselves with this information so you can accurately account for the marine life that you see in each blue hole. Now unless anyone has any other questions we should get started."

"I thought we were going on a treasure hunt," said

Beth with a confused look on her face. "Why are we bothering to take pictures of the marine life?"

"I must have forgotten to tell you. What was discussed with the McNeil's and Dr. Lounsbury is true. I'm actually doing a survey of the blue holes but also looking for treasure at the same time. I do have a contract with the Bahamian Department of Marine Parks and this is in part how we're able to fund the expense of the treasure hunt; it's also the perfect cover on an island of nosy people, and not too many islanders care about our time spent researching marine life on the island. I just didn't inform the Marine Parks' folk sort of like I didn't inform Dr. Lounsbury and the McNeil's of everything that we're hunting for," John flashed a sly grin at Beth.

They loaded the remaining scuba gear in the van along with lunch, ready to depart. John and Grant hoisted double scuba tanks into the van along with a metal detector and other gear.

"Those don't look like what we use," said Laura.

"The doubles?" responded John. "Yes, they are different. The extra air allows Grant and me the maximum bottom time, and the manifold, with an isolation valve, is for extra safety. Should we ever have a catastrophic failure of one tank or regulator, we can isolate it and use the other. It's like diving with two complete systems for technical diving," John explained.

"Neat!"

The van pulled onto the highway and headed south to Lignum Vitae Blue Hole. It seemed like it had been a week since they were on the highways of Andros, so much had already happened at the field station, and they had only been on the island for two days. On both sides of the road, the thick Androsian forest loomed above the road. A few homes, painted in bright yellows, blues, and greens, dotted the roadside as they passed by. The construction of most of the structures was makeshift and more shack-like than home-like. In the yards, a few abandoned boats sat unused and in a desperate state of disrepair. Goats were penned near homes, and dogs seemed to sprout from every yard.

After twenty minutes on the Queen's Highway, they turned right on an unmarked logging road. The road, crudely paved, was full of potholes, and cut a straight path through the thick Androsian jungle. Shallow creeks filled with stagnant water flanked both sides of the unkempt road. Within a mile, they turned right again onto an even narrower road. It was more of a path, overgrown, and judging by the vegetation, used very little. Vines and branches scraped by the sides of the van; clipped vegetation flew into the open windows and landed on the floor in small growing piles of greenery. Soon they turned again and found an old faded red pickup truck with big balloon type tires blocking the road. A stout man approached, carrying a rifle, and walked up to Grant on the driver's side.

"Road's closed today," the man said abruptly. He wore a red bandanna around his head, and an aged-white mustache carpeted a thin upper lip. A large shark's tooth dangled loosely around his neck on a thick gold chain. He was shirtless, with a muscular build, and reeked of an acrid scent. Turning away without waiting for a reply from Grant, he walked past the old truck blocking the road and began to talk with another man further up ahead. He wore a wide-brimmed felt hat with a brown band and sported a hideous scar on his arm.

"Grant, back up and get us out of here, now!" John said. Grant quickly tossed the transmission into reverse and got them out fast.

"What's wrong, John?" Jeff asked as they tumbled down the road and away from the guards.

"Those are TSL employees." John's voice was low, rushed.

"What?" Beth asked, looking behind her nervously.

"You mean TSL's at the same blue hole we were going to dive this morning?"

"Looks like it," John replied.

"How can you be sure?" Eric asked. "I mean, just because someone has a gun, that doesn't mean they're out here looking for treasure. Does it?" "I'm positive," John said with a sober look on his face, "I recognize one of the men."

"I recognize him, too," Justin responded, "and that black Jeep Cherokee further up the road is probably the one we saw at the airport two days ago."

"Which man do you recognize?" asked Laura.

"That one, wearing the hat," said Justin pointing.

"Who's he?"

"Winfrey!"

10

TURTLE HEAD

Grant reversed the passenger van off the sandy lane and then drove forward along the narrow pothole-filled logging road. The jungle-like vegetation growing close and thick on each side of the road screeched along the sides and top of the van. In several places pine branches hung low over the road and scoured the van like giant brushes in a car wash. In the distance a statuesque great blue heron fished in marshy shallows and cocked its head sideways, as if preparing to catch a frog for breakfast.

"So that was Winfrey?" asked Eric while Laura craned her neck for a better view. "What bad luck. I can't believe he's at the same blue hole we'd chosen."

"Yeah, and I wouldn't want to mess around with that guy holding the rifle either," stated Jeff.

"I definitely didn't like the looks of those guys," added Beth, who was sitting between Jeff and Justin on the far back seat. "Maybe this treasure hunt isn't such a good idea after all."

"I think it was just a coincidence that they showed up

here," said Justin. "I certainly doubt we'll run into them again."

John sat quietly in the passenger's seat, resting his elbow on the edge of the open window; with his chin propped on his thumb and index finger, he momentarily stared off into the distance as if deep in thought.

"What in the world was Winfrey doing here today?" Grant asked.

"How should I know?" John responded abruptly. "He was supposed to be off the island."

"How would you know that?" Beth inquired.

"Because I have the coconut telegraph of the islanders on our side and they inform me each morning of the whereabouts of Winfrey and the TSL yacht. This morning, it was spotted anchored near Mastic Point. But then Winfrey turns up at our chosen site," John explained.

"I think Justin's right and it's just a coincidence," Grant replied. "What else could it be?"

"I don't know," John said.

"Who's helping you?" Laura inquired. The air blowing into the van puffed her sandy-blonde hair into her eyes and she quickly twirled it behind an ear. "I thought you and Grant were the only ones looking for the treasure."

"We are. But I have old friends here on Andros. They're sort of my watchdogs. Nothing much happens around here that they don't know about."

"So you have people spying on TSL," Eric asked.

"I know their whereabouts, if that's what you mean. But no, I don't have anyone hiding in the dark and tripping over trash cans to listen in on their conversations!" John answered. "Please keep in mind that these people are searching for a real honest-to-goodness treasure, probably worth millions of dollars, and they do mean business!"

"Well, maybe we're making a big deal out of this.

Perhaps Winfrey changed his mind and left part of his crew behind. Your friends saw the yacht heading north to Mastic Point and assumed that Winfrey was on board," Grant concluded.

"Maybe," John said in a more relaxed tone. "That makes sense. I'll talk to them later today and see what they say."

"You know, I think it's time for a reality check here," Beth said, feeling a little unnerved. "What're the chances of us running into these guys again? If they mean business, then I don't want any part of it, especially since they're carrying a gun."

"The chances of us running into them on this big island again are remote with the added protection of my friends. I'll just make sure that they keep a closer watch on them," John explained. "And, as far as the gun goes, out in these parts with wild boar…it's actually not a bad idea!"

"John, do the islanders know what you're hunting for?" asked Laura.

"No, like I explained earlier, as far as anyone knows, I'm conducting a legitimate blue hole survey for the Bahamian Department of Marine Parks. If the islanders knew I was looking for treasure, then they would be watching me instead of Winfrey. And as far as David Winfrey is concerned, with the Rockwood logo on the van, a group of students was going to dive a blue hole this morning and our presence was no reason for any alarm."

"So, I'm a little confused," said Beth. "Why would your friends on the island keep an eye on Winfrey if the only thing they think you're doing is surveying blue holes?"

"Because I asked them to. The simple fact is they are good friends and they don't like Winfrey and his gang. They know he's up to something and they won't rest until they find out what it is. This is their island, their home, and they don't like pushy strangers coming in and creating problems."

"I guess that makes sense," said Beth. "The cab driver who drove us from the airport to the field station said pretty much the same thing."

"You mean Basky," said Justin.

"Yeah, he said that he and his friends would watch out for us. He must've been referring to your friends, John!"

"It's a big island with a small population," added Grant. "I'm quite sure they're one and the same."

"What if Winfrey finds the treasure today?" Laura asked.

"Nothing we can do about that," John responded, "but we can tell from their movements if they find the treasure. If they never return to the location of Lignum Vitae, and remain on the island, then we can probably check that one off our list, too."

Reaching the Queen's Highway, Grant stopped the van and John pulled out a map from his backpack, unfolded it and began to scan the squiggly lines. "Looks like the next blue hole we haven't explored is Turtle Head. This site's not exactly on the top of our list, but it's close by and we'll need to search it sooner or later. Maybe we can still salvage the day."

"Sounds good to me," Grant said. "Just give me the directions."

"Hang a right here and I'll tell you when to turn," John said.

Grant turned the van southward and with the increased speed on the smooth road more air wafted into the van and quickly made conditions tolerable in the Bahamian heat. He then fumbled with the tuner to the van's radio, and soon the lyrics for Tom Petty's song, Runnin' Down a Dream, spilled from the speakers and filled the van. After a few miles they came to the opening of an overgrown path, cutting east and nearly invisible from the main road. Grant slowed and turned onto another abandoned logging road. Initially, the van blazed through the opening, its bumper like a bulldozer mowing down small saplings. Then, past the entrance, the lane widened. Two narrow trails, like footpaths, headed off into the distance, framed by the usual thick vegetation. In the middle of the road, plants formed a knee-high mat that scraped under the bottom of the van. In places, poisonwood trees grew so close that the van's side mirrors clipped leaves as they passed by. The sun, now almost directly overhead, baked down on the non-air-conditioned van like the heat in an oven, and the air, with only a whisper of a breeze, was suffocating as the van crept along at a snail's pace down the pothole-filled trail.

John reached down to the left side of his seat, pulled a small lever and swiveled the passenger seat so he was facing the kids. "So tell me, back in the dining room when the McNeil's were discussing your involvement, I heard them mention the EcoExplorers. Can you tell me what they were talking about?"

"That's the name of an outdoors club Mike formed outside of the school," Laura began. "He got tired of the school's fear of liability, so he formed his own club. But it's not just about doing sports, like if you go rock climbing, it's to catalog the plants on a cliff, or spelunking is to search for bats and stuff. So it's like sports with a purpose."

"Mike seems like a sharp fellow," John said.

Beth propped her elbows on the back of the seat in front of her and explained: "Everyone likes the McNeil's. Mike's also a scuba instructor and offers courses to students through a local dive shop in Charlottesville, Virginia. Molly is big into horseback riding. She has three horses at their small farm in the country. The McNeil's are kind of like parents but way cooler! Mike's our biology teacher back home and Molly teaches science to the other students that are with us this week. And somehow they manage to make it all interesting."

"I see," John said. "Sounds like a club I would have joined at your age. So you're from Virginia and know each other from high school, I gather?"

"We'll, we've kind of grown up together," replied Laura. "Justin's my fraternal twin; I'm five-minutes older. Beth's been my best friend since elementary school and we play on the same soccer team. And, Jeff, well he's a computer nerd that happens to be an okay scuba diver." Laura smiled as Jeff playfully thumped her head from the back seat.

"Nothing wrong with being smart," John said, winking at Jeff.

Grant had reached a crossroad. He swiveled his seat forward, stopped, and looked both ways. He turned to John, waiting for directions. John looked at his map and thumbed to the right like a hitchhiker catching a ride. Off in the distance, near a marshy creek, the canopy of pine trees was covered with snowy egrets squawking in a throaty chorus. Jeff zoomed in with his digital camera and took a few pictures through the side window of the van. Soon, coming to another path, Grant turned left, drove into a small circular clearing and parked the van.

"Looks like the end of the road," Grant said. He opened the door and stepped out.

"End of the world, you mean," Laura jested.

"Looks like a scene out of Jurassic Park," Jeff joked.

"Yeah, I feel like there should be a band of velociraptors waiting to pounce on us from the bush," Justin said.

"Look!" Beth said pointing. "I can see the blue hole over there"

John stepped out of the van and opened the side door. The EcoExplorers piled out and hiked down a narrow path to the edge of the water. The blue hole cut an oval circle out of the vegetation with a large V-notch in the side where they stood. The notch, observed from the air, made the blue hole look like a turtle's head. Large mats of algae covered the surface like the pattern on an intricate quilt and the pungent marshy aroma reeked of rotting vegetation. Along the narrow rocky shoreline, colorful orchids grew in profusion, adding contrast to the monochromatic greenery. Birds, hunting for insects, chirped in the undergrowth while the hot sun angled higher in the sky.

"It kind of looks like a dark and watery eyeball without a pupil," said Eric.

"Some of them are small like this one," John said. "I haven't dived in this one yet. Who knows, maybe we'll be the very first to explore it."

"Wow, that's a pretty cool thought," said Justin "Maybe you can write it in your report that the EcoExplorers were the first divers to ever explore Turtle Head!"

"Ouch!" Laura said slapping her arm. "These doctor flies never let up."

"Better put on your wetsuits for protection. Set up your gear, stage it near the water's edge and then we'll have a short dive briefing. You may get a little toasty before you dive, but at least the flies can't bite through neoprene," John explained and they headed to the van.

"Spider!" screamed Laura as they walked back along the short path.

"Relax, Laura," Justin said, but she was already at the van.

John stopped, looked and then asked Justin, "Would the irony that the spider built its web on a spider lily be lost on your sister?"

"Definitely!" Justin said. "Ever since she was little and got tangled up in a spider web with a big spider crawling on her face, she's hated them."

Soon they wiggled into wetsuits and carried their

scuba gear from the van to the edge of the blue hole. Justin brought the underwater metal detectors and several dive lights for John, while Jeff fiddled with his digital camera and its underwater housing. Grant got a cooler out of the back of the van, began to hand out ice cold water bottles and then lugged the heavier double tanks he and John would use to the blue hole. Laura gave the spider lily and its eight-legged inhabitant as much space as the narrow path allowed. John stepped to the edge of the blue hole with an inflated inner tube that had a small dive flag attached to the top on a short flexible pole. He uncoiled several feet of yellow line that was secured to the inner tube and attached the opposite end to a small bush. Then he feathered out a larger coil of line that had a weight on the end. Finally, he reached in a small bag, removed an underwater strobe light, switched it on, attached it to a red mark on the line and tossed it into the blue hole. The line sank out of sight and pulled the inner tube several feet off shore, where it bobbed like a cork.

"What's all that for?" Laura asked.

"It's easy to get disoriented in a blue hole, so the strobe light marks the exit. It's not such a big deal at this one, but if you surface on the opposite side of a big one, it's no fun having to swim across it to get out. I generally just use a compass, but Grant told me only Jeff dives with one," John explained.

"Yeah, that makes sense."

"Okay, if I can have everyone's attention for a dive briefing, we can get started," John said, in a louder voice so that Jeff could hear from the van, where he was still fussing with his camera. He wiped sweat from his brow while Jeff walked over and set his gear down on the grass next to the blue hole. A sound like a bell rang out when Jeff's regulator clanged against the aluminum tank. "All right," John continued," let's all first descend down to the halocline. Since you haven't seen one before, you'll find it very interesting. It should be at about sixty-feet. Then—"

"What's a halocline," Laura asked. "I remember you mentioning it to Mike in the lodge, something about how you would make sure we stay above it."

John nodded and explained:

"Andros is honeycombed with tunnels that run beneath the island to the sea and they're filled with salty seawater. Here in the blue hole you have about sixty-feet of fresh water sitting on top of the sea water below. The halocline is the mixing zone between the salt and fresh water. Some of these blue holes are influenced by the tides. Out in the ocean sometimes whirlpools can form, but inland I think only one called Pimlico has a whirlpool. Those whirlpools are probably a fairly good explanation of a Lusca monster that has generated some of the island folklore that doesn't really interest me. Anyway, there's hydrogen sulfur in the halocline, so you'll get a little dose of a rotten egg taste if you venture in."

"Yuck!" Laura said and scrunched her face with disgust.

"Now, the halocline is several feet thick and the sun does not penetrate through it. I'll be below it with Grant, the dive lights and the metal detector," John continued. "Grant said he has seen you all dive and suggested buddy teams. So I'd like Eric, Laura and Beth to buddy-up as one team and your search depth will be twenty-five feet. Jeff and Justin, you are the other team; your depth will be forty feet. Once you have seen the halocline, fin over to the wall as a group. I want one team to go right and the other left; circle the entire blue hole at your assigned depth. Meet up back here where the strobe light is blinking. Look for signs, anything that might resemble something that has been lowered into the blue hole. Some blue holes have shelves that can run in sporadic patterns along the wall. So don't be squeamish if you need to probe into the muck with your hands. Jeff, I'm so glad you have your camera and please take lots of pictures. And Beth, here's my digital." John passed the camera to her. Contained in a clear plastic waterproof housing, it had a few knobs and dials sprouting from the sides and top. "Please take this on the dive and get a few shots of any marine life that you see. It's quite easy to use in automatic mode and with the bright sun today you can just use the available light and ignore the strobe." He gave Beth a quick lesson in the camera's usage, then turned to the group:

"Any questions?"

"Yes! Can we get started?" Jeff said, with shiny rivulets of sweat coursing down his face. "I'm about to roast."

"Let's go," John replied. "We'll all feel better in the water."

Soon they all splashed in. Below the surface the sun's rays streamed down toward the bottom in shimmering, wavy patterns. The cool water found its way inside the wetsuits and was a welcome change from the heat on the surface. Descending down the wall, greenish-brown mats of algae, jostled by the turbulence of rising bubbles, jettisoned tiny particles that soon made it look like a snowstorm in the water. Reaching sixty-feet, they floated above the halocline that stretched across the entire blue hole like a huge undulating brownish cloud. Beth ventured in a short ways and Jeff took her picture.

John and Grant turned on their dive lights, descended through the halocline, and disappeared from sight. Twin trails of bubbles streamed toward the surface, marking their approximate locations, as they breathed through their regulators. Large bubbles coming from the depths resembled jellyfish, undulating and dancing in the water column. Then, as the air bubbles continued to expand forever upwards, they broke into showers of smaller bubbles and rushed towards the surface. Beth, Laura, and Eric finned over to the wall, ascended to twenty-five feet, turned right and began to tour the blue hole. Jeff and Justin turned left, ascended to forty feet, and finned effortlessly along in their weightless state, enjoying the dive.

Under a ledge, a small scattering of stalactites sprouted from the rock, hanging as a vivid reminder of the vast amount of geological time that had come and gone. Since stalactites only form in dry air, their silent creation happened during the past ice age when the water level in the oceans, and blue hole, was much shallower. Jeff hovered close, framed the amazing creations with his digital camera, and the flash of twin strobes recorded the image. Justin signaled okay to Jeff with his hand and they continued along the wall.

Beth, Laura, and Eric finned along the wall on their circuit. Laura and Eric held hands as they looked for any interesting details. Beth snapped a picture of the twosome as she familiarized herself with the workings of the digital camera. In the distance, a large ledge jutted out from the wall with large mats of greenish-brown algae draped over it like a blanket thrown over a sofa. Eric moved in for a closer inspection. He fanned with his hand, into the muck, stirring up plumy clouds of dark brown sediment. The visibility was reduced to nearly zero, so Laura and Beth watched from a distance. Eric was soon inside the large brown cloud, and all the girls could see were his yellow fins. For a moment, even his fins disappeared into the opaque water, then he reappeared and turned both of his hands upward, signaling, "Oh well, nothing."

Far below the halocline not a single ray from the bright Bahamian sun, hovering overhead, could penetrate through the depths of the thick halocline. John and Grant descended, with the craggy wall in sight. Dive lights stabbed into the inky blackness surrounding them. Out in the gloomy distance a blind cavefish cruised along, oblivious to their presence. At one hundred twenty-five feet, they found the bottom nearly level, dotted only with a few scanty peaks and valleys. In places, a thick layer of brown sediment covered large fallen branches and disintegrating leaves. Grant switched on an extremely bright light and hovered several feet above the bottom. John switched on a strobe light attached to a short stick and thrust it into the mucky bottom to mark the beginning of their search. Then he started to make sweeps with the metal detector from the inside wall of the blue hole outwards; always staying close to the wall, their plan was to circle the entire blue hole and return to the strobe. Grant hovered above John and held the powerful dive light.

Several minutes into their search the metal detector rang out with an audible beep and blinked its red light, announcing that there was a metal object below. John stopped, unclipped a scoop from his BC, and began to dig into the detected area. Inches into the thick and gooey sediment the distinct ribbed pattern on the side of an old soup can emerged from its silent grave. The dive light reflected on the shiny surface as he reburied the worthless trash and moved along, finishing his sweep. Later, they ran into a passage leading back into the bowels of the island. Water was flowing out of the opening, signaling that the tide was coming in. The current was strong but not so fierce that it kept John from inspecting the opening. Checking his air gauge first, he entered the wide mouth of the cave, which sloped gently downward. Within several yards, he came across the ghostly remains of a dolphin's skeleton. The poor mammal must have lost its way in the cave from the ocean, got disoriented, somehow managed to get this far, and drowned. The image of the animal's final breath made John reconsider going any further, so he turned around, and he and Grant finished their sweep around the blue hole when they returned to the blinking strobe.

He gave the thumbs up, signaling the end of the dive, and they both headed to the surface.

Beth, Laura, and Eric completed their circuit, running into Jeff and Justin near the strobe light on the yellow line. All of them ascended, slowly. At fifteen feet, they hovered for five minutes, giving their bodies the necessary time to disperse the extra nitrogen from their bloodstream that they acquired while at depth. When they broke the surface, the sun beat down on them and the audible chorus of insects and birds surrounded them like an orchestra.

"What a dive!" Beth said, excitedly floating on the surface. "The halocline was so incredible—and a little spooky, too."

"I wonder what it's like below?" Laura asked of no one in particular.

"Dark, murky, and not very interesting; you didn't miss anything," John said as he and Grant finned their way over to the shore.

The divers reached the V-notch and began to climb out. Soon the edge of the blue hole was stacked with tanks, fins, masks, dive lights, a metal detector and cameras. John talked about the junk can he found, the blind cavefish and the unfortunate demise of the dolphin.

"Ouch!" Beth said, smacking a doctor fly.

"Yeah. They seem to especially love wet skin. We better load up and get underway before they make lunch out of us," Grant suggested.

They carried their gear along the path back to the van and stacked it inside. Then they wiggled out of their wetsuits and stacked them on top of the mound of scuba gear. Laura retrieved the inner tube with the dive flag for John and avoided a certain spider lily when she walked along the path. The van rumbled to life, filled with the aroma of wet neoprene, and they began to make their way along the narrow road.

"Well, now you know what a blue hole is like. We've eliminated one more from our list, and I say that's good progress for the day. Can I count on all of you to work with me again tomorrow?" John asked.

"I'm in," Jeff said, and the others nodded in agreement.

The return trip back was filled with stories of their blue hole experience. Justin handed out sandwiches from the cooler Stilly had packed earlier. Laura sat close to Eric. Beth and Justin talked about their experiences on the dive and Jeff talked nonstop to John about travel, treasure, blue holes, and dive sites in the Bahamas. Grant plugged his iPod into the van's sound system and soon they were all singing along to the sounds of Jimmy Buffet.

The singing abruptly stopped when an explosion, like a gunshot, caused the van to lurch sideways.

11

SABOTAGE

Grant quickly brought the van to a stop.

"What was that?" screamed Laura.

"That was the sound of trouble," Grant said gloomily. "The front tire just blew out." He climbed out of the van and checked the condition of the tire. Several strips of rubber littered the road and the van was sitting on a bare wheel rim. "Dr. Lounsbury thinks he saves money with the cheap retread tires, but I disagree. I think we're in for a long hike out of the jungle!"

"Why?"

"We don't have a spare."

"No spare?" Laura asked, astonished.

"Well, we have a spare, but it's flat, I mean, it has a slow leak and there's no way to pump it up out here in the middle of the jungle," Grant said in frustration. "We've all been too busy lately at the field station, and Newby was supposed to get it repaired."

"Can't we call for help on your cell phone?" asked Laura.

"What cell phone? There's only limited service here

on Andros and there're not many requests for coverage out here," Grant said sharply. They all climbed out of the van and looked at the damaged tire.

"I've got an idea," Jeff said, walking back to the side of the van. "I might have it in my save-a-dive kit."

"Save-a-dive kit?" Laura asked.

"Yeah! You know, stuff like O-rings and tools so simple repairs on your scuba gear can be fixed on-site so you don't miss a dive," Jeff replied. Fumbling in his dive bag, he removed a small plastic box, opened the lid and rummaged through the contents. "Here it is!"

"What is it?"

"It's an air chuck for car tires that attaches to the low-pressure inflator hose from your regulator. We could put the spare tire on, fill it with air and drive until it gets low again. We still have plenty of compressed air remaining in the scuba tanks. So, maybe it'll be enough to get us back to Rockwood." Jeff smiled broadly, a bit pleased with himself.

"We could give it a try," Grant said, walking to the back of the van for the tool kit. Soon, with tire iron in hand, he crawled under the van and began to remove the spare from its berth.

"Come on Justin. Let's give them a hand," John said. "How's it that you happen to have an air chuck with you Jeff?"

"I keep one in my save-a-dive kit for bicycle tires and to inflate inner tubes when we go tubing on the James River back in Virginia. It beats using a hand pump," Jeff explained.

"Wasn't it Laura that called you a computer nerd?" John asked.

"Well, she's just jealous because I'm smarter," Jeff said.

"I heard that," Laura said, and flashed a scowl at Jeff.

Soon they had the van jacked up and the spare in place, and using Jeff's air chuck, filled the tire with enough air to begin their journey to Rockwood. Their progress was slow along the overgrown road; they had to stop often to refill the tire. But they made it back in the late afternoon, pulled up to the dive shop and began to unload their dive gear.

"Now remember, no discussion whatsoever with anyone outside this group about hunting for treasure or about running into the people from TSL," John said, looking from face to face. "Everyone understand?" He stepped out of the van. "Keep your conversation to diving the blue hole and the search for marine life. Show them the pictures that you took today with the underwater cameras and that's it."

Molly could be seen through the front window walking towards the van and was only steps away.

"How was your blue hole dive?" Molly asked, greeting the adventurers.

"It was great," Beth said. "A long drive but well worth the trip. We got to see the halocline and I took some underwater pictures of the blue hole with John's digital camera. I'll show them to you in the lodge later."

"We had a flat tire on the way back…a blowout actually," Justin added, pulling an empty scuba tank from the van. "It was a little touch and go there for a while when we found out the spare was also flat, but Jeff came up with a great idea." Justin then explained the rest of the story.

"Sounds like you all had a real adventure," Molly said. "Glad you made it back in one piece."

"How was your day, Molly?" Laura asked.

"We had a very nice outing. The Androsian Batik Factory is always fun to visit and then we explored the caves at Morgan's bluff. That was Mitch's favorite place; he climbs like a monkey." Molly chuckled and sipped water from a bottle. "Oh! I bought you all a gift, too."

"Gift! What gift?" Laura asked, excited.

"Well, I left a package in the lodge behind the bar. So

go and see for yourselves," Molly said.

"Thanks, Molly," they chorused, continuing to unload the van. Soon they all dispersed in various directions to shower, hang wet suits on the rinse deck to dry and prepare for the evening.

Later, Laura and Beth, freshly showered, entered the lodge before dinner and found Carmen and Nicole sitting on the sofas talking with Mike and Molly. Newby, on top of a stepladder, was busy changing a bulb in the light fixture hanging overhead. Debbie was sitting at the bar, her hair completely braided in cornrows with colorful beads on the ends. Jane was still in the process of having her hair braided as a lady with practiced hands worked while humming a tune. Both girls wore colorful batik dresses with seashell and starfish patterns.

"Wow! Check out you two!" Laura said. "You look like natives of Andros."

"We bought the dresses today at the batik factory," Jane explained. "Mrs. Henry, these are our friends, Laura and Beth."

"Nice to meet you girls," she said with a friendly smile. Her face was weather-worn from years in the sun and her gray hair was braided. "I'm almost done here, want to be next? It's fifty-cents per braid, as many as you want."

"Um…maybe one or two," Laura said feeling obligated.

Beth pulled a brown paper package from behind the bar, opened it up and peered inside. The colorful patterns of Androsian batik fabric stared back at her. She pulled out printed cotton dresses with large island flower patterns and similar button down shirts for the guys. "Wow, these are really beautiful," Beth said, and both girls thanked Molly.

"You're most welcome," Molly said. "You may want to try them on for size so we have time to exchange them before the dance Wednesday night."

Laura and Beth left the lodge and walked to their cabin. In the alleyway between the kitchen and the staff cabin they noticed Stilly feeding the five field station dogs their supper.

"I think the island look is kind of growing on me," Laura stated.

"I can't believe I just heard you say that! You who wouldn't be caught dead wearing clothes like this," said Beth, laughing. "At least that's what you said at the airport when we arrived."

"I know," Laura replied, "but, after a couple of days here, like they say, when in Rome do as the Romans do, or in our case like the Bahamians do! And I liked the way that Jane and Debbie looked dressed with braids."

"That's pretty cool," added Beth.

"I can't wait until the dance," Laura continued. "I hope Eric will like the way that I look in my new island dress with the one or two braids I told Mrs. Henry I would get."

"You seem to be really interested in him."

"Yeah! I'm beginning to like him," Laura said.

Laura slipped into her navy blue dress with large white island flowers over her head and looked into a full length mirror on the back wall. She seemed to approve.

"Wow, you look great!" said Beth.

"You, too," Laura said admiring the similar dress in green Beth had just slipped on.

"Maybe Justin will even notice me Wednesday night."

"I thought you liked Grant and were mad at Justin."

"Justin acts differently to me when Jeff's around; like with that water fight fiasco yesterday, he's more apt to pick on me," Beth explained. "Grant, I like, but he has a girlfriend who lives here on the island. Kind of the same problem you have getting interested in Eric."

"I didn't expect to come to Andros and like a guy, but I could probably fall for him, which kind of scares me, since we are only here for the week," Laura explained. "Now as far as Justin goes, just remember he wouldn't pick on you if he didn't like you."

"Think so?"

"Know so! Wear that dress Wednesday night and get your hair braided…maybe an orchid in your hair to finish the look. I'm sure Justin won't be able to take his eyes off you," Laura said.

Beth turned, smiled into the mirror, spun left, then right, to let the dress fan out around her legs as the vision of the dance filled her head.

Back in the lodge the girls got a few braids before dinner while the rest of the EcoExplorers chatted about the day's activities. After dinner Carmen suggested they all walk down the road to get ice cream before the evening's lecture in the classroom. Out on the Queen's Highway, in front of the field station, the procession advanced south toward a small store. Up front, Mike and Molly walked with Carmen and the other staff members. In the middle, Beth was talking to Mitch, Steve, Jane and Debbie about the blue hole and the things they saw. At the back, Justin, deep in thought, silently and slowly walked along with Jeff by his side.

"What's eating you?" Jeff inquired. "You've been quiet ever since we got back from the dive today."

"I don't know," Justin said.

"Could you possibly be a little more vague?" Jeff responded. "Let me guess! You don't like Eric hanging out with Laura. Right?"

"Yup! You got it."

"Okay. So they're walking on the beach. Dude, you have a gorgeous sister, and you know guys are going to be interested in her. If I was Eric, and she liked me, I would definitely give up ice cream to go walk on the beach and be alone."

"Oh, I know. I'm not really worried about them not getting ice cream or walking on the beach," Justin said. "She was just recently in that relationship with Kevin and I think she may be rebounding on Eric. She's just opening herself up to get hurt."

"And what are you going to do about it?" Jeff asked.

"Nothing, absolutely nothing," said Justin. "There's not a thing that I can do but worry. Hey come on," he said, abruptly changing the subject. "We better catch up with the others."

Up the road they reached a small rustic store with a wide-covered porch. Everyone except Beth was already eating ice cream; she was playing with a basket full of puppies.

"Aren't they cute, Justin?" Beth said. She cuddled a small black puppy with brown spots that was licking her face. "This one looks like Loona."

"They all look like the field station dogs, only younger," Justin said while the others left to walk back toward the field station.

"I wish I could take them all home with me."

"Don't you want any ice cream?" Justin asked.

"Sure! I just got distracted by the puppies."

Justin bought two ice cream sandwiches and handed one to Beth.

"Thank you," Beth said.

"You're welcome. Those braids in your hair makes you look like an island girl."

"Thanks!" Beth said, and smiled. "I'm sorry I snapped at you last night. I thought you were playing another joke on me about Grant and his girlfriend."

"It's okay," Justin said. "I guess I shouldn't have started that water fight. I've been a little uptight since we got on the island…I mean with everything that has been going on since we've arrived. Has Laura said anything to you about Eric?"

"A little," Beth replied.

"Beth! You're best friends, come on, girls share everything," Justin said.

"She likes him, Justin. Anyone can see that," Beth

explained. "It's not a big deal."

Later that evening, in the classroom, Carmen lectured about the island's botany. Surprisingly, for such a detailed topic, she made it interesting and held their attention for most of the forty-five minute lecture. Near the end, John Dettor entered the classroom and took a seat in the back. Carmen continued:

"Now, as you know, part of your group went out today to dive a blue hole and Beth took photographs with a digital camera. We have the digital projector setup, and if Beth is ready we can take a look before we complete the lecture for the evening."

Beth turned on the digital projector and Stilly clicked off the lights. They went through pictures of gearing up and preparing for the dive. Then Beth showed several pictures of fish, the large mats of algae hanging on the walls of the blue hole and Eric's yellow fins sticking out of the cloud of muck.

"Now my last shot is of Laura. You can see her at sixty-feet, half hidden by the halocline and—"

Beth's words were cut off as a loud explosion rocked the field station, followed by a strange jet-like roar, then a repetitive banging and thumping sound. Each EcoExplorer and the field station staff jumped, startled by the sudden disturbance. Grant yelled for help and his cries could be heard coming from the direction of the dive shop. Stilly fumbled with the light switch and a few desks crashed to the floor as the classroom immediately emptied.

Inside the dive shop, a cloud of dust hung in the air with a deafening hiss coming from the back room. A hose had ruptured from the dive compressor and was violently venting air as it menacingly smacked the wall. The flailing hose would duck toward the floor and send a fresh cloud of dust from the bare dirt, then rise and smack the wall again—and again. Grant was on the floor and a large beam from the wall pinned him down. Jeff,

Justin and Newby grabbed the beam and hoisted it off of him. They gave Grant a hand up; he stumbled outside, coughed a few times and brushed the dust off his clothes. John Dettor grabbed a board and pinned down the hose while Eric shut off the valve.

"I was just beginning to fill the scuba tanks," said Grant. "The storage bank was low, so I fired up the compressor and it just blew. The metal tube leading into the bank of storage bottles smashed into that beam, and before I knew it, I was on the floor with it on top of me."

"What's going on?" Dr. Lounsbury asked, out of breath, having run from his office.

"Compressor blew a tube and knocked a beam out of the wall," Newby explained as Grant regained his composure.

Dr. Lounsbury turned to Grant. "Are you all right?"

"Yeah, nothing's broken. Just scared the heck out of me," Grant said.

"What would make it blow out like that?" Dr. Lounsbury asked.

"I don't know," Grant said. "I'll have to take a look to see what happened."

"If you need parts we'll have to order them first thing in the morning so we can get them in by this coming weekend. The field station will be at full capacity next week, all scuba divers, and we cannot be without the compressor," Dr. Lounsbury explained.

"I'll let you know if we need anything," Grant said.

After the excitement had died down and most of the group had headed off, Justin, Jeff, Grant, Eric and John stayed behind in the shop. Grant inspected the compressor and rubbed his head in disbelief.

"You know what?" Grant said.

"What?"

"Look at this." He pulled up a length of tubing that ran from the output on the compressor to the first large tank in the storage bank. "This tube was crimped right here where it blew apart," Grant said as he pointed it out to the others.

"Why would there be a crimp in the tube?" Justin inquired.

"Don't know. Shouldn't be," said Grant "There's no reason for that hose to be damaged unless something hit it with the edge of a heavy object and it certainly hadn't been hit by one of us."

"OK, so it wasn't hit or crimped by one of us. That can only mean one thing," John said from the back of the group. "Someone came in here today when we were gone and sabotaged the compressor. Someone is trying to keep us from diving!"

12

RAT CAY

Early the next morning after breakfast, the EcoExplorers loaded Day Tripper for their scheduled outing. Nicole and Carmen readied the boat and scurried around the field station, busy tending to their morning duties. Mike and Molly loaded their field lab materials and Jeff fussed with his digital camera and underwater housing. Newby had just finished installing a new propeller on Kontiki that had gotten lost in the shallows of Pigeon Cay during the dive trip to King Kong. When all were aboard the boat Newby waded over, started the two outboard motors, maneuvered out of the channel and soon had them skimming along the surface of the water. The day, clear of rain clouds, and the ocean, calm with a mirrored surface, reflected the sun as it peeked from behind billowy white cumulous clouds soaring above the Tongue of the Ocean.

Eric and Laura sat together with their feet dangling over the bow and chatted about snorkeling, and Beth and Justin discussed the dive they would make later in the afternoon. Jeff talked to Nicole about underwater photography and scuba diving. Mike and Molly told stories to Carmen about past trips. Newby, quiet and alone at the helm, stood firmly planted, expertly piloting the boat toward their destination.

"Look!" Debbie said, as a bird hovered over the water.

"Oh! Wow! That's an osprey," Molly said.

The osprey dove almost straight down and made a great splash into the azure water between the boat and shore. Then with several flaps of its large wings it took to the air with a fish dripping wet and wiggling in its talons. Flying with the fish head first, to streamline it for wind resistance, the great bird headed toward shore to perch and enjoy its meal.

"That was so cool," Mitch said. "That would've been a great picture, Jeff."

"I know, only problem is, once my camera is in the housing it's only good underwater. Pictures above water would just be blurred," Jeff explained.

Arriving at a sandy beach, Newby cut the twin engines, and the boat glided into knee-deep water. Nicole jumped out, plunged into the shallow water, and with mooring line in tow, soon had the boat firmly anchored into the sandy beach; she waded back, splashing her way through the shallow water.

"Welcome to Rat Cay," Nicole said. "Let's unload the boat and stage our gear on shore, up by the tourist trees."

"Why do they call them tourist trees?" Jane inquired.

"I know that one. If you look at the bark, it's peeling, and the skin of the tree is all red, like a sunburned tourist," Debbie explained.

"Oh I get it."

"So if you don't want to look like a tourist tree, put on plenty of sun block today," Nicole suggested. "Especially the back of your necks that will be exposed, uncovered by your wetsuits." She grabbed a large cooler packed with their lunch, took it off the boat and waded back through the knee-deep water with Carmen and the others. Newby decided to stay on Day Tripper and get a nap, enjoying a break from the field station work and the ongoing list of things that needed fixing.

The small island was not much higher than the shallow water that surrounded its windswept shores. Up close to the tree line, dried turtle grass, washed up from the last high tide formed a line that ran around the cay on either side and continued out of sight. Doctor flies, tenacious and sneaky, swarmed around the group as they changed into their wet suits for snorkeling. Up in the forested area, hermit crabs crawled en masse, so numerous that the entire forest floor seemed to undulate from their sheer numbers.

"Those crabs kind of remind me of spiders," Laura whispered to Beth who rolled her eyes.

"If everyone will settle down," Molly asked, "we can begin. Mike and I have brought students here for years, and this is one of my favorite sites to snorkel. Today, now that you've had some practice, we're going to begin our reef fish survey that we'll be working on the rest of the week. REEF is an environmental educational foundation that was started by Paul Humann. As some of you may have noticed in the lodge, Paul's books are invaluable tools to assist in identifying all of the marine life that you will observe here on the Andros reefs." Molly held up a set of the Reef Coral, Reef Creature, and Reef Fish identification books. "Now, the surveys are quite simple. I have dive slates here for you to use and on each is a long list of the fish names. What you do is snorkel along, identify and then list the fish that you see. If you don't know the name of a particular fish, just look it up on these cards." Molly showed groupings of colorful cards, held together in rings, depicting a color image of each fish and its common name. "Once you know the name of the fish, you make a mark on your slate. Note if you saw one; a few would be from two to ten; many would range from ten to one hundred; and if you see them in abundance, more than one hundred, just mark accordingly. Then tonight, in the classroom, we'll fill out a scansheet and mail them in to the REEF organization. All their data is available on their web page."

"So," Molly continued, "what I like to do here, and the cay is small enough to allow it, is to circle the entire little island. You should have a snorkeling buddy. Anyone is welcome to follow Mike and me, or you can venture forth on your own if you like. The area around the cay is very shallow, so you can stand up just about anywhere. Remember not to stand on the coral. You should find octopi here like around Pigeon Cay, lots of fish, sea stars--and watch out for the spiny sea urchins. Don't forget to count the fish. Try to be back to the boat in about ninety minutes and then we have a special lab planned for you."

"Lab! Sounds like school work to me," Mitch said.

"Well, you've never seen one of my field labs. I'm sure you'll be amazed and surprised at what I'm going to show you today. By the time you get back from snorkeling and see the lab, you'll be amazed at what you've missed," Molly explained

With masks, fins, and snorkels in place, each of the EcoExplorers entered the shallow water and finned off in different directions. Mike and Molly were out in front, leading the way around the cay. Despite years of bringing groups to this location, they found that each trip was a new adventure, and they never tired of the underwater wonders that they discovered and shared with others. It also reminded them of the time when they first met at the field station and the beginning of their relationship.

This trip was no different. With trained eyes, they both spotted octopi peeking out from beneath crevices in the rocky bottom, sea stars, spiny urchins, goatfish, and on a level plane, they found three sting rays partially covered in the sand. Pausing, they estimated the numbers in a large school of yellow goatfish, made a notation on their slate and continued. If they could hear underwater, they would've heard each other laughing with delight at the wonders before them.

The EcoExplorers saw most of the same creatures the McNeil's saw and spotted a flamingo tongue snail on a sea fan. Eric pinched Laura in the leg and they stopped, stood in the shallows and splashed water into each other's face, laughing hard. Laura later spotted a flounder on the sandy bottom and looked to her fish identification slate to find its name. After eliminating a few possibilities, she noted it as a peacock flounder and moved along, looking for more fish.

Beth and Justin, very interested in the marine life, took their time and observed carefully. They finned over to the far reef, or shelf, and peered down into the deeper water. Sponges and sea fans covered the craggy terrain. Justin dove beneath the waves about fifteen feet and cruised along, enjoying the silent serenity of the depths. Beth followed and found she could hold her breath for longer than he could. Back closer to the shore, they found Elkhorn coral and a sand shark glided along the sandy bottom in relaxed motions, undisturbed by their presence. Fish were abundant here, and they spent several minutes counting the various species and identifying their names and making notations on their slates.

Jeff finned along with Carmen and Nicole, more interested in photography than counting fish. Debbie, Jane, Mitch and Steve followed the groups, making a few free dives to the bottom. Then Debbie and Jane moved closer to the shore and Mitch and Steve headed further out so as not to recount the same fish. After more than an hour the EcoExplorers met back at the beach where the boat was moored. Eating lunch in shady places, they discussed the highlights of their recent assignment and all of the fish species they had found.

"Okay," Molly said when lunch was over. "I have gathered a clump of tubular thicket algae here for our lab. So gather around and I think you'll find this very interesting."

She sat on a large beach towel and began to work. Wearing green rubber gloves, she opened the cover to a clear plastic pan, partially filled with water; a large clump of algae was on the bottom. She took the algae and gently pulled it into little pieces until she found what she was looking for.

"Oh wow," Molly said. "You never know exactly what you'll find. Here's a baby sea star." They gathered for a closer look at the tiny sea star. No more than a centimeter across, it crawled slowly across her glove.

"I have magnifying glasses here in little trays, if I can get him in one," Molly continued. She put a little water in the clear plastic tray, and attached a small magnifying glass to examine the contents. "Now, here we are. Take turns." Molly passed the viewer to Jane. "And you can all have a close look."

"Wow, it looks just like the big ones, and its arms are moving," Jane said.

"Let me see," Beth said, and Jane passed the viewer to her.

Molly continued to work on the piece of algae and filled two more viewers with sea stars. Then she found a few small fish: grouper and stop-light parrotfish. Soon they all had viewers filled with various marine creatures which they passed around the circle.

"I had no idea that there was so much to see in just a little clump of algae," Mitch said.

"That's what always amazes me about the ocean," said Molly. "Every little nook and cranny is filled with marine life. You don't realize it while you are snorkeling, but you do swim over the majority of what is down there without ever noticing it."

After they had viewed the marine life in Molly's pan, she returned it to the water. Then they woke Newby while loading Day Tripper and returned to the field station so the scuba divers could explore another inland blue hole. The rest of the group was headed up Bollard Creek to snorkel along the mangroves and, they hoped, to find sea horses.

"Hey Beth, don't let the Lusca monster bite you in the blue hole," Mitch teased from the deck of Day Tripper when she splashed down into the shallow water.

"Very funny," Beth replied. She stooped, knee-deep in the water, cupped her two hands together and scooped water onto Mitch.

"Lucky aim," Mitch said, wiping his face with the back of his hand while the boat moved back into deeper water.

"Luck? Skill!" Beth proclaimed and Laura smiled.

Newby started up the engine and motored away from the beach where John Dettor's crew were waiting to explore the next blue hole on the map and get back to the hunt for Hornigold's treasure.

13

BEN'S BLUE HOLE

Laura and Beth splashed through the shallows to the rinse deck, where Justin, Eric and Jeff gathered their scuba gear for the afternoon's blue hole dive. Day Tripper motored off in the distance toward Bollard Creek. Dr. Lounsbury waved to scuba divers as he entered his office. Stilly sat on the beach deck with the cab driver, Basky, both engrossed in a game of chess and surrounded by lazy napping dogs.

"Glad to see you back a little early!" John Dettor said approaching. "I just heard the boat."

"We were out at Rat Cay for a field lab and did a fish survey," Justin explained.

"Similar to what we're doing in the blue holes. Now, Grant and I just finished loading tanks and gear into the van, so whenever you're ready we'll be off." John was clearly anxious to get underway.

"How did you fill the tanks?" Eric asked, remembering the damaged compressor from the previous night.

"Grant had some tanks already full and the rest we

had filled by a dive shop down south at Small Hope Bay. So we've got enough air for today, and the compressor, with a little luck, should be back online this evening," John explained.

"That's awesome!" Justin said as John began to walk toward the dive shop. "We'll be with you."

The EcoExplorers and Eric then met John and Grant at the van, loaded their gear inside and took seats. Grant drove out of the shadowy palm-covered lane, turned right, and headed north on the Queen's Highway. As the van rumbled across the bridge at Bollard Creek, the divers waved to their friends aboard Day Tripper, who had almost made it up the creek as far as the bridge.

"Where're we headed today?" Jeff inquired, the humid breeze wafting through the open window rippling his hair.

"We're going to dive Ben's Blue Hole," John said. He turned a page in a notebook that he had studied ever since they had left the field station. "It's a little off the beaten path, but still, it's a process of elimination and I think it's worth a look. And who knows, each dive brings us that much closer to finding the treasure."

"Justin told us about how the compressor got damaged and it sounds like you think it was intentional. Do you think the men from TSL will continue to try and stop us?" Beth asked.

"We'll be more careful now that we know they are trying to slow us down," said John. "We put a padlock on the dive shop door before we left so no one can get in without the key. I also talked last night with some of my friends on the island and they promised to keep a sharper eye out for their movements. I think we'll be okay as long as we keep our wits about us."

They rode along, chatting about the scenery and the morning's trip out to Rat Cay. John silently studied some papers while Grant drove the van and turned on the radio. A Calypso song filled the van as background music to their conversation.

"Hey John, what was Andros like back when you first came here?" Justin asked.

"It hasn't changed much in some ways, and in other ways, it has changed a lot," John said. Swiveling his seat to face Justin, he folded a map in his lap and the bifocal glasses perched on the end of his nose gave him a dignified appearance. "There's still a spirit here among the islanders and once you get to know them, well, they're just like family; they'll do anything in the world for you. As more people have moved in, the spirit still exists, but it tends to stay more to the places where the locals gather. I guess what I'm trying to say is that the people used to rely on themselves more, which to me is the spirit of self-sufficiency. It's funny how you remember little things over the years; they seem insignificant at the time, but they become the storybook in your mind and your connection to the past. I remember one evening in particular we were eating a fresh batch of souse down on the beach at Obediah's—"

"Souse?" interrupted Justin.

"Yes, souse! Hasn't Stilly made his souse for you?" John asked, surprised.

"Never heard of it!"

"Stilly loves those field station dogs so much he probably saves it for them," John chuckled. "Anyway, souse is a soup which is meat-based with water, onions, lime juice, celery, and peppers. It has a very rich and spicy flavor. Although some of the more superstitious islanders might avoid it and think it's cuckoo soup so—"

"Cuckoo soup?" Laura interrupted and leaned forward in her seat.

"Ah yes," said John. "The dreaded cuckoo soup is a love potion whose strength depends on the addition of certain questionable ingredients. The saying goes that a dose of the broth can make you fall in love and want to marry just about anyone or anything. Basically, the legend goes that you fall in love with the first thing you see after eating the soup. An islander once told me a story of a young man who was invited to lunch and served a bowl of cuckoo soup. Not wishing to offend his hostess, he flung the soup out an open window first chance he got. One of the family pigs ate it and within minutes was oinking up a storm, grunting out a marriage proposal to the goat." They all laughed, and Justin joked:

"Maybe we can get the recipe. Then we could make some for Jeff so he could finally get a date!"

"Oh shut up!" Jeff snapped; his face grew crimson while the others laughed some more.

"Anyway, like I was saying," John continued. "That evening, years ago, on the beach at Obediah's was just incredible. The sun was setting; the souse was superb, especially when washed down with a little rum punch. Everything was locally grown, locally harvested and fresh-caught. The beach fire and tiki lights illuminated a calypso band playing lively music. That's the spirit I'm talking about because we had everything we needed-- food, friends, music, a warm fire--and we were basically self-sufficient and without a care in the world. If I could go back to a time on this island, I think I would go back to that evening. You'll be going down to Obediah's tomorrow night; he makes the best souse on the island. But don't tell Stilly I said so." John winked.

"You know everything about this island!" Laura said.

"Not really. Just been around a bit," John responded, and looked down in his lap at the map. "Grant, our turn is coming up right there," he said, pointing to a little break in the forest at the side of the highway, and swiveled his seat forward.

Grant slowed the van and turned. The road, like most of the Androsian logging roads, was overgrown, and they had to plow their way through the jungle of vegetation. The van screeched and groaned as it rubbed against the overhanging branches, vines, and tall grass that covered the lane. Ben's Blue Hole, located closer to Queen's Highway, was a shorter drive back into the dense jungle than the previous sites. The blue hole soon came into view from the logging road, which had easy access to the water's edge. Grant pulled the van up close; they all got out and began to unload the dive gear.

"Someone's recently been here," John said looking at fresh tire tracks in the sandy soil.

"Well they couldn't have been scuba divers," Grant explained. "It looks like a vehicle pulled in here and backed up to the blue hole. Only a few foot prints and no signs of scuba gear being staged on the ground. Probably someone came back in here for an evening picnic, or it was maybe even used like a lover's lane."

"Wow! This blue hole is much bigger than the one from yesterday," Laura said walking over to the edge with Eric. She picked up a rock and tossed it over the water. It plunked in with a splash. Concentric rings in ever widening circles stretched out from the middle of the splash, undulating across the surface. A pair of blue-winged teals took flight from the blue hole; disturbed by the divers, they fussed indignantly with a cross between nasal bleats and evenly spaced quacks.

"Yes, this is more typical of the blue holes on Andros," John explained. "Let's keep the same buddy teams as yesterday."

"Can I dive with Jeff and Justin today?" asked Beth feeling like a third-wheel as Laura paid more attention to Eric. "Maybe Eric would like to use your digital camera."

"Okay then, if that's ok with everyone, then Jeff, Beth, and Justin, you dive the same search profile as yesterday. Go down no deeper than the halocline, then move over to the wall and begin to make a circuit of the blue hole and work your way up, circling the wall. See anything that looks like treasure, you know what to do."

Soon they wiggled into wetsuits and started to sweat under the hot midday Bahamian sun. With scuba gear in place, they splashed into the welcomed cool water of the blue hole to begin their dive. John and Grant immediately descended deep below the halocline and disappeared, apparently heading to the bottom. Eric and Laura leisurely finned down the wall, to about twenty-five feet, and began to make their circuit. Jeff, Justin, and Beth descended slowly, observing the thick mats of greenish-brown algae that hung from every outcropping on the wall.

Beth spotted a small unknown fish and signaled to Jeff. He pointed his digital camera, twin flashes illuminated the scene, and a new image was quickly being written from buffer to memory card. Descending further, they noticed a small cavern and a large fish hovering in the opening, as if guarding the entrance. Justin turned on his dive light and shined it into the back to see what he could find. The back wall was covered with sediment, and the narrow walls of the cavern ended not more than twenty feet from the entrance.

Beth, wanting to experience the halocline again, pointed her thumb down to Jeff and Justin. They all descended close to the wall until they came to a brownish layer that undulated across the expanse of the blue hole. The water was clear, but the blue hole was large enough that they could not see to the other side. Beth finned across and enjoyed the thrill of skimming through the various upper layers of the halocline like an airplane rising and falling between different layers of clouds in the sky. Beth turned on her dive light and disappeared below the dark, murky halocline. The brownish layer engulfed her and Jeff and Justin watched from above.

She spent several minutes ascending and descending, from the clear fresh water above, then back into the darkness and salty water below. Each time she checked to see that Justin and Jeff were still close by. Justin noticed a small intriguing swirl of whitish sediment just above the halocline, and spent a few minutes examining it in the water column. Jeff kept a close eye on Beth and when she came back into view through the halocline, she seemed to be fighting her way out.

Jeff thought at first that maybe some undercurrent was just making it tough for her to ascend, and then she began to frantically wave her arms in distress.

Jeff quickly finned to Beth's side and noticed that a stout piece of rope had gotten wrapped around the first stage of her regulator, holding her down and stopping her ascent. He reached behind her and untangled the rope; Beth swam freely and a little further above him.

Interested, Jeff tugged on the rope and felt resistance on the other end. Beth, curious as well, moved back in close and helped Jeff pull on the rope, but whatever was attached to it was barely moving. Through the gloomy halocline, the shadowy black outline of a large object loomed closer. Jeff grabbed tight on the rope with Beth and they pulled harder. This time, the weight of the object brought both him and Beth down shoulder-deep into the murky halocline while the object itself floated slowly upward and in their direction.

Jeff saw first the back of what appeared to be a man's head with hair undulating in the murky halocline. He thought that maybe John or Grant had run out of air, had gotten caught in the rope and drowned while trying to make an emergency ascent. He pulled again on the rope. The body pivoted face-forward to him and he immediately backed away, startled by what he saw. The body rotated in front of Beth and she found herself face to face with neither Grant nor John, but the hideous, disfigured and half eaten face of a dead corpse.

14

DEAD MAN'S HOLE

Beth's face was closer to the gruesome corpse than a slow dance partner when she started to scream through her regulator. She punched and kicked it with all of her strength as she tried to get away. A strong kick with her fin sent the ghastly body back down towards the bottom of the blue hole. She watched as it slowly slipped away and disappeared into the ghostly depths. The startling encounter played tricks on Beth's mind, and suddenly the undulating halocline was like a thousand hands prowling over her body trying to tug her below. Beth bolted toward the surface. The only thing that seemed to matter now was to get out of the horrific blue hole. But within an instant into her ascent she crashed into something hard and the strike to her forehead knocked her senseless.

Jeff caught the blow of Beth's head on his lead weight belt. She had collided with him not knowing that he hovered a short distance above her. Jeff looked below at Beth who was obviously stunned from the collision: she had gone limp. From her forehead what appeared to be black ink oozed into the water. Jeff was confused then remembered that since all red light is filtered out of the water below fifteen feet, Beth was not spurting ink, but blood.

Beth regained her senses, kicked at Jeff not knowing who or what she had collided with and continued on to the surface at a dangerous speed, leaving a trail of blood behind. Jeff immediately took off after her. He knew that he had to reach her fast before her swift ascent become dangerous. Jeff caught her within a short distance and started to purge the air from her over-inflated BC, slowing her down as they continued together in an upward path.

Beth fought him as if it was for her life. She kicked him and punched at him, all the while screaming through her regulator and venting a cloud of bubbles. Finally, Jeff maneuvered behind her, latched onto the tank valve, vented the remaining air from her BC and arrested their ascent at thirty feet. Jeff moved them over next to the wall of the blue hole so that they would have a visual reference in the water column for the remaining ascent to the surface. Beth calmed down during their safety stop when she recognized Jeff. As they neared the surface, the inky black oozing from Beth's forehead was blood red.

"Get me the hell out of here!" Beth yelled, after spitting the regulator from her mouth as they broke the surface. She ripped the mask from her face and pitched it behind her. Beth finned to the shallow shelf at the exit point and Jeff helped her out of her BC. She then crawled out of the water with her fins still on, bent over the ground and started to vomit.

"Beth? It's going to be okay," Jeff said.

"What's going on dude?" Justin asked, perplexed as he exited the water.

"There's a dead body down there! Beth's gear got tangled in a rope in the halocline. I untangled her and then we pulled on the rope. The other end was tied to a corpse. It was a gruesome site man, totally freaked me out," Jeff said, obviously shaken by the incident. "Beth had bolted for the surface, then ran into my weight belt and cut her forehead. I tried to slow her down so she wouldn't injure herself further. She just about kicked and punched the life out of me."

Justin removed his mask, fins and scuba gear and put it up on dry land. He climbed out of the blue hole and kneeled down beside her. "Beth, are you all right?"

"That totally freaked me out! I had to get out of there. My head's killing me. How's it looking?" Rivulets of blood trickled down her face.

"You cut yourself pretty good above your right eye, just below the hairline," replied Justin. "I'm no expert, but I think you're going to need a few stitches. The medical kit's in the van. Let's go over and see if we can get the bleeding stopped." Justin helped Beth remove her fins and pulled her to her feet. They walked together towards the van.

Jeff recovered the mask Beth had tossed into the water, removed his own gear and lumbered out of the water. At the same time, Eric and Laura reached the surface, followed by Grant and John, who finned over to them.

"What's going on?" Laura asked.

Jeff quickly recounted the details of the encounter while they listened intently.

"You found a dead man in the halocline?" John asked, perplexed.

"Yeah, it's down there and disgusting. It's maybe fifty-feet out from here and in the halocline," Jeff explained, pointing with his hand out over the water.

"How's Beth?" Grant asked.

"Justin just took her to the van to get the bleeding stopped."

"I'm going to go and see if I can do anything for

Beth," Grant said. "John, perhaps you should go down and take a quick look and verify the corpse."

Grant got out of the water with Eric and Laura while John descended back to the location in the halocline that Jeff described. Grant put his gear on the ground and walked over to attend to Beth.

"How're you doing, Beth?" Grant said when he reached the van.

"Jeff's lead weight belt is about as hard as his head, but I think I'll live. But my head is throbbing!" Beth said. Justin had taped a bandage over it and the bleeding had slowed.

"Did you ascend too quickly?" Grant asked.

"No! I mean, I began to, but Jeff slowed my ascent and…I don't think there's any way I could be bent."

Laura reached the van and looked at Beth. "You look like hell. You okay?" "I just escaped from hell! I'll be okay, I think," Beth said, rolling her eyes.

"Justin, you and Laura stay here with Beth and keep an eye on her," said Grant. "I'm going to gather up the dive gear and as soon as we're loaded we'll head for Rockwood." He headed back to the blue hole.

"How's Beth?" Jeff asked.

"She's fine. Justin bandaged her up and the bleeding seems to be under control. How about you?"

"I'll get over it," he said. "But I'm going to be hurting for a while. Beth kicked and punched at me while I was trying to slow her down. She hits with an awesome punch!"

"Would you and Eric help me gather up the gear and load it in the van?" asked Grant. "We'll leave as soon as John is back."

Jeff and Eric did as asked and were soon down the path and out of sight.

"Find anything?" Grant asked in a low voice once John surfaced.

"It took me a little while, but unfortunately they're

correct. I found the body below the halocline. This is not an accidental drowning. He has a single bullet hole in the side of his head and there's a rope tied around his waist and anchored to something heavy down below. We better alert the authorities," John paused, lowered his eyes, seemed distant. "But let's be discreet about this, Grant. I don't want to unnecessarily alarm them any more than they are. And as far as I'm concerned, they're now out of the treasure hunt."

"What should we tell them?" Grant asked.

"We'll tell them that we appreciate all of their help and efforts; it's just become too dangerous and I don't feel that after the incidents over the last few days we can guarantee their safety," John explained.

"Is there more to this than you are telling me?" Grant asked, suspiciously.

"That's it for now, keep the rest quiet. Now let's go and see to Beth."

They walked back to the van and loaded their gear. Grant started the van and headed to the field station. Soon they reached the main highway and headed south to the field station. Rumbling across Bollard Creek Bridge, Grant slowed the van, turned onto the driveway and drove up to the lodge. Stopping, with a cloud of dust trailing behind, he beeped the horn three times to announce their return and signal to all the trained staff at Rockwood that there was an emergency. Dr. Lounsbury ran from the director's cabin. Mike and Molly, who had just returned from the trip up Bollard Creek, instantly hopped off Day Tripper into the water, splashed through the shallows and made their way to the van. From the lodge, Carmen and Newby approached, while others came from various directions all over the field station.

"What happened?" Dr. Lounsbury asked, his eyes signaling his concern.

"Beth and Jeff discovered a corpse in the blue hole,"

Grant explained. "Beth unfortunately got tangled up with it. She ended up with a nasty gash on her head."

"Beth! Are you okay?" Molly inquired. She stepped into the van and began to evaluate her condition.

"I'm all right but my head is killing me!" Beth said.

"Let me take a look at the wound," said Molly, and Beth pulled back the bandage, exposing the two inch gash. "You're definitely going to need stitches. Laura, please take Beth to your cabin and see that she gets into dry clothes. Dr. Lounsbury, if you'll drive the van we should take Beth to the clinic at Fresh Creek. As soon as you're back, we'll be leaving. Don't tarry. Boys, unload the van so we can leave without delay." In response to Molly's orders, the van turned into a bee hive of activity. The guys got busy with gear, Laura and Beth went to their cabin and John Dettor walked to Dr. Lounsbury's cabin to use the phone.

Despite what was happening around him, Mike couldn't resist letting a smile cross his face as Molly took charge, assigned tasks to so many and had them marching in cadence; a quality that he admired so much about her.

Laura soon returned with Beth in dry clothes and they climbed into the van with Molly. Dr. Lounsbury started the van and drove away in the direction of the clinic. The guys waved from the rinse deck as they washed and hung the scuba gear to dry.

"Where's John?" Jeff asked.

"Not sure. Maybe he's in the kitchen with Stilly." Grant said.

"No! I was just there and didn't see either one of them," Jeff replied.

"Then I don't know. But John did ask me to relay a message to you. He asked me to thank each of you for your help, but considering today's events, he believes that it's become too dangerous for you to continue with the treasure hunt," Grant said.

"Why? What does the discovery of the body today have to do with it?" Justin asked.

"He didn't say."

"Come on Grant, you can tell us!" Justin said.

"Look! I asked him but he told me to tell you that you're out of the treasure hunt and that's it."

"We'll that's seems odd, just like that" Justin commented.

"He didn't say anything in the van, so maybe he plans to talk with you later," Grant suggested.

"I hope so; I thought we really had a shot at finding the treasure!" Jeff said, feeling let down. "And I know he still needs our help!"

Jeff, Justin and Eric finished the work that Molly had assigned them and returned to their cabin to shower and dress for the evening. Jeff sat on a bunk and fumbled through his bag for clean clothes; he pulled out an EcoExplorers T-shirt with the logo blazoned across the back. Justin stepped out of the shower, toweled off and dressed.

"You know, there's got to be more behind John's decision than what Grant told us," Jeff said as he pulled the wrinkled T-shirt over his head.

"Yeah, I agree. John seemed really concerned the other day when Winfrey showed up out of the blue," Justin added.

"And with his partners carrying rifles," said Jeff.

"Like my first encounter with Winfrey in the airport bathroom when he came looking for Stein. Winfrey threatened him then with a gun and forced him to leave with him. Remember? I saw them drive away together with two other men in his Jeep. You don't suppose that the body you found today was his, do you?"

"I don't have any idea whose body that was in the blue hole. I never saw Stein at the airport and the remains of the corpse were too decomposed to tell, anyway," Jeff said.

"John dove back down to take a look. Maybe he recognized who it was. What do you think?"

"I think John has his reasons for calling off the hunt and is primarily concerned about your safety. That's the bottom line. He's in charge and I think you should do as he says," Eric said.

"I think he owes us an explanation," Jeff said.

"Well, think what you want. I for one believe that Winfrey and his pals have already caused enough problems this week. Who knows what else he's capable of? John told you up front what a devious type of person he is. He thought we'd be safe because he believed Winfrey was hunting for the treasure off the island, but then as you pointed out, Winfrey just showed up by surprise and without warning. John is right. We should all go back to doing what we came here for and forget about the treasure hunt. The treasure probably doesn't exist anyway!

The three left the cabin and walked along the winding palm-tree-lined path to the lodge. Inside, the mood was a bit somber, with some still discussing the incident earlier that day at the blue hole. Mitch trumpeted the conch to let everyone know that Stilly had dinner prepared, but it lacked the usual gusto he put into his self-appointed task. After a quiet dinner they all sat around the lodge, talking and waiting for the evening lecture.

The field station van pulled to a stop outside the lodge. Doors opened and then slammed shut. Dr. Lounsbury held the door to the lodge for Beth, Laura, and Molly, and followed them inside, letting the screen door creak shut behind them.

"Wow, how many stitches did it take?" Mitch asked as he stared at Beth's cut above her eye.

"Nine! The doctor also thought that I might have a slight concussion. He numbed me up pretty good and gave me some pain meds to take. So besides being about to starve to death and tired, I think I'll be okay." Beth smiled wanly. "The doctor did say that I'm not allowed back in the water for the rest of the trip, so I guess diving and snorkeling are out for me."

"Well, at least you can come along with us on the boat," said Justin.

"Not tomorrow. The doctor said I have to be under observation for twenty-four hours. So Molly is staying behind with me in case I have to go back to see the doctor. He said being out on the boat is too far from medical care."

"That sucks," Justin said.

"Really, a day on the beach in paradise reading a book and getting a tan…I think I'll manage," Beth said.

"Hey, wait a minute. Keeping an eye on Beth sounds like a job for her best friend," Laura protested and looked at Molly.

"Well, Laura, you can stay if you want to, but if Beth is not acting like herself you will need to get Dr. Lounsbury to drive her to Fresh Creek to see the doctor," Molly said.

"No problem!" Laura said.

"Dinner's in the kitchen when you're ready," Stilly said from inside the doorway.

Molly, Beth, Laura and Dr. Lounsbury ate, then they all gathered in the classroom and Nicole lectured for the total forty-five minutes on how Andros was formed from a geological perspective. She discussed current issues and problems with blue holes and how increasing population was putting additional burdens on the islands' fragile ecosystem. When she was done, Mitch showed images on a screen with the digital projector of the sea horses they found and photographed that afternoon along Bollard Creek in amongst the mangroves.

After the lecture, Laura and Eric moved on to the beach deck. Mike and Molly headed towards the water to take a short moon-lit walk on the beach before bed. The others dispersed in various directions. Jeff, Justin, Nicole and Stilly stayed behind in the lodge and struck up a game of dominoes. After a few rounds were played, distant sounds were heard from outside the building followed by a loud, high-pitched shrill of a bark.

"What was that?" Justin asked.

"Sounds like the dogs caught another wild boar!" Jeff said.

"I don't know about that," replied Nicole. "I need to stretch my legs so I'll go outside and see what's going on." Nicole grabbed the flashlight from the fireplace mantle, walked through the classroom, then through the lab and out the back door.

It was now completely dark. Nicole swept the beacon of light from her flashlight around the field station and walked in the direction of the Queen's Highway. The noise heard from the lodge had disappeared, leaving only the sounds of the palms as they swayed slightly in the wind and the distant clatter of a car passing over the metal grating of the Bollard Creek Bridge. Nicole determined that whatever had made the racket had left and decided to head back. She turned when she reached the dive shack and tripped over a large object laying hidden in the dark, then she fell to her knees in the sand. She picked herself up and shined the flashlight on the unknown object. Lying unmoving on the ground was Stilly's dog Loona. Nicole stared in horror at the lifeless body of the black dog.

The game had continued in the lodge and Stilly won another round. The screen door opened and Nicole stepped inside. She slowly entered the lodge sobbing, her usual vibrant eyes now filled with tears.

Stilly, noticing her first, jumped to his feet. "What's the matter Nicole? Are you okay?"

Nicole began crying and stammering. "I-I can't believe that anyone would hurt her," she explained and sobbed deeply.

"Hurt who?" Justin asked.

"L-loona! Loona is dead," Nicole said. A shiny rivulet of tear streaked her face.

"Loona," Stilly whispered out loud in disbelief.

"I'm s-so sorry Stilly," Nicole stammered looking into his watering eyes. "I found her near the dive shop." She stepped next to Stilly and held him tight. Then, slowly breaking their embrace, Stilly turned his face away from the group and walked towards the door.

"Did you see what could have happened to her?" Jeff asked.

"No, it's too dark and there wasn't anyone or anything else around," Nicole said.

"Stilly? What can we do to help," Justin asked.

"Nothing," Stilly replied. He inhaled deeply, paused midstride and kept his back to Justin; he momentarily held his breath, as if a dam of tears was about to break free. "But thank you. This is for me to do and for me alone," he said. Stilly walked out of the great room and disappeared into the dark shadows of the dim moon-lit night.

15

THE DEATH OF MAYNARD

Early the next morning the mood over breakfast was somber when they learned about the loss of the field station dog, Loona. Stilly was absent and Dr. Lounsbury helped cook breakfast with Ooma and Nicole. Beth skipped breakfast and afterwards the beach became a hive of activity as the EcoExplorers loaded Day Tripper for the day's outing. Eric loaded his snorkeling gear and then sat quietly on the beach beside Laura, who was entranced by the sun, distant puffy clouds and the turquoise water of the subtropical Atlantic. Eric, not interested in the scenery, turned onto his side and started drawing squiggly pictures with his finger in the cool morning sand.

"How's Beth doing today?" he asked, and then brushed away the abstract images he had just created.

"She didn't sleep well last night. Had a nightmare," Laura said.

"Nightmare?"

"Yeah, she woke mumbling and in a sweat. She told me about the blue hole dive after she bumped into the dead dude. To Beth it was like a thousand hands were suddenly about to tug her below. Then she bumped into Jeff's weight belt and that only added to her being freaked out. I think all the scary movies she watches and maybe the concussion didn't help her nightmare, either. Molly is checking on her now."

"You're a good friend to stay with her today, but…."

"But, what?"

"Well, I just wish you were going with us today," Eric said in a tone of hesitation. "I'll, I'll miss you."

"You will! I'll miss you too," Laura said. She turned toward him, glancing at his face and noting his look of disappointment. "I think it's best that I stay behind today and keep Beth company. She's my best friend and I want to be here for her."

"I know. You're doing the right thing. It's just that…"

"Just what?"

"Well, I really wanted to spend the day with you. This week is going by so fast, I feel like we're running out of time."

"I know, Eric, I've really enjoyed hangin' with you too, but I'm not ready to get in another relationship at this time."

"Why's that?" he asked, reaching for her hand.

"I was recently really involved with someone back home. He hurt me deeply," Laura said, staring out across the water. Feelings and memories from the past relationship quickly washed over her. No one had filled her heart so completely before. And no one had broken it so completely, so callously. She was crushed when she found out that Kevin was lying to her. She was totally humiliated when her friends told her that he was seeing someone else without her knowing. Laura pulled her hand out of his grasp.

"What's the matter?" Eric asked.

"Nothing. I just need to go and check on Beth."

"Did I say something wrong?"

"No, I'm just worried about her," Laura said, in an attempt to cover up her feelings. Laura stood and brushed the sand from the back of her shorts. "Eric, this is all moving too fast. I need some time to think about what's happening between us. Please try to understand. I really like being with you. You've renewed some feelings in me that I thought I'd lost. But these feelings are really scaring me. Like you said, we only have this short week together. I'll return to Virginia and you'll move on to wherever. I can't allow myself to get hurt again."

Eric stood, wanting to say more, but Molly was walking in their direction.

"I've just seen Beth and she's doing all right. Her head hurts a bit and she had a bad nightmare last night," Molly said.

"I know; it was a rough night for her. I was just telling Eric about the hands pulling her down and stuff," Laura said.

"I appreciate your staying behind today to be with Beth. But if you'd rather go on today's outing, I'll be more than happy to stay in your place," Molly suggested.

"No, I gotta be here for my friend," Laura said. "She'd do the same for me."

"Looks like the boat's about ready to leave," Molly said looking toward the boat then back to Laura and Eric. "Well, Dr. Lounsbury will be around Rockwood today. He'll be in his office or in the lab. Don't hesitate to ask him if you need anything. And if you suspect Beth is not acting like herself, get Dr. Lounsbury to drive her back to Fresh Creek to the see the doctor."

"I will."

"Eric, we better get moving. The boat is loaded and they're waiting for us," Molly said. "We should be back before dinner."

"Okay," Laura said.

Molly walked to the boat, but Eric stood by for a

moment longer, not knowing what to say. He stared at Laura, desperately wanting to express his feelings. He tried to think of the right thing to say, but it was hopeless. They were waiting on the boat for him and she had to go. Laura turned away and headed towards the cabin.

"I'll see you when you get back," Laura said, glancing back in his direction.

"Okay. Sure." Eric said, more quietly than excitedly.

He jogged over to the waiting pontoon boat, splashed through the shallow water and climbed aboard. Laura waved goodbye to him from the beach as Day Tripper pulled away. Soon they were skimming across the tranquil water and disappeared behind a line of cays just off the shore of the field station. Laura walked barefoot along the sandy ground, dappled with palm fronds, to the front of their cabin. Inside, Beth was lying quietly on her bunk, awake.

"So, another day in paradise, how's it going?" Laura asked.

"Um, all right, I guess," Beth explained in a monotone.

"But you should've gone with the others" Beth continued, having just heard the boat leave.

"What, and let you have the place to yourself? No way! Looks like you're stuck with me today. So, why don't we find a nice spot to lie on the beach and get some sun? There's a bunch of books over in the lounge. We could pick something out to read, fix ourselves a little picnic and just spend the day doing nothing. What do you say?"

"I guess that would be all right," Beth said, sitting up on her bunk. "I did want to return home with a tan."

Both girls changed clothes, grabbed beach towels and lotion and headed to the lodge. Inside they began to browse the small bookcase full of used paperback novels that guests leave behind for others to read.

"Nothing much here," said Laura after a few minutes of searching through the books on the shelves. "Let's see if there's anything interesting on the bookcases in the classroom." The girls moved into the next room and began to look.

"Beth, I'm glad to see you up and around," Dr. Lounsbury said, entering the classroom from the lab, wearing a long white lab coat over a tropical patterned shirt. "How are you feeling?"

"I'm feeling all right, thanks." Beth replied. "We've decided to take it easy today, lie on the beach, read a book and get some sun."

"That sounds like a great plan. I noticed you were picking through the books. Did you find something interesting to read?" Dr. Lounsbury asked his glasses perched precariously on his nose.

"All of the books in the lounge are the typical paperbacks we have back home. Most we've already read," Laura said. "The cab driver, Basky, told us that he thought there was a book about Bahamian legends," Beth said. "I kind of got interested after hearing Stilly's tales around the beach fire the other night. I don't suppose you have that book here do you?"

"Well, actually, I believe I do. My library is in the back of my cabin. If you'll follow me, we can go and see what we can find."

Inside Dr. Lounsbury's cabin, there was a large teak desk along the eastern wall, overlooking the beach and ocean. Piled on top were large stacks of folders and research papers. Next to his desk stood a table that held a computer, printer and a fax machine. Numerous prints and paintings covered the walls depicting various scenes from around the island. A sizable map, yellowed and torn with age, was placed on an easel in the office corner.

"Back here is my research library," Dr. Lounsbury fondly stated, leading the girls through the doorway and into the dimly-lit room.

The walls were lined with books from floor to ceiling, tightly filling all available space on the shelves. Constructed of Androsian mahogany, the shelves lined four sides of the room with a large rectangular shaped table in the middle. "On this side of the room, and both sides of the doorway, you'll find books on botany, biology and geology. On the opposite side are books relating to the history of the Bahamas and Bahamian politics. The back wall contains books and research papers about reef ecology, which is an ongoing study here at the field station."

"Wow!" exclaimed Laura. "This is quite a library. I didn't realize that there was so much information about the Bahamas."

"Well, I've been building this library now for over thirty years. The library was actually started by Ross Rockwood when he owned the property, and I've been adding to it ever since. I've tried to purchase every title published about the Bahamas. Some of these books are very rare, and I have a few under lock and key because they are the only surviving copies. In fact, even though the head librarian would not admit to it, my collection here is more complete than the collection at the main library in Coakley Town."

"That's amazing," Beth said. "This whole library is amazing. Dr. Lounsbury, could you show me where to find the book about the legends of the Bahamas?"

"Oh yes, of course. I think that book is, no, wait a minute, it's over here," he said. He walked around the table, reached up and pulled the volume from its place. "Here you are," he said, handing the book to Beth.

"Thanks!"

"Is there anything else that you're looking for?"

"Pirates!" Laura said.

"They're over here with the history books. Some of these books are documented history and others are, well, just tall tales," Dr. Lounsbury said with a sly grin. "So, please help yourself to whatever you'd like to read and I'll get back to my research in the lab. I should be there for most of the day. Don't hesitate to ask if you need anything. Stilly's not feeling well today after losing his beloved Loona last night and it's his day off. So please help yourselves in the kitchen. There should be plenty of food in the refrigerator to make sandwiches and snacks are in the pantry. The field station is yours."

"Loona?" Beth asked while Laura's eyes anxiously darted between Beth and Dr. Lounsbury.

"Yes, I suppose they didn't want to say anything after your accident yesterday, but unfortunately, Loona was found dead by the dive shop last night," Dr. Lounsbury explained.

"Oh no!" Beth said and her eyes watered. "I liked that dog."

"We all loved Loona and she'll be missed," Dr. Lounsbury said and put a hand on Beth's shoulder. "If you need anything today, you know where I'll be. And, Laura, if you think Beth is not acting like herself from the concussion I want you to find me right away."

"I will."

"Thanks!" both girls said as he left.

"What else did I miss yesterday evening?" Beth asked. Laura explained what Grant had told the guys on the rinse deck about being out of the treasure hunt. They discussed it for a bit and then began to scan the expansive volumes of books for anything that looked interesting. Beth pulled out a chair and sat down to open the book of legends. Laura stood in front of the bookshelf, peering at the various titles on pirating.

"So much for our day of fun in the sun," Laura said, with her back to Beth as she searched the shelves.

"Well, I don't know about that," Beth said. She opened her book and a musty scent wafted out. "Let's spend an hour or so in here, fix some lunch, and then hit the beach."

"Sounds like a plan," Laura said, wanting Beth to focus on anything but yesterday's incident. Laura pulled a few books off the shelf and stacked them on the table. "I want to see if there's any information about Hornigold. I would like to know something about him since we were hunting for his treasure."

"Let me know what you find."

Laura pulled out a chair and sat directly across from Beth. Both girls sat quietly flipping pages in their books.

"Oh, here's something about Hornigold," Laura said.

"Well what does it say?"

"It's not very long. Do you want me to read it to you?"

"Sure go ahead, I'm listening," Beth said, continuing to flip through the pages of her book.

"The earliest documents state that Hornigold was a pirate that hunted the waters of the West Indies and along the American coastline sometime after the War of Spanish Succession in seventeen thirteen. They think he may have served on an English privateer during the war and probably turned to piracy sometime after the Spanish were defeated. Hornigold was a pirate captain based in New Providence Island around the year seventeen sixteen. He and another leader, Thomas Barrows, declared New Providence as a pirate republic and appointed themselves as governors of the island. Hornigold trained hundreds of men as pirates and commanded numerous sailing ships of all shapes and sizes.

"Hornigold left New Providence Island with Edward Teach, who would soon be known by many as Blackbeard, and one of his crew. They captured a French sloop and made Teach captain. In seventeen seventeen, they plundered six ships off the American coast and also pirated in the Caribbean. By the year's end Hornigold and Teach had captured a French Guineaman off the coast of St. Vincent's laden with gold, jewels, and other treasure. After dividing the loot, Hornigold gave Teach the ship which he renamed Queen Anne's Revenge. They then separated and went their own ways."

"Wow, sounds like the type of treasure that was listed in Hornigold's manifest," Beth said, looking up from her book. "That must have been a really adventurous time, being a pirate back then."

"I know. That would've been so cool. Hey, there's one more paragraph," Laura said, and she continued to read. "During the same year, King George I appointed Wood Rogers as royal governor of the Bahamas. Tipped off on the British plan to reclaim the island, Hornigold waited and welcomed him. He arrived around the month of July in the year seventeen eighteen, bringing with him a royal commission as 'Captain General and Governor-in-Chief of the Bahamas Islands.' At that time there were more than two hundred ships moored in the harbor and hundreds of pirates. Rogers brought with him an Act of Grace, a king's pardon for all pirates who turned themselves in before September five, seventeen eighteen, and were willing to swear an oath to refrain from future pirating. Hornigold, together with hundreds of other pirates, retired from their pirating ways and were pardoned by the king. Rogers befriended Hornigold and hired him, and he became one of Rogers' most trusted agents. Rogers sent Hornigold out to capture pirates unwilling to stop their pirating activities. In seventeen nineteen, Hornigold traveled to Mexico on a trading voyage. His ship struck an offshore reef and everyone on board apparently perished."

"So that's what happened to Hornigold! I would bet anything that's why he never returned to reclaim his treasure," Beth added.

"Probably. Take a pardon and keep your treasure, not a bad deal if you can get away with it. I guess his treasure was lost for good until John's friend rediscovered his logbook and manifest in the chest in Nassau."

"He certainly was an important figure during the golden age of piracy," Laura added.

The girls continued reading their books for a while when an astonished look began to spread across Beth's face.

"Hey, take a look at this!" Beth said, passing the book of legends to Laura.

"What did you find?"

"It's an old poem titled 'The Death of Thomas Maynard.' Wasn't that the name of Hornigold's crew member that died in the blue hole when they hid the treasure? I remember the name Maynard from John's documents."

"I don't remember. Why don't you read the poem and see what it's about?" Laura said, passing the book back to Beth.

Death of Thomas Maynard
Poor Thomas Maynard
Dead he be,
Los his soul
Cross the bottomless sea
Where the sperrits be holy,
an the devil be free.
Poor Thomas Maynard,
may e' rest in ease.

"I think he might be talking about Andros," Beth said, pausing her reading. "Remember, when Jeff was telling us about their discovery? He said the Spanish name Christopher Columbus gave to this island is the Island of the Holy Spirit. And I also remember reading the Spanish name again in Hornigold's logbook. Then he mentions crossing the bottomless sea. Hornigold also wrote something about sailing across deep water. New Providence is the next closest island and the Tongue of the Ocean separates these two islands."

"Possibly," Laura replied, then smiled and joked, "If you just paid attention in class like you do to this pirate stuff, you' be first in the class!"

"Yeah, right."

"Well read on, you've got my attention."

This be a tragic tale
of death an hidden' treasure.
With numbers a' pirate booty,
too big to measure.
I no it be in' true,
I ain't fibben to thee.
I tell this ol' story to you
for I'm the last to be!

"Did you hear that?" Beth asked. "The poem is describing a hidden pirate treasure. I can't believe it."

"This is unreal. Read on!"

Into land we rowed
Early n' the day,
Into the snarle' wilds
Of a place called Lucifer's Cay.
Followed the creek, a western route,
then spots ye a narrow passe.
Sunken' sludge up to me boot,
that was hidden by tall marsh grass.

The crew and me we waded through
an found a distant beach.
Sun now touching the tips of the pine,
this place we're about to reach.

We be carryn' along a seaman's chest,
a well fashioned box.
Wrapped n' iron strapping

and chained w'tri padlocks.
Me see'n the chest in port,
aye, it sat on the guarded dock.
Took two men to bear its weight,
as heavy as ballast rock.

We came upon this hid'n place,
a passage to death I'm told.
Me hear the stories of evil things,
and legends to unfold.

Now the natives say that
it's the gate to hell,
where the monster named Lusca,
a devil demon dwells.

Here a mishap befallen him,
on that horrid sultry day.
Where'n Thomas's wretched soul,
would soon be swept away.

A missed step of the foot
on a slipp'ry limey wall,
and into the dark watery pit
did poor Thomas fall.

Thomas struggled for his life,
He bested to escape.
But instead poor Maynard
was knockin at Lucifer's gate.
The Lusca now a heavy breath inhaled,
came a swirlin' water spout.
Then the struggling crewmate Maynard,
was gone without a shout.

The Captain stood standing
hallowed he began to pray.

Poor Thomas Maynard's soul
God save he that retched day.
Then he swung his mighty sword,
and promised to all a great reward.
For those that finish the work by dusk,
and follow through without a cuss.
To fasten the chain around a tree,
and lower the box into the deep.
Aye, great is the treasure if be found,
for many a clue is laid around.
But he who reads this tale beware,
best stay away from Lucifer's Lair.

"Wow, that's an amazing tale," Laura said, when Beth finished reading. "Could you imagine being swallowed up by that Lusca monster?"

"Come on, Laura. You know there's no such thing as a Lusca monster. The monster stuff was probably written to scare others away from trying to find the treasure."

"Well, there could have been. The people on this island certainly swore by it."

"The people on this island are very superstitious, and the old stories about such things as Lusca and the Chickcharnies have been passed along forever. They believe in it because they've been told to believe in it. I'll bet you anything that not one soul on this island has ever seen anything remotely similar to their fabled creatures, at least if they're in their right mind! What's important here is not the monster tales or even the death of Maynard. I think it's the clues in the poem that might help lead us to the location of the treasure."

"I'm sorry Beth, but you just lost me here. I don't remember anything in the poem telling us where the treasure is," responded Laura, confused.

"The poem states in the last passage that for many a clue is laid around! Why don't you find a pad of paper and a pencil from Dr. Lounsbury's office? Let's write down all the clues that are written in the poem."

Laura walked through the doorway, eager to keep her friend busy and her mind off the events from yesterday's dive. She returned a few moments later with the materials.

"I'll read all of the clues to you that I can find and you write them down. Okay?"

Beth started at the beginning.

"Bottomless sea. That we already believe is the deep waters of the Tongue of the Ocean. Sperrits be holy. That's from the Spanish translation for what is now Andros. The words treasure and pirates booty too big to measure. So we know that the poem is describing what we're looking for, right? For I am the last to be!"

"Well, if you're right, the author must be the only survivor from the pirates that carried the treasure," Laura added. "Remember the history of Hornigold said that he perished with all of his crew near Mexico in seventeen nineteen."

"That's right," replied Beth. "So maybe the pirate who wrote this knew he was the sole survivor, and wrote this poem to tell others how to find Hornigold's treasure!" She continued:

"Maybe he was one of the pirates who refused to give up his trade, was caught and knew that he was to be hanged by the neck." She rubbed her hands around her neck and acted like she was choking. "The next clue is a place known as Lucifer's Cay. Maybe we can find it on a map. That would give us the location of where they camped and the starting point of their journey. Next clue is they hiked along a western route."

"If they headed west, they must have started on the east coast and hiked inland," Laura suggested.

"Right! And that leads us to the next clue, which is they spotted a narrow pass where they crossed to a distant beach."

"So basically, they followed the creek to a sandy beach. That could be anywhere," Laura said, rubbing the pencil on the side of her head. "And the marshy area described in the pirate's poem is all over Andros."

"Ok, that's true," Beth said. "But there are more clues here. Let's see what else there is."

"Sun now touchin' the tip of the pine, this place we about to reach! That describes the time of day that they were about to get to the blue hole. When the sun was positioned just above the pine trees. Wouldn't that be like three or four in the afternoon?"

"Probably."

"Next he describes a dark watery pit. Isn't that a pretty good description of a blue hole?"

"We already know that," Laura added. "Are there any other clues describing the location?"

"No, that's it. But it does state that they lowered the treasure into the pit with a chain. That was not described in Hornigold's logbook."

"You're right. So maybe if we could locate the chain, that is if it's still there, then we would know that we're at the right location."

"And the treasure should be hanging on the other end!" Beth said, glancing around the room.

"So what do we do next?" Laura asked.

"Let's make a copy of the poem on Dr. Lounsbury's copier. Then we can take our notes and the poem over to the lodge. There's a large map of Andros in the classroom. Maybe we can find some of the clues on it."

"Great idea, Beth. Even if we find just one clue, it'll really help narrow down John's search area."

Beth and Laura copied the poem and returned the book to the shelf.

"Come on, let's go look at the map," Beth said, walking out the screen door.

Laura and Beth walked quickly to the lodge and then into the classroom. The large map of Andros hung down in front of the limestone wall next to the blackboard.

"Here's our location at the field station," Beth said, pointing at the map, and continued:

"The first clue in the poem we haven't found is Lucifer's Cay."

"Let's see," said Laura. "Here's London Creek, Stafford Creek, Bollard Creek and down here is Fresh Creek. That's it for creeks and no Lucifer's Cay. It has got to start on this side of the island."

They continued to go through their list, searching to find anything on the map that related to the names in the poem.

"Nothing," Laura said in frustration. "I'm not seeing Lucifer's Cay on this map."

"I know. I'm not either. I was so sure that we would find at least something on this map that relates to the poem. But nothing."

"Well, it was a good idea, but maybe the poem is just a poem, and we're trying to make a connection where there is none. All of this happened a long time ago and—"

"Long time ago!" Beth interrupted. "Laura, that's it, that's it, come with me."

"Beth what are you—" Laura stopped short as Beth quickly left the classroom and headed back to the director's cabin. Laura didn't catch up until they reached the screen door.

"What're you doing?" Laura asked.

"When you said a long time ago, it came to me," Beth said, entering the director's cabin. "The problem is that the map in the classroom is a recent map, a twentieth century map. The poem was written in the early eighteenth century. We're looking for clues that were written almost three-hundred years ago. The names of places have probably changed. There's a really old map of Andros sitting on this easel. We need to go through our list of clues again but this time with a map from that period of time."

"Why don't we take the map and lay it flat on the library table? It will be easier to look at it that way."

Beth grabbed the framed map and carried it into the library with her. They laid it down on the table and started to examine it.

"Look here," Beth said, pointing to the upper left hand corner of the map. "It says here that this map was printed in England and is dated seventeen fifteen. The map was printed just a few years prior to Hornigold sailing to Andros."

"I can't read this, Beth. The print is handwritten and faded."

"There's a magnifying glass on Dr. Lounsbury's desk. Maybe that will help us," Beth said.

Laura returned with the magnifying glass and started to examine the map. "Let's see. There were four creeks on the other map. Yeah, here they are. At least that hasn't changed!"

"Look for Lucifer's Cay. It should be somewhere around the neck of the creek," Beth said, looking over Laura's shoulder.

"Here it is!" Laura said, excitedly pointing to the location. "It's near the mouth of this creek."

"Let me see," Beth said, and asked Laura to hand her the magnifying glass. "You're right, Laura. I can't believe it! Now let's see if we can find another twentieth century map of Andros and copy it. That way we can identify the locations on the antique map and transfer the information onto the modern map, just like John Dettor did."

Laura got up from the chair and walked over to the bookshelf. She reviewed the selections and then pulled an atlas off the shelf and laid it on the table. Turning to the table of contents, she looked up the Bahamas and then found Andros.

"We can make a copy of this map," Laura said,

carrying the book to the copier. She returned with the fresh copy.

"All right, now we're in business. Mark an X at the location on the copy and then write the name beside it."

Laura sat down and marked the first clue onto the copied map.

"They headed west from Lucifer's Cay until they reached a marshy place and a freshwater creek. They must have hiked parallel to the creek. I would imagine that most of the terrain close to the creek would be marshland."

"You're probably right. There certainly appears to be a considerable amount of wetlands on this island, at least from what we've seen driving along the logging roads."

"Looking at this map, it would be too wide to cross this swampy area until they came across this narrow passage way up here, which is the next clue in the poem. They must have found a shallow passage somewhere around here. Mark this spot on the map as the possible crossing point. Then, it says they found a distant beach. By that time it was afternoon, and they were getting close to the blue hole."

"Do you see anything close to there that looks like a blue hole?" Laura asked.

"Yes, there are a few small bodies of water shown on the map in this area. But I don't see anything marked as Lucifer's Lair. However, the map is very faded in this area. It's getting rather hard to read."

Laura stood up and looked at the map once again. "Try using the magnifying glass,"

"Look here!" Beth said. "You can see that there's a hole in the map right here." She moved in for a close look. "I can still make out a few letters. On the one side of the hole, you see three letters, LUC. Then over on the other side, you can see two other letters, IR. If you put Lucifer's Lair into the lost space, then it makes sense. This has got to be the location of the blue hole. And if this is the blue hole, then we've found the location of the treasure! I can't believe it1 I can't believe we've pieced together the clues that will lead us to Lucifer's Lair!"

"Wow! You're right Beth. We've just discovered the hiding place of Hornigold's treasure!"

16

OBEDIAH'S

Beth and Laura basked in the sun, enjoying their afternoon and anxiously awaiting the return of the boat so they could share the news with Justin, Jeff, and Eric. The day was pleasant and the subtropical breeze gently rippled the calm waters in the lagoon. Around four o'clock Laura looked up from her book, cupped her hand over her eyes, and peered toward the ocean. Barely audible at first, then more distinct, she heard the faint whispery sound of an outboard engine.

"I think I hear their boat," Laura said, while Beth sipped iced tea through a slightly bent straw and peered over her book.

The drone of an outboard engine, mixed with exuberant conversation, grew louder as the boat came into view. Entering the channel in front of Bollard Creek, it turned toward the beach and motored for the shore. Gliding up until the bow grazed the shallows, Newby cut the motors, and the pontoons soon scraped on the shallow bottom and stopped the boat several feet from the beach.

"Beth! How're you feeling?" Molly asked, splashing through the water with the others and up onto the shore.

"Much better…I think I just needed a day to rest," Beth replied, sounding more like her usual self.

"You missed a great trip," Justin said. "We saw a massive school of silver sides in a small cavern back in the reef. There must have been a million, and when I swam through them, they parted like a big cloud. It was really cool."

"Sounds neat," Beth said.

"How're you doing," asked Justin.

"We've enjoyed our day just lounging around on the beach. And until you arrived it was peaceful and quiet," Beth joked.

"Very funny," Justin said, but he was happy to see her humor had returned.

Beth motioned with her finger for Justin to come closer while the others began to disperse to the rinse deck and cabins for showers. He knelt down on Beth's colorful beach blanket, and she whispered in his ear.

"We need to talk with you, Jeff and Eric, as soon as possible," Beth said, anxious to tell them about her discovery.

"What about?"

"Not here. Get Jeff and Eric and meet us down the beach," Beth explained.

The girls walked a little ways along the beach and waited. Beth unzipped her backpack when the guys arrived under the shade of a large Australian pine.

"So what's up?" Justin asked.

"While you were gone, Laura and I did some research on Hornigold in Dr. Lounsbury's library and we think we've found where the treasure was hidden," Beth said.

"What? No way!" said Eric.

"What'd you find?" asked Jeff.

"We were looking for a good book to read in the lodge when Dr. Lounsbury invited us over to his really awesome library. He had the book about the legends and tales of the Bahamas. You know the book that Basky told us about in the taxi? In the book was this poem—"

"Poem?" Justin interrupted, perplexed.

"Just hang on a sec and hear me out," Beth replied. "In the book there's this poem about the death of a pirate named Maynard and—"

"Maynard, wasn't he mentioned in Hornigold's logbook?" Justin asked interrupting Beth again.

"No, duh!" Beth retorted, and knitted her brow at Justin. "The poem described how Maynard died in a dark watery pit called Lucifer's Lair and—"

"Lucifer's Lair, that was in the—"

"Will you quit interrupting and let me finish," Beth tersely stated; Jeff and Eric quickly agreed. "As I was saying, the poem is about Maynard, and how the treasure was hidden at Lucifer's Lair. We looked at an old map of Andros that Dr. Lounsbury had in his office and found something amazing." Beth pulled some papers from her backpack and continued:

"Here's a copy of the map. At first, we couldn't find it, but look here…we discovered that there's a hole in the map." She pointed at the copy. "On this side are the letters LUC and on the other side are the letters IR. There's a space missing in the middle where the hole is and where the rest of the letters were. If you place the missing letters into the center, you have LUCIFER'S LAIR."

"Wow, I can't believe it," Jeff responded, his voice rising as he peered at the paper.

"We then made a copy of a modern map," Beth continued, pulling another page off the bottom of her little stack. "Of course the old map is different, but we enlarged the copy of the newer map and if you overlay them, you can see that it's a pretty close match." Beth held them up to the light. "In fact, that's the only blue hole in the area. It's now called Pimlico, but it matches up with what was described in the poem as a 'pit' that was once named Lucifer's Lair."

"Let me see," Eric said, lining up the pages and looking for himself. He smiled excitedly. "You're right Beth, maybe this is where the treasure is hidden."

"Maybe," Jeff said. "But how do you know the poem is about Hornigold's treasure?"

"Just read this," Beth replied. She handed Jeff the poem. "I copied the page that mentions Lucifer's Lair. The poem dates back to the early seventeen hundreds, around the time that Hornigold must have hidden his treasure here on Andros. It's got to be the location. There are just too many coincidences."

Jeff studied the poem carefully, and then said, "You're right Beth. Have you told John and Grant?"

"No, we looked for them, but Ooma told us they would not be back until later today. I think they'll be at the party tonight. Maybe we can tell them then."

"Yeah! Once John sees this, maybe we can dive the blue hole with him tomorrow," Justin suggested.

"I'll go, but you know I can't dive," Beth said as the vivid image of the corpse in the halocline swirled in her mind. "But I can count treasure!"

"I hope it comes to that, Beth," Justin said. "Well, let's get Grant and John aside at the party tonight and see what they say."

"There you are," Molly said, approaching with her hair still wet from the shower. "You should start getting ready for the party. The van leaves at five thirty, and that gives you," Molly said, looking at her watch, "about an hour."

They dispersed to their cabins to shower, change, and get ready for the party. Close to five thirty, Newby backed the Rockwood van up to the lodge and waited. The boys arrived first, freshly showered; they had changed into shorts and sandals, and they wore the batik shirts that Molly had purchased for them earlier in the week.

"You guys look great," Molly said, as she and Mike walked to the van and climbed in.

"Thanks again for the shirts, Molly," Justin said.

"You're welcome. Glad you like them," Molly said.

"Let's see, is everyone here?" Dr. Lounsbury asked, walking to the van with Carmen and Nicole.

"We're waiting for the girls as usual," Jeff answered.

"We're here," Beth said, arriving at the van with Laura, attired in her long green Batik dress. She wore a white shell necklace around her neck, several braids dangled on the left side of her head, and on the right, just over her ear, perched a yellow orchid.

"Wow!" Justin exclaimed. "You look…amazing."

"Thanks, Justin!" She took a long moment to look over Justin, then quipped, "As my mother always says, you clean up pretty good yourself." She took a seat in the van beside him.

The other girls got in the van and Newby headed out the lane to the main highway, then south toward Obediah's for the fish bake and dance near Small Hope Bay. As they rode along, they discussed the highlights from the day's activities; the van arrived before they knew it at a small wooden sign on the left side of the road. "Obediah's" was all the rustic sign stated from the top of a rickety post in the middle of a small flower bed outlined with conch shells. Newby turned the van onto the palm-covered lane, drove up in front of a spacious home, and parked amongst a collage of vintage vehicles. A long porch ran the length of the house and was covered with rocking chairs and two swings suspended from the ceiling. They got out and walked up two steps. Carmen knocked on the screen door. From somewhere in the back of the house a dog started to bark, and a young boy appeared at the door. "Party's out back," was all he said in a high-pitched voice, opening the door.

"Hello, James," Carmen said, greeting her little friend.

"Hi," he replied in a long drawn out tone. He grabbed Carmen's hand and led her through the house to a porch in the back.

"James, I haven't seen you all week. Where've you been?" Carmen asked.

"Mamma's been feeling poorly this week, so I had extra chores to do," James explained in his bubbly Bahamian accent.

"Welcome, welcome," a stout man said, as they all exited the house and walked onto the spacious porch in the back. "I'm Obediah Daggett. Welcome to our home. My, my, I've never seen such beautiful women in all my days," Obediah continued in a gravelly voice, looking at the group. He was dressed in long tan trousers with a long-sleeved fisherman's shirt; leather sandals covered his feet. A shiny silver buckle in the shape of a sailboat was attached to his handcrafted leather belt. Around his neck were stout gold chains that dangled freely and bounced with every movement. He had an oval face and wrinkled leathery complexion. His dark skin was accentuated with silver-gray hair, eyebrows and beard.

"Obediah, it's so good to see you," Carmen said. "James told us that Mrs. Daggett is feeling a little under the weather."

"Oh, she be fine and dandy now. Had a little touch of something or another, but the medicine woman came by and gave her some remedy. Um, boy did it smell something terrible. You could tell because she scrunched her nose up with every dose. She drank it though, and it either cured her, or she's just pretending, so she don't have to drink no more of that stuff," Obediah explained, laughing heartily.

"Well, I'll go talk to her in the kitchen shortly," Carmen said, and then introduced the other guests.

"Nice to meet you folks, and Mike and Molly, it's sure good to see you again. Please make our home yours while you're here. We have the band getting ready to play, the fish is baking on the grille, souse is cooking, the dance floor is in place, and I'm expecting some more folks to arrive. What more could the good Lord give us on this fine day?" Obediah asked of no one in particular. "James, you show our guests around, and I'm going to check on the cooks back in the kitchen."

James led the group down the steps to the sandy ground. To the left a five-member Calypso band tuned instruments. Out in front of the band was a large dance floor. Sheets of plywood were placed in a large rectangle, lined with conch shells, and torches with orange flames lapped at the sky. Over to the right, a woman in a long dress tended to a grated pit, raking coals in the fire, cooking. Long tables were set up with fruits, vegetables, drinks, punch, and all the utensils for dinner with condiments. Toward the beach three Bahamian fishing smacks, or boats, were pulled up close to the tree line. A few men mended fishnets and watched children splashing in the shallows. Out over the Tongue of the Ocean puffy subtropical clouds hung in the sky and reflected on the calm water. The sun, beginning to set over the island in the west, cast a warm and reddish glow on the clouds.

"Wow, looks like a Hawaiian luau," Debbie said. "I should've brought a grass skirt."

"Obediah's cookouts are the best. We come down here every Wednesday night and many of the locals come as well," Carmen explained.

Debbie and Jane walked to the water's edge, took their sandals off and waded into the shallows. Some of the local kids started to quiz the girls about where they were from. Soon the guests had scattered and dispersed, blending into the surroundings. After a while the sound of metal on metal rang out over the beach party; everyone stopped what they were doing and looked in the direction of the back porch. Obediah was running a metal stick around the inside of a triangular metal bar, making a sound similar to a bell.

"Dinner is served," Obediah announced his voice loud as the bell. "We have fresh fish and conch, vegetables from our garden, souse, and fruit. So, help yourselves. There be plenty for everyone."

A line gathered at the table near the fire pit. Plates were soon filled with steaming fish, bits of conch, a variety of vegetables, locally grown fruit and bowls containing souse. Finding places either at tables or blankets on the sand, they enjoyed Obediah's feast. Many went back for seconds, especially for souse, and more locals arrived throughout dinner. Then the calypso band began to play. Two native islanders, wasting no time, got onto the dance floor and began to dance. Their colorful dresses shifted and twirled around their bodies, as they contorted and danced in rhythm to the music. Then a few of the men got on the floor and joined the women. Before long the dance floor was covered with a colorful throng of dancers, twirling around the floor creating a kaleidoscope of swirling colors.

"Want to dance?" Justin asked Beth.

"I don't know island dance," Beth replied.

"Neither do I but let's give it a try anyway," Justin said, pulling her onto the dance floor. They began to dance like the others.

Mike and Molly entered the fray and, to the amazement of all, actually seemed to have it down to perfection. Jane and Debbie got up with a tentative Steve and Mitch and tried a few steps of their own. Eric and Laura moved in and danced in their own unique way. Jeff was watching from a distance as he finished his last morsel of dinner when a hand reached out and grabbed his.

"I'm Mrs. Daggett," a slender woman with gray hair said, introducing herself to Jeff. "I always get to dance with whomever I want since I can never get Obediah on the dance floor. Complains that his knees be hurting

him, but truth be known, the man ain't got no rhythm,"
she said, laughing. Jeff introduced himself.

"You like to dance?" Mrs. Daggett asked.

"Um, well, I'm not very—"

"Good, come with me," she said, tugging on Jeff's
arm and leading him right into the middle of the dance
floor.

"Oh, we have a special treat this evening, folks," the
lady singer announced, as the music died down. On the
dance floor the crowd parted, leaving only Jeff and Mrs.
Daggett in the middle. "I see Mrs. Daggett is on the
dance floor this evening, feeling much better," she said
to the cheering crowd. "Now, for you newcomers, this
will be a special treat. Mrs. Daggett is one of the
islander's best dancers, and she always picks someone
from the crowd to dance with her." The band started up
again, and Mrs. Daggett began her dance. Jeff, standing
in the middle of the dance floor, pushed his glasses up
on his nose and seemed startled. He was frozen in place.

The music, with a rhythmic calypso beat, seemed to
move Mrs. Daggett in practiced steps around the dance
floor. She twirled close, grabbed Jeff's hand, and pulled
him along with her as Jeff clumsily tried to keep up with
her and mimic her steps. He tried a few steps of his own,
and then she brought him close and helped him through
some moves. Soon the others joined back in, and the
dance floor was alive with a writhing colorful mass of
dancers.

"You dance all right, just need some practice," Mrs.
Daggett said when the song stopped.

"Thanks," Jeff replied.

"Here, I want you to have this," she said, pulling a
shell necklace over her head and putting it around Jeff's
neck. "Didn't mean to embarrass you earlier. It's
customary to invite a newcomer to dance. Makes
everyone feel at home, and they have a better time." She
smiled kindly at Jeff.

"It's okay, it was fun—and thank you for the necklace," Jeff said. She walked back into the house, and Jeff headed to the food table for a drink of water.

"You did all right for your first time," Grant said with a smile when he approached the food table with John, then he chuckled. "It wasn't quite as smooth when she had me out there."

"That's quite a woman," Jeff said and sipped water.

Grant nodded and then changed the subject. "John and I just finished fixing the air compressor."

"Did you need any parts?"

"Nah, just a bit of island ingenuity and now we can fill tanks again."

"That's awesome," Jeff replied, then lowered his voice conspiratorially. "We've been hoping you guys would show up this evening. We've got something we need to discuss with you."

John did not seem to hear Jeff at first, appearing instead to concentrate on filling his plate with food. "Did you try the souse?" he asked Jeff.

"Yeah! It's awesome," Jeff said.

"Obediah makes the best," John said, then stopped filling his plate and looked carefully at Jeff. "So what's on your mind?"

Jeff took a deep breath. "Well, today Beth and Laura spent time in Dr. Lounsbury's library researching Hornigold and discovered some really important information. It's about the treasure. I think Beth should tell you herself. Maybe after you eat, we can all meet down on the beach and talk about it."

"Now, I'll be happy to talk with you guys, but you know my mind is set and you're out of the treasure hunt," John replied, reiterating what he had told Grant back at the blue hole. "Please understand it's for your own safety."

"Maybe you'll reconsider after you hear what Beth has to say," Jeff said. He turned and walked over to find the others. John followed Jeff with his eyes, then scratched his chin. Jeff had clearly left him wondering.

Soon John and Grant finished their meal and walked down to the edge of the water. Eric and Laura walked over, and then Beth, Justin and Jeff arrived.

"This is quite a party," John said. "Remember that spirit I talked about in the van the other day. This is it! Good food, good people, music and a setting sun."

"I could sure get used to this kind of living," Jeff said.

"Beth, Jeff told me that you have something to tell me," John said, changing the subject.

"We found the location of the treasure today!" Beth said her voice tinged with excitement. "You found what?" John asked, surprised and perplexed.

Beth explained how she and Laura found the poem about Maynard in Dr. Lounsbury's office earlier in the day, and with a hint of melodrama in her voice, she mentioned a blue hole named Lucifer's Lair that was also noted in the treasure documents. And then, she showed him the copy of the old map and how the letters of Lucifer's Lair could fit in the space she found. She showed him the copy of the poem and the new map of Andros with the newer name of Pimlico for the blue hole in the same location as the old one. When she was done, John stood silent and still, scratched his head and closely examined the documents that Beth had produced.

"This is absolutely amazing, but there's only one problem with your theory," John stated.

"Problem? What problem?" Beth asked, now crushed that John was about to shoot down her research.

"Well, Grant and I have already searched this blue hole. There's no treasure there," John said.

"But it's got to be there," Beth reasserted.

"I'm afraid that we did a thorough search of that blue hole, and we didn't find a thing," John explained again. "I'm sorry."

"But you're always searching below the halocline. Maybe, just maybe, the treasure's in the blue hole, but more shallow," Beth said.

"You know, Beth does have a point, John," Jeff began in Beth's defense. "The treasure, if lowered to be recovered later, might have been placed close to the wall of the blue hole. Maybe it's still there and not on the bottom."

John shook his head. "That treasure has been down there in the water for almost three centuries. The wooden chest with metal strapping that the documents says it was stored in would have disintegrated by now. The contents would have spilled out and fallen to the bottom of the blue hole."

"In that case why did you have us looking around the blue hole on the upper shelves, or outcroppings?" Justin inquired. "And what about the dead man? Did he have anything to do with the treasure?"

"The police are investigating and I haven't heard anything from them yet," John explained. "Now as far as your search pattern, I was trying to cover my bases with your extra help."

"Well, did you go into Pimlico and look on each and every shelf in the blue hole?" Beth asked.

"We most certainly did, young lady and—"

"John, you know what," Grant said interrupting him. "When we dived Pimlico, we spent a lot of time below the halocline. The metal detector battery died and when we searched the shallower regions, it was without the detector. Remember?"

"I do remember, Grant, but I don't recall seeing any likely locations where a treasure could have been hidden above the halocline. I'm sorry, but it's just not there."

"Well, I'm not convinced," Beth bravely asserted; her eyes riveted on John.

"I agree with Beth," Justin said. "I think we ought to go back and take another look around at that blue hole tomorrow."

John held up a hand and stated sharply, "Now wait just a minute. This is not a democracy here. I call the shots. I told Grant to tell all of you that as much as I've appreciated your help, I don't want you involved anymore. You've got some sound research here Beth, but we eliminated that blue hole and—"

"John, let them go out one more time," Grant said in their defense. "It can't hurt. And if we spot anything that even remotely looks like trouble, we'll bag the dive."

"We could leave early. Then if we find it, we could be in and out before anyone else even knew we were there," Jeff suggested.

"Now wait just a minute—"

"Please, John, please," Laura said, interrupting him.

"So this is how it's going to be, all of you ganging up on the old man?" John said, scratching the top of his head. "I tell you what—"

"We can go!" Jeff almost yelled.

"Hang on, and let me finish, please," John continued. "If, and only if, the McNeil's and Dr. Lounsbury agree to your going, and if you can leave at first light in the morning, I'll go out against my better judgment, and take another look in this blue hole. Now, Beth, I thought that you were under observation after the bump you got on your head? Won't you have to stay behind?"

"No! I mean it's been twenty-four hours so the observation period is over. And I want to be there when you find the treasure." Beth wouldn't take her eyes off John.

"Find the treasure, just like that," John responded, a smile darting to his mouth. You're sure of yourself aren't you?"

"Yup!"

"Okay, get your permission, and if it's a yes, we'll be off at the crack of dawn for Pimlico," John relented.

Jeff, Justin, Beth and Grant walked over and found

the McNeil's and Dr. Lounsbury talking with Obediah and his wife, Mrs. Daggett. They asked about the blue hole dive in the morning, and they were surprised that Beth would even consider wanting to go. Beth explained that she just wanted to go along, she would not dive, and she didn't want the others to miss out just because of her. They relented and said that Friday would be a group day, so this would be the last of their blue hole dives. They returned to the others, who were patiently waiting on the beach, and gave them the thumbs up.

"Okay, it's set then." John said. "We'll meet at the dive shop at first light in the morning."

17

LUCIFER'S LAIR

A misty fog had rolled in during the night, covering the Rockwood grounds. Long sweeping branches of the Australian pines undulated in the light wind and swayed with the palm fronds above the rooftops of the field station. Jeff, Justin and Eric approached the shop at daybreak carrying their scuba gear, eager to get underway. Beth and Laura arrived a few minutes later carrying the lunch they had gathered from the kitchen. Grant backed the van up to the dive shop. John arrived; they all lent a hand to load the van and were soon on their way.

The van's headlights illuminated the dense fog that seemed to reach out of the forest like big fingers on a wispy hand. The terrain, now familiar to everyone, passed in a blur as they traveled along the deserted Queen's Highway. They chatted with excitement about the upcoming dive and the possibilities of finding the lost treasure. John navigated from the front passenger seat with map in hand, directing Grant, who soon slowed and turned west onto an old logging road. The vegetation looked different in the eerie glow of the early dawn. One could even imagine creatures lying in wait in the dark shadows of the forest like the fabled chickcharney.

Reaching a turn, John motioned left. They headed south. Within a few miles of slow driving down the logging road, they came into a small clearing visible on the driver's side. The blue hole was located just a few hundred yards from the logging road down a shallow, grass-lined trail. The blue hole cut a two-hundred foot oval out of the thick vegetation with its clear, blue-tinted water. They unloaded all of their scuba tanks and dive gear from the van and carried it over to an open grassy area, close to where they would enter the water. Beth and Laura, the bubble watchers, put on light cotton pants and long-sleeved shirts to cover themselves from the relentless doctor flies, while the divers donned their wet suits and prepared for the first dive.

"I certainly hope we have better luck than last time," John said, and winked at Beth.

"It has to be here." Beth said with confidence. "I wouldn't have tried to persuade you to come here again if I didn't believe that the treasure was here!"

"I hope you're right," Grant said.

"Yeah, because if you're right, we'll all be famous," Jeff said, and wiggled into his tight wet suit.

"OK, you all know the routine by now, so our briefing will be short," John said. "Grant and I, as usual, will dive deep and search the bottom and the wall below the halocline. I'd like you guys to search along the wall and shelves, or outcroppings that potentially could have caught the treasure. Don't try to explore the entire blue hole on your first dive. We have the whole morning to search this site. Just take your time and be thorough. And remember, if you find anything, leave it undisturbed."

"Good luck," Laura said as she waved her crossed

fingers toward them.

Grant and John entered the water with dive lights blazing and waterproof metal detector in hand, dove deep, and disappeared below the halocline. Jeff, Justin and Eric descended to sixty feet and began to explore a section of the shelf that jutted out around the blue hole. As they moved along the wall horizontally in a search pattern, they fanned each projecting shelf, using their hands as fans, clearing the algae and muck from the shelf down to the hard rock. The fanning created opaque clouds of sediment, so thick that they were forced to feel with their hands for any loose objects that they now could not see. With nothing uncovered, they moved on to the next shelf. Eventually their air gauges—after nearly an hour's worth of work—started reading low and they signaled with thumbs up to end the dive. On the surface the sun had angled higher, the fog had lifted and Grant and John, who had already completed their dive, were resting on the grass-lined shore talking with Beth and Laura.

"See anything?" John asked as the three divers submerged and finned their way over to the shore.

"Nope! Nothing but a bunch of brown muck," Justin said when he removed the regulator from his mouth. "But we were only able to search about half of the wall."

"We'll keep looking. Let's make sure that we've covered every inch of it," said John, now up on his feet and switching tanks. "We either need to find it, or convince a certain persistent young lady that it's not here."

"You're talking about me?" Beth said.

John smiled and said, "You know, not to dash your hopes, but sometimes the best research cannot reveal the one possibility we haven't even discussed."

"What's that?" Beth said.

"Maybe somebody has already recovered the treasure." John said.

"Like who?"

"Well, if I found it and did not want to turn it over to the government, I would keep it quiet and no one would ever be the wiser. Then the question of who could have potentially recovered the treasure would become impossible to answer. But I only see several possibilities for how it could have been recovered."

"Hornigold?" Beth asked.

"That's the best answer or someone at the time who knew about the treasure, hence the poem. If that's not the case, then I don't see any real possibility of it being recovered until after the invention of hardhat diving and then scuba that would have made it possible to search with long stays underwater and at depth. The natives certainly wouldn't have found it. They were too superstitious about the fabled blue holes and stayed out of them. Early pioneering scuba divers on Andros could possibly have blundered into it and kept it quiet, but there's never been a mention of it in any way from the islanders and they would certainly know something about it if it had happened." John paused and looked at the faces looking at him. "And even for us when we're pretty sure that we know where it's located, with authentic historic documentation and the use of modern tools such as scuba and underwater metal detectors, the treasure still remains elusive today."

"I can't imagine going home without finding it," Beth said, her tone uncharacteristically quiet. Her exuberant hope from yesterday's research was fading.

After the surface interval of approximately an hour required between repetitive dives, the two dive teams re-entered the water. Grant and John returned to the bottom again to work the lower walls; the boys began to search another unexplored section of the shelf, halfway around the blue hole and twenty feet higher than their earlier search. Large mats of algae hung off the wall like tinsel on a Christmas tree. Jeff disturbed some of the stringy algae, and large strips peeled off the wall, sinking into the depths of the blue hole.

While Justin worked his way over to another shelf, Eric searched a crevice directly above and slightly to the right of him. Jeff decided to observe the wall from a broader view and swam out until he could see as much of the wall as possible. He scanned the entire view from just below the surface to the top of the halocline; with over one hundred feet of clear visibility, he could see a large area. Then something unnatural caught his eye. A little farther up and over to his right was what appeared to be a straight line of rust-colored algae running from the surface and abruptly ending halfway down the wall. Jeff kicked over to it for a closer inspection. He reached into the algae. His hand touched something that felt stiff and rigid, like the wall of the blue hole. He cleared the algae from a small area and waited until the water cleared enough to see the object. It appeared to be the rusted remains of what was once stout links of chain.

"Chain," Jeff mused to himself. Understanding the magnitude of what he had found, he followed the antiquated remains of the algae-covered chain straight down to its last link. It ended directly above a large outcropping, a projecting ledge close to where both Justin and Eric were searching.

Jeff signaled to Justin and anxiously waved him over. Curious, Justin finned over and Jeff maneuvered Justin's hand onto the exposed ancient chain. It took a moment for him to understand the significance of what he was touching. Then the reality of the discovery washed across his face and he pointed straight down. Jeff signaled okay. They both dropped down to the ledge below and began to fan the shelf furiously with their hands.

After a few moments, they stopped and gave the sediment and algae droppings a few moments to clear. Then they moved in close and felt along with their hands. Jeff swept his hand across a section of the shelf. He found nothing but a handful of mucky sediment. After a few attempts, Justin reached in and grabbed something that felt hard and round. He pulled it out. The Bahamian sun rays that streamed through the water illuminated the shiny surface of a gold doubloon. Justin had to blink his eyes several times—then realized that the first piece of Hornigold's treasure was found. Jeff began to hoot and holler through his regulator. Eric saw the coin and did the same.

Jeff then reached for the coin and signaled with his thumb up to end the dive. Eric and Justin flashed an okay signal. Then Jeff pointed to his chest, pointed a thumb downward, flashed the coin and pointed again below. Justin understood that Jeff would get John and Grant while he and Eric surfaced to tell Laura and Beth. Jeff descended and finned away from the wall; he soon found bubbles rising from beneath the halocline. Without a dive light, he passed through the halocline. Clear visibility turned to pitch black once he passed through the thick layer of sediment. Far below he could just make out the faint illumination of a moving light. Descending in the direction of the light, Jeff finned directly in front of John and Grant and was nearly blinded by the sudden bright luminance of the dive light.

John and Grant were startled to suddenly see Jeff appear in front of them in the murky gloom. Then Jeff, seeing nothing but the blinding light, held the gold coin in his hand answering all of their questions. John saw the brilliance of the gold luster of the coin and hooted through his regulator.

John signaled thumbs up, and they finned over to the wall to begin their ascent. Back through the halocline they ascended to the shelf where Justin had found the coin. Jeff showed Grant and John the chain. John reached into the muck with his hands and felt around, appraising the situation. Soon surfacing, they were greeted with absolute pandemonium of hoots and hollers.

"I can't believe it!" John said. "It was right here and we had missed it. I was so convinced that the treasure would have fallen over time to the bottom."

"Let's see it!" Beth said from the shore, knowing they had recovered a coin. She and Laura were so excited they almost fell into the blue hole. Jeff swam over and handed her the coin.

"Beth!" John said. "If it wasn't for the research you and Laura did we might have never found this treasure."

"I can't believe it!" Beth said, looking at the wet gold coin. She and Laura cheered and hugged each other while jumping up and down.

"Wow! The last person to see and touch this coin was probably Hornigold. That's just awesome!" Laura said.

"Almost three-hundred years ago!" John said.

"Wow!"

"You know I never cared much for myths and legends—just too unscientific for me. Even if I had read that poem, I'm not sure I would have put together the puzzle like you girls did. I must say I'm mighty proud of you both, well, all of you for making an old man see things in a new light. Thanks!" John said.

"Bet you'll start reading about myths and legends now!" Beth winked at John and he winked back.

"Now we need a game plan," John said. "Let's work in two teams. Go back down and fan all the muck away from the treasure with your hands. I felt into the sediment and I think the dilapidated chest is sitting on top of the treasure. So, Grant and Eric, why don't you start as team one. Go down and fan as much muck away as you can. Take Beth and Laura's fins down with you and use them as fans. Then surface and we'll send team two, Jeff and Justin, down after we give the site about a half an hour to settle. We'll keep that up until the treasure is clear of the muck and then begin photographing in place. Jeff, when we get to that stage, I want you to stay at depth and photograph everything we do, both up-close and again from a distance. I've got mesh bags for the treasure and lift bags to hoist it to the surface. I'll go back down below the halocline with the metal detector and make sure nothing slipped off that shelf and landed below. Everyone understand your job? Any questions?"

John finned over to the location of the treasure with Eric and Grant. While they began to fan the muck away using their fins, John descended directly to the bottom and searched with the metal detector in case any stray coins had spilled into the depths of the blue hole below. Finding nothing, he ascended back to the wide shelf at twenty-five feet where a gloomy cloud of sediment, from Eric's and Grant's work, hung like a brown fog bank over gold that was glinting in the filtered sun. Upon closer inspection John saw a pile of wooden boards and rusted metal strapping sitting on top of numerous gold and silver coins. He fanned at the sediment a bit and then surfaced.

"Pretty awesome sight, isn't it?" Grant said when John surfaced.

"Awesome it is indeed! And it puts us all in elite company making such a discovery," John said.

"Huh! What do you mean?" Grant said while John finned to the shore, passed his gear up to the others and climbed out of the blue hole.

"Think about how it feels to make such an incredible discovery like Hornigold's treasure. Well, that's the same feeling that Columbus must have felt when he discovered America. That's the same feeling you would get uncovering an ancient Egyptian tomb. You can't buy this feeling and you can't experience it in some amusement park riding a rollercoaster. You can only feel this way from making an incredible discovery." John paused for a moment, smiled, and continued: "That's why I say it puts us in elite company—you have experienced something that very few people ever get to experience. And now you know firsthand what people like Columbus must have felt like when he discovered America."

"Wow! That's incredible," Laura said.

John nodded and said, "The site is looking clearer after team one fanned the majority of the heavy sediment away. Let's take a break and soon team two, Jeff and Justin, can go down and continue the work. The way it looks, just a few more dives and we can begin to remove the treasure. Jeff, take your camera this dive and let's begin documenting the treasure sitting on the ledge and make sure to photograph the remains of the chest too. I want photographs of everything we see and do."

Soon, Jeff and Justin descended to the ledge and continued the work of fanning away the sediment while Jeff took pictures. Then a half an hour later Grant and Eric were back on site and had most of the muck cleared of the treasure. One last dive by Jeff and Justin and the site was virtually free of all sediment, revealing stacks of gold and silver sitting below the wooden boards and heavily rusted metal strapping.

"That's about it," Jeff said when they returned from their last muck clearing dive. "By the time the sediment clears this time we should be ready."

"Excellent! I've been thinking about our recovery and this is my plan," John replied. He was sitting in the sun, eating an apple. "Jeff, I want you to stay as cameraman to document everything we do underwater. First, I'll go down with Grant and Eric, we'll move the chest off the treasure and leave it on the shelf."

"Aren't we going to recover what's left of the chest?" Justin asked.

"Not today. That can't be recovered until preparations are made in a conservation lab to protect the wood and metal. That work can be expensive and takes years to do correctly. So, until that's in place the chest is best left right here in the blue hole," John said. "So, once we have moved what's left of the chest we'll begin to fill these mesh bags with treasure." He pointed to several large bags on the ground. "Then Grant and Eric can bring up the first lift. I want two divers handling our precious cargo. Once they surface, Justin, you come down and we'll bring up the second lift and break for lunch. Now, everyone's used a lift bag before?"

"I haven't." Justin said. "But I saw Mike use one when we were diving King Kong earlier in the week."

"It's really quite simple. Just clip it to the mesh bag and fill it with air from your regulator. Then when it begins to lift, you just ascend with it to the surface. If it starts going too fast as the air in it expands, you can just vent a little out to slow it down," John said. "The lift bags will lift one-hundred pounds each, and I estimate that the treasure is several hundred pounds, so a couple of trips should do it. Any questions?"

No one responded. They got to work.

Down on the shelf Jeff hovered above Grant and Eric and took pictures while John helped to clear the remains of the chest off the treasure. Then they started to fill two mesh bags with stacks of gold and silver coins. A silver box emerged from beneath silver coins, then an ornate jewelry box that they placed in the bags. John clipped a lift bag onto one mesh bag and filled it with his regulator. As it began to lift off the shelf, Grant and Eric ascended with it to the surface. Justin then descended, and he and John brought up the second bag while Jeff took pictures.

"I can't wait to see it!" Laura exclaimed once they surfaced.

Grant and Eric were in chest deep water by the edge of the blue hole where the first lift bag still floated. John, Justin and Jeff finned over with the second bag and they soon had them both hoisted on dry land. Over lunch, as

John began to talk about the treasure, they inspected the coins and excitedly awaited the opening of the silver and jewelry boxes.

"Laura, if you will do me a favor, I've got a large plastic pan in the back of the van. Would you bring that over here," John said. They all sat on the ground around the treasure bags, eating sandwiches under the sun that had long since burned off the early morning fog.

"Here you go," Laura said when she returned with a gray pan about as large as a bread box. She set it down beside John.

"Thanks! Now here's a copy of the manifest and it states that the silver box was filled with pearls the size of filberts. Anyone know what filberts are?" John said.

"Hazelnuts," Jeff said.

"That's right," John said, then removed the silver box, placed it in the pan and opened the lid. Inside dozens and dozens of large pearls saw the light of day for the first time in three-hundred years.

"Wow!" Beth said reaching in she pulled one out for closer inspection.

"That's amazing!" Eric said.

"And now the manifest says this jewelry box should be filled with diamonds and gemstones," John explained and placed the box in the plastic gray pan. As John gently opened the lid, a colorful mixture of diamonds and gem stones sparkled in the sun. The moment took them all away; caught up in the excitement of the discovery, they all cheered wildly.

"This has got to be worth millions," Justin said when the excitement died down a bit.

"At least," John said. "And that's only the intrinsic value in the gold, silver and diamonds. With the provenance that this belonged to Captain Hornigold, it's worth even more. And this is only about half of the treasure. There's more to come up!"

"So what'll you do with it now," Justin asked.

"Ah! Good question," John said. "First, I'll find a secure space that we can lock away the treasure for safe keeping. Eventually, it'll be turned over to the Bahamian government, but not until the world knows it exists. That way I can more likely guarantee that it will be displayed in a museum and not auctioned off," John said.

"You know, I can almost imagine those pirates and Hornigold here, putting the treasure chest into the blue hole. And this must be where Thomas Maynard was killed by the Lusca Monster," Beth said

"Now I can tell you without a doubt that Maynard was not killed by Lusca. Whirlpools aren't known to form in the inland blue holes, but I suppose under the right conditions it could be possible under an extreme change in tides and the water tables have changed in three hundred years of time. That's your Lusca monster, nothing more than a change in tides creating a funnel of water like a bathtub when it is drained." John paused and smiled a tight, knowing smile. "But it is a skillfully crafted story that would keep superstitious people like sailors away, not to mention the local folk from looking too close at blue holes. Pirates are known to be crafty."

After lunch, the guys strapped on the last of the tanks and submerged to recover the remaining treasure. The girls carried the pan of diamonds and pearls to the van. In the distance they heard a vehicle scraping through the overgrown logging road. The sound became louder as the vehicle approached the blue hole. Beth and Laura closed the van door and walked back to the blue hole, looked for the guys, and listened from the water's edge. Soon they heard a vehicle stop, the engine cut off, and doors opened and banged closed. Not sure what to do, the girls quickly made a dash for cover in the thick growth at the jungle's edge a short distance away from the treasure.

Someone approached slowly, still back behind the

bushes so the girls could not see. The intruder walked out into the sunlight and stood right by the treasure still in the mesh bags. Laura saw him first with a rifle: a large man sporting a wide-brimmed felt hat with a brown band.

"Oh no!" Laura said, crouching lower and well hidden behind the bush.

"Who's that?" Beth asked.

Then both girls noticed the infamous scar on his arm, turned to each other and whispered, "Winfrey!"

18

LUCIFER'S SNARE

Three men followed Winfrey into the clearing next to the blue hole. One, a muscular, bald- headed man, wore a stout gold chain around his neck with a white shark tooth dangling at the end; he sported numerous colorful tattoos of sailor art, visible on his arms and neck through a sleeveless white T-shirt. The other two were dark-skinned islanders. They were both younger, comparable in height and size, standing about as tall as Winfrey's shoulder. One wore his salt and pepper colored hair long and the other cropped short and neat. Both men were dressed in black jeans and T-shirts and had pistols holstered on their belts.

"What're we going to do?" Beth whispered to Laura, peering through an opening in the thick vegetation that cloaked their presence.

"I don't know," Laura said quietly, "but somehow we need to warn the others."

"There's nothing we can do at the moment without giving ourselves away. They're trapped in the blue hole and warning them is not going to help. They'll soon have to come up anyway, and they'll be carrying with them the last of the treasure."

"But we can't just sit here and do nothing. That's my brother and our friends down there," Laura said, beginning to stand.

Beth grabbed her arm and pulled her back down behind there cover.

"Are you crazy? What're you going to do against four men with guns? We need to stay put and out of sight. Maybe an opportunity to help will come along."

"I see someone has gone to the trouble of recovering the treasure for us," Winfrey said, letting out a hearty and maniacal laugh. He reached down and pulled a doubloon from a mesh bag for examination. "Now that's what it's all about…gold!" He tossed the coin to one of the others. "Might as well go ahead and carry these two bags to their van."

Two Bahamian men carried the bags of the heavy treasure over the pathway to the vehicle, slapping doctor flies as they went. On the surface of the blue hole the bubbles coming up from the depths were small, indicative of divers deep. Slowly, twin billowing circles of bubbles grew larger on the surface as two of the divers ascended. Then, the bubble pattern held constant, while a safety stop was made, and finally got larger as they neared the surface. It felt like an eternity to the girls in hiding, waiting for someone to return. Jeff and Justin breached the surface, pulled their dive masks off and turned around looking for the girls, but only found the stainless steel barrel of Winfrey's rifle.

"I want to thank you for recovering my treasure," Winfrey said, pointing the rifle menacingly at them.

"What?" Justin said astonished by this sudden change of events, a cold shiver rocking his body. His eyes darted, searching for Beth and Laura.

"It's a small world," Winfrey said, then smiled as he recognized Justin. "Who would have ever imagined that the young man from the airport would end up being among the people that found my treasure? How convenient, and you've even brought it up for me. Now out of the water, both of you." He raised his rifle and continued as Justin and Jeff climbed out:

"Out! And bring the bag over here to me. Don't try anything stupid or you'll end up as fish bait!"

Jeff and Justin lifted the heavy bag up to Winfrey. They briefly glanced around for signs of the girls. Once on shore, they were instructed to remove their dive gear and wet suits, and then they got into their dry clothes under Winfrey's watchful eye. The two men returned from carrying the first load of treasure, and at gunpoint commanded Jeff and Justin to carry their bag to the van. Then they collected all of the dive gear and equipment, loaded it into the back of the van and took seats as ordered. Grant, John and Eric surfaced next, and started talking about the treasure when a deep voice interrupted.

"John Dettor? We finally get to meet in person; what perfect timing. This is such a pleasant surprise." Winfrey spoke in a mocking tone, his smile wide and gleeful. He brandished his weapon.

"Winfrey!?!" John yelped. Instantly he was concerned for everyone's safety, as numerous thoughts and possibilities coursed through his mind. "Where are the others?" he asked, darting his head from side to side.

"In the van. All three of you, out of the water and don't try anything!" Winfrey ordered. They finned to the edge of the blue hole and glanced at each other without saying a word, each expressing confused looks on their faces. They handed up the last bag of treasure and exited the water. Winfrey kept his rifle pointed at them.

"You'll never get away with this, Winfrey!" John said. "This treasure is not yours."

"You're wrong! This treasure is mine." Winfrey said. "Now, I strongly suggest you do as you're told, unless you'd like to become a relic yourself for someone to discover someday." Two of Winfrey's men reappeared, gathered the last bag of treasure and disappeared down the trail. The bald-headed man watched from nearby, like a security guard waiting to react; sunglasses hid his eyes.

"Eric my boy, job well done," Winfrey said, placing a hand on Eric's shoulder. Eric pushed away and stepped back from him. "Eric's been keeping me informed of your progress." Winfrey's smile widened gleefully once again.

"Eric?" John said incredulously. His face suddenly flushed red with anger; he seemed dumbfounded by the revelation of betrayal.

"I, I can explain," Eric stammered. "Winfrey threatened me and made me do it. I didn't have any other choice. He said he was going to kill my—"

"That's enough!" Winfrey interrupted. "There'll be plenty of time for you to explain to your friends what a snitch you are. But right now, it's time for us all to leave and I want no more talking!"

Led at gunpoint, they marched along the path and to the van where Jeff and Justin were already seated, waiting nervously. John, Grant and Eric soon joined them after changing out of their dive gear and into dry clothes, remaining silent as ordered. They climbed through the side door and into the empty seats.

"Where's the two girls that have been helping you?" asked Winfrey. "I see their dive gear is here in the van."

"The girls decided to stay behind. One of them had the unfortunate opportunity of seeing your handiwork, Winfrey, up close and personal on an earlier dive. She's still pretty shaken up from it."

"Ah, yes, you must be referring to my buddy Dr. Stein. Well, unfortunately he outlived his use and needed to be removed from the ranks. If you're not careful, you and your friends could be joining him too! Maybe we'll make it into a blue hole club with free memberships for a lifetime." Winfrey laughed.

Jeff glanced at Justin with a serious look of concern. "How could we have gotten ourselves mixed up into such a mess," he thought to himself. He could still visualize the remains of what was once Dr. Stein floating lifeless in the middle of the blue hole and now knew that Winfrey was the one that had murdered him. He felt like he needed to throw up with his nerves now becoming untangled but swallowed hard and held it in. Would they be next?

"You two," Winfrey said, calling his associates. "Go get your scuba gear out of the Jeep. I want you to go back down and make sure all of the treasure has been recovered. Meet us at the yacht when you're done."

Winfrey slid into the driver's seat, turned the van around and drove. The bald headed man sat with the rifle trained on John and the others from the front seat swiveled backwards. Screeching back through the vegetation, Winfrey drove around the parked Jeep and was soon down the trail and out of sight. The two men, who stayed behind, pulled on wet suits, talking to themselves at the same time about the treasure and how they would both be rich and what they would do with their share. Then suited up, they dove into the water and descended into the depths and out of sight.

Beth scanned the area and slowly stood with her hand shielding the sun from her eyes.

"They're gone," she said.

They walked over to where the treasure had been minutes before, peered across the blue hole again and saw only bubbles rising from the depths of Lucifer's Lair.

"I can't believe Eric betrayed us and now Winfrey has them all as hostages," Beth said.

"I know! And to think I was falling for that creep," Laura said. "I suppose it was all just a game for him."

"Those divers won't be down long." Beth said. "I'm sure they'll quickly realize that the guys already brought up the last of the treasure and come back to the surface."

"What're we going to do? Winfrey took them in the van," Laura said with tears clouding her eyes. "We're stranded out here in the jungle and those men will be back soon."

"Maybe not!" Beth exclaimed. "I'll bet you anything they left the keys in the other vehicle." The girls ran down the trail and found a black Jeep Cherokee parked in the middle of the dirt road. As they opened the driver's side door, the chimes immediately answered their question.

"Let's gather up all of their stuff and toss it in the Jeep," Beth said.

"You mean leave them out here?"

"Absolutely! Dr. Lounsbury can call the cops after we get back to the field station. They'll send someone to pick these goons up and take them to where they belong."

"Yeah, jail," said Laura, and added, "Come on, let's get out of here."

They tossed the men's clothing and gun belts into the back of the Jeep, leaving nothing behind. Beth started the engine, put it in drive, turned around and sped away.

The logging road looked different to her from the driver's seat. It felt somehow closer, denser, and in places impenetrable. Beth made as much effort to speed out of the jungle and find help, but the rough conditions of the washed out, overgrown, and pot-holed road together with the low visibility due to the overgrown terrain made it slow going.

"Stop!" Laura yelled, as they passed a turnoff to their left on another road. "I think that was our turn."

"No," Beth responded. "I'm sure it was further up. I remember a large wetland next to where we turned."

"Are you sure? All of the roads look the same to me."

"Trust me. That's not it. We still have a ways to go yet." Five, then ten minutes passed and several miles, when they reached a familiar swampy area and Beth turned onto another dirt road. "Now, this should run straight to the main highway. Shouldn't be too long now!"

"Yeah, especially the way you're driving. Slow down, you're driving too fast! Oh no! Beth, watch OUT!!!" Laura screamed.

A strange bedraggled creature suddenly jumped out of the swamp and darted across the road directly in front of them. Beth slammed on the brakes trying not to hit it; they skidded to the left and off the narrow road, splashed into the mucky swamp and crashed into a stout tree. Two thunderous pops and both air bags deployed as the grill smashed in and the hood crumpled from the impact.

"You okay?" Beth asked.

"Yeah, I think so! Remind me to never ride with you again."

"Very funny!"

"What was that thing?" Laura said.

"Looked kind of like a dog but not!"

"I know it was really creepy looking. Like something out of Stilly's stories!" Laura said. "You think it's still around?

"I hope not. We have enough problems to deal with!" Beth said, looking around for any signs of the creature.

"Oh no! Check out your stitches."

Beth centered her face in the rear view mirror and saw that although her stitches were intact the wound was bleeding from the impact with the airbag. She looked at Laura and just shrugged her shoulders.

"How're we going to get out of this mess?" asked Laura.

"Maybe we could put it into four-wheel drive, back it up and get it onto the road."

"Okay, let's give it a try. I've got my fingers crossed."

"Well, cross your toes too," added Beth.

Beth restarted the Jeep and the tailpipe, positioned just below the surface, bubbled exhaust through the gooey muck from behind. She shifted a lever and the four-wheel drive light illuminated on the dashboard. She gunned the engine; they shot backward briefly, but then the wheels began to spin. Large clods of dripping black sticky-muck flew into the air and rained down onto the roof and hood of the Jeep. The spinning tires were barely moving them along, and soon, they came to a complete stop several yards back from the tree and parallel to the roadbed just above them. Wheels did little more than spin as Beth shifted back and forth from forward to reverse, trying to create a rocking momentum.

"Um, this is not a good place to park," Laura said.

"Park? We're stuck!"

"Duh! You're hardly ready to make a living mud-bogging?"

"I'm doing my best."

"Best! You've got us stuck in the middle of nowhere and my brother is out there with that madman, and I don't know what's going to happen to him and—" Laura said.

Beth motioned for Laura to settle down. "Look, I'm sorry. This is not easy for me either. We'll think of something." She opened her door. The swamp was just inches below the door well; she climbed up onto the mud-covered hood and looked around. The dripping wet muck reeked of pungent rotting leaves.

"What're you doing?"

"Looking for a way to get us out of here." Beth studied the situation. She scanned the area, calculating in her mind any possible way to get the Jeep out of the swamp.

"I've got an idea," Beth said, noticing a tree across

the road and a winch mounted on the front bumper.

"I'm not sure I can deal with any more of your ideas today," Laura replied, while Beth climbed back in the front seat.

"Jeep has a winch, and there's a tree over there," Beth said pointing to it.

"You think it'll pull us out?"

"It's either that or we walk. I need you to pull the cable over to that tree. I'll give you some slack. Climb up on the hood, grab the cable and jump over onto the road."

"Why me?" Laura asked.

"I'll do it if you want, but this is our best and probably only chance of getting us out of this mess!" Beth said with her voice getting louder from frustration.

"Look, don't snap at me! I'm not the one that got us stuck out here," Laura retorted.

"Laura, we need to get a grip. Come on. We have to do this as a team—and please stop complaining. You're just making our situation worse!"

"All right, give me some slack in the cable. I'm climbing out on the hood," Laura said.

Beth turned on the wipers and with twin streams of water squirting, she soon could see through two mucky half-moon clearings on the windshield. She then pushed a button on the dash, activating the winch. Laura collected a few loops of slack on the slippery hood and then jumped off onto the dry roadbed. As the winch reeled out more cable, Laura walked across the road and hooked it around the tree.

"Stand aside in case the cable breaks," Beth yelled from the Jeep. She had watched her father back home do this a few times and that was what he had always said to her. A snapped cable flying wildly could actually sever you in half, her father would say.

Beth pushed another button and the winch began to pull in the slack. Once the cable was taut, Beth turned the steering wheel hard to the right, put the Jeep in drive and eased on the accelerator. The Jeep inched forward and slid sideways, barely clearing the aged tree they had hit. Slowly coming out of the muddy swamp, the vehicle tipped on its side at a dangerous angle, and then began to pivot straight and level. Grazing a tourist tree, the Jeep was soon relieved of its right rear-view mirror and scraped heavily along its entire right side. Then the tree the cable was wrapped around made a cracking-pop sound and angled over slightly toward the ground and over top of the Jeep, dropping limbs and leaves on the roof. Beth gunned the engine and with a shower of mud managed to get the Jeep back up onto the road again. Suddenly, the tree snapped and crashed down onto the right rear corner of the Jeep, crumpling the roof and shattering the rear windows—and barely missing Beth.

"Beth? Beth!!! Are you okay?" Laura yelled from behind the tree, pushing through branches to get to the Jeep.

"I'm fine, I think, but the Jeep's not," Beth said through widened eyes; she twisted in her seat and observed the damage and crushed-in roof right behind her head.

"Well, at least we're back on the road. You did it!" Laura cheered.

Beth instructed Laura to unhook the cable. Pushing the winch button, she let out slack in the cable. Laura then unhooked the cable from where it remained around the fallen tree. Laura let it fall to the ground and the cable was reeled back in underneath the foliage.

Beth inched the Jeep along the road, pulling it slowly away from underneath the fallen tree still resting on top. Then as she drove forward it rolled off the crushed roof, crashing onto the old logging trail blocking the road behind. Laura climbed through the debris and back into the vehicle, and then they continued their journey down the logging trail. After a few more miles on the dirt road, they finally reached the Queen's Highway. Beth looked right, then left, and seeing the road clear, stomped on the accelerator. The Jeep shot forward onto the pavement leaving twin trails of dirt and smoky rubber behind, heading fast toward Rockwood.

.

19

CONFESSION

Beth blasted the Jeep's horn as soon as they squealed off the Queen's Highway and onto Andros Drive at Rockwood. She did not let up, sounding the alarm until the Jeep skidded to a stop by the entrance to the lodge. By then Mike and Molly were running out of the lodge, as did the rest of the EcoExplorers, and the field station staff came from different directions. All the resident dogs immediately surrounded the Jeep, yapping and barking, adding to the excitement. The sea breeze blew the cloud of dust surrounding the vehicle inland, revealing a heavily damaged Jeep completely covered in mud. The hood was crumpled and the grill smashed in, the right rear corner of the roof was crushed in and the right side mirror dangled loosely from a single wire, swinging like a pendulum below the door window and over a heavily scraped and beaten Jeep body. Wispy steam hissed from the radiator like a snorting dragon. Then to the surprise of all, Laura and Beth climbed out. At first, the assembly of cohorts stood and stared at the wreck of the vehicle without saying a word. Then Dr.

Lounsbury broke the silence.

"What in the world is going on? Where did you get that Jeep and what did you do to it?" Dr. Lounsbury inquired incredulously, his eyes wide. "And where're John, Grant and the others? Is anyone hurt?"

"You've got to call the police at once!" Beth replied breathlessly. "The guys have all been taken hostage at gunpoint!"

"Hostage? What are you talking about?" Molly inquired, her brow knitted in a concerned frown.

"We were out at the blue hole when—" both girls began at the same time.

"When Winfrey showed up with a rifle and three other men!" Laura added.

"They took the guys." Beth started to explain when Laura jumped in:

"Yeah, and the treasure, and left with Winfrey and a bald-headed man in the van and—" She continued, bedazzled:

"Then when the other two men who stayed behind went back in for a last dive, we took their things and stole their Jeep and drove straight back here."

"Okay, slow down girls, one at a time," Mike suggested, waving a hand at them. "What's this about a rifle, and Winfrey and a treasure?"

"Well, Winfrey, who's the boss, was hired by TSL to find the treasure, the treasure we found this morning at Pimlico blue hole and—" Beth said.

"You found what? What's TSL?" Mike interrupted.

"Treasure Seekers Limited is the name of the other group that was competing with John Dettor to find Hornigold's treasure. You know the one described in that old book Justin found in his backpack? Well, we've been kind of looking for it in the blue holes this week," Beth said.

"You've been looking for treasure? When have you been looking for treasure?" asked Mike. "I thought you were assisting in a blue hole survey with Grant and John Dettor!"

"Um, well, we were doing a survey too, but also looking for the treasure," Laura explained, her eyes darting to Beth.

"Where're they now?" Mike asked.

"I don't know," Beth said. "But I do remember overhearing Winfrey when we hid in the jungle. He was thanking Eric for keeping him informed about what we were doing. That creep was a snitch! Then Winfrey left his other two men behind to dive and check for any remaining treasure. Then we overheard their conversation when they were suiting up about how rich they were going to be and they would split up the treasure when they returned to the TSL yacht after they were done."

"Any idea where this yacht might be?" Mike asked.

"No! But after Winfrey left with the guys in the van, we threw the divers' guns and clothes in the Jeep," Beth said.

"Guns and clothes?" Mike repeated.

"Yeah! They had pistols in holsters. We threw their stuff in the Jeep and left them out there," Beth said.

"Where's their stuff? Let's see if there's any identification." Mike walked to the driver's side of the Jeep, opened the mud encrusted door, and began to rummage through the clothing that was bundled in the back seat. It was just as the girls had described: two pairs of shirts and trousers, each with a holstered pistol attached to their belts. Mike also found two wallets that he handed to Dr. Lounsbury.

"Newby, check the glove compartment for registration," Dr. Lounsbury said.

"Here's the license plate number," Mitch said after he wiped away the swampy black muck from the plate. Dr. Lounsbury collected the registration from Newby, noted the license plate number of the Jeep, and with the two wallets dashed to the director's cabin to call the Andros police at Fresh Creek.

"So what exactly happened to this Jeep," Mike asked radiator still hissing steam.

"Um, erm, we kind of had some complications getting back," Beth said, her eyes twirling toward Laura.

"All right, I think it's time you both start at the beginning and tell us everything you've been up to this week," Mike said, arms crossed, towering above the girls. "Let's go into the lodge."

"But, b-but, we should be out looking for the guys," Laura said, looking toward the Queen's Highway, her mind drifting, her thoughts unsettling.

"I'm afraid it's a police matter now," Mike said.

"I want to know about the treasure!" Mitch said, while holding his hand out to his side, still dripping mucky-black from wiping the license plate. Molly gave him a look. Mitch went off to the rinse deck, and everyone else moved into the lodge.

Questions were showered at Beth and Laura about treasure, blue holes, guns, Winfrey and everything they had done over the last several days. Then Mike put an index finger from each hand into his mouth and silenced them all with an ear-piercing whistle.

"Now that I have your attention, I'd like you all to take a seat," Mike said while Mitch walked into the lodge and sat with the others on the four couches. Even the field station staff, Ooma and Stilly, sat; Mike paced; Molly took a seat at the bar. "I heard some things outside that would suggest a lack of candor, deception and lies. Now, I want to hear your story from the beginning. I'll expect nothing less than absolute truth from you two. Also, more importantly, keep in mind that the safety of the others could very well hinge on your statements. Molly, please take notes. And everyone else, I'll not tolerate interruptions. So start explaining!"

The screen door opened and Dr. Lounsbury entered

the lodge. "Excuse me, Mike, before you begin, just so you all know, the police have sent officers to pick up the men the girls left stranded at Pimlico. Bahamian customs will have records of the yacht and they are tracing the Jeep that was rented here on the island. They've alerted the coast guard, and the island is being searched for any signs of Winfrey, the yacht or the field station van. I'm quite sure that the boys will be close by. Don't worry; I know they'll be found soon." Dr. Lounsbury took a seat beside Molly at the bar.

"Dr. Lounsbury, you may need to call the police back and let them know that there's now a tree lying across the road. We had a little problem getting out of the jungle," said Beth. "I think they'll need a chain saw to get through."

"Thank you for that, Beth, but I'm quite sure that the Bahamian police are used to the problems of driving the back roads of the island."

"Now I think Laura and Beth have some explaining to do," Mike said sternly, and sat in front of the bar on a high stool. His arms were crossed, his brow knitted; he looked directly at Beth and Laura. The girls looked at Mike, eyed the floor and then looked at each other. Then over the next forty-five minutes, Beth and Laura, trying not to interrupt each other too often, spelled out the entire escapade, from the meeting in Stilly's office with John Dettor, to exploring the blue holes, recovering the treasure and arriving back at Rockwood in the mud-covered Jeep. Eyes around the great room periodically shifted towards Stilly, and Stilly seemed to fidget a bit in his chair.

"So, let me see if I've got this straight," Mike said in a no-nonsense tone when they were done; he stood and began to pace around the four sofas in the great room. "You all met with John Dettor in Stilly's office the night before John had breakfast with us and asked us if you could assist him in a field study in the blue holes. You already knew about the treasure hunt at that time, but conveniently chose not to mention it. Is that right?" Mike asked.

The girls looked at each other, shifted on the couch, and started to say something when Mike spoke again:

"Then on the very first blue hole you were going to dive, you ran into this Winfrey character, and the man that you described being with him now was there armed with a rifle, but you all shrugged it off as just being a coincidence. Later that day, you made a dive in another blue hole, and then returned to the field station with photographs of marine life to cover up the real reason for the outing. I remember seeing your pictures in the classroom that evening just before the compressor blew. Dr. Lounsbury and I were suspicious of the compressor incident at the time and thought it could be vandalism. Grant said it was a faulty connector. Only problem was the connectors are super strong stainless steel and Grant never produced the faulty part. Sometimes you students feel adults are stupid because we're willing to give you enough slack to hang yourselves. Remember, experience is the best teacher," Mike said.

The girls were mute on the couch, wanting to speak, but words were elusive.

"Then, the very next day, you explored another blue hole, and Beth this time, you unfortunately got tangled up with the corpse of a murdered man," Mike said.

"Murdered? I didn't know he was murdered!" Beth said, suddenly finding something to respond to.

"Do you think a dead body floating in the middle of a blue hole out in the middle of the Andros jungle, with a rope tied around his torso, just happened to be there?" Mike asked. Molly flashed him a scowl.

"I, I—" Beth stammered.

"Then less than forty-eight hours later, you, Laura and the boys are back at it, hunting once again for treasure. And Eric has been informing Winfrey all along about your whereabouts and then the man conveniently happens to show up, then takes the treasure and everyone hostage with whereabouts unknown. Meanwhile, you and Laura steal a Jeep and destroy it on your drive back to the field station. There are two men now being hunted by the Andros police and you have their guns and personal belongings. Does this sound about right to you? Have I got your story straight now? You're sure that you've included all of your deceptions and 'meet-ups' with shady characters?" Mike asked.

"Well, we just wanted to help John Dettor recover the treasure for the people of Andros. I mean he's not in it for financial gain. He just wanted to beat TSL to it to save it from being auctioned to the highest bidder, and he needed our help," Beth said.

"Such benevolence at your expense and risk I cannot buy," Mike retorted.

The girls looked at each other and Mike, then eyed their friends around the room, but no credible reply came to their minds. Silence in the great room of the lodge hung like a cloud full of tension.

"I've got something I want to address," Dr. Lounsbury said, shattering the silence; he began to pace while Mike sat. "I don't want to sound like I'm chastising an employee in front of others, but I believe we all deserve an explanation from Stilly. After all, John Dettor is your friend, Stilly, and you invited these youths to the table!"

Stilly looked into Dr. Lounsbury's eyes, Mike's, Molly's, and Laura and Beth's, then said, "I never wanted the kids involved in this treasure hunt. The first night when the new kids arrived they asked me about Hornigold after the beach fire. Back then, I knew that John, with Grant's help, was searching for the treasure. The only other people who knew anything about the treasure were the folk from TSL. The students showing up and suddenly asking about Hornigold and his treasure was a big surprise. John asked me to arrange a meeting with the students after the robbery so he could find out what they knew. He explained everything to them and they told John about the treasure documents they had and then about the theft. To my surprise, he asked them to join the treasure hunt. I objected, but John suggested that the kids could make up their own minds." Stilly paused as if to catch his breath, then continued, his eyes darting from Mike to Dr. Lounsbury:

"Then, after finding the corpse in the blue hole, I thought that was the end of their involvement and John made that perfectly clear. I was as surprised as anyone else when they pulled up today in the Jeep. I wasn't around the field station yesterday after I buried Loona. They left this morning before I knew where they were going."

"Well, Stilly," Dr. Lounsbury responded with a frown. "If there's ever a decision between the safety of the students versus a loyalty you may feel towards a friend, I'll expect you to always put the students first." Stilly nodded, and Dr. Lounsbury knew that he meant it. "Now the police will be here soon to question the girls. They'll collect the pistols and the men's wallets, and they asked that no one touch the Jeep. Is that understood?" They all nodded in agreement.

"Now's not the time to get into it, but I hope you girls understand the gravity of the position you've put everyone in. I know you're only a part of the blame, but your deception is intolerable. I have to say that I'm very disappointed in both of you," Mike said, worried for the safety of the boys and angered by their dishonesty.

"We're sorry, Mike. We never thought it would come to this," Laura said. She and Beth, feeling small on the couch, let their eyes hug the floor. "And if it wasn't for Eric telling Winfrey—"

"So you think this whole mess is Eric's fault? What about the roles that you played in it with deceptions and lies! You see, this is what happens when you don't consider the consequences of your actions. You kids never think that you're at fault or that something's ever going to happen to you." Mike's voice rose in anger.

"And another thing—"

"Mike," Molly interrupted, "I think they've been through enough for one day. There'll be plenty of time to discuss this later. Right now, I think we all need to stay focused and upbeat for the safe return of the guys."

20

HOSTAGES

Winfrey drove the van down the old logging road like an off-road racer, speeding recklessly through the Andros jungle back to the Queen's Highway. He turned and drove north. His associate held a rifle aimed at their hostages, who sat quietly in the back of the van with wide-eyed anxiety. Not a word was spoken during the drive. The noise of the van engine mixed with the humming sound of the tires against pavement drowned out the sounds of their wildly beating hearts. Eventually, they sped past the field station in a blur, rumbled over the Bollard Creek Bridge and continued north.

Another ten minutes flew by and miles later, Winfrey turned off the Queen's Highway and drove down a sandy lane that led to an abandoned sisal plantation. Winfrey stopped the van and got out, unlocked a padlock with chain that guarded the property, relocked it after he had driven through and then drove on. The lane eventually turned and wrapped close behind the back of an old manor house and around to the front, facing a small inlet that led out to the ocean. Directly in front of them was a large, elegant yacht moored to a rickety and makeshift wooden dock. The sleek white yacht stretched over one-hundred twenty-five feet along the waterfront. *Intrepid*, painted in black bold letters on the sharp-angled bow, was a modern motor yacht with two decks separated by dark-tinted windows. The upper deck was open in the back behind the bridge and captain's quarters. On an angular ship's mast above the yacht, antennas spiked the sky, radar spun, and the American flag flapped in the breeze.

A tight stand of Australian pines swept across the overgrown yard and shaded the two-story derelict structure, long since deserted and now in shambles. The shutters hung at odd angles against broken glass windows. The roof, partially caved in, nurtured vines that covered the exterior walls like thick wall paper and sprouted out of every possible opening, growing towards the sun. Winfrey parked the van in front of the yacht and barked:

"Okay, I want each of you to grab what you can of the treasure and carry it over to the yacht. And if I hear a peep out of any of you, you'll regret it." Winfrey got out of the van, walked around to the side and pulled the twin side doors open. The bald-headed man climbed out and walked several yards away, turned to face the van and menacingly brandished the rifle. "Dettor, you carry that plastic pan with the gems, and the rest of you grab a bag and follow me."

John collected the pan, while John and Eric hoisted one bag of treasure, Jeff and Justin another. They followed Winfrey across the sandy lane, over a gangplank and onto the yacht at the middle of the starboard side. They deposited the treasure bags on the stern area of the main deck. The yacht had a spacious deck, open on the sides but covered on top, directly behind the forward galley.

Lining the sides of the deck against the bulkheads

were lockers for dive gear, and on the top of each locker, scuba tanks were set up on BC's and regulators. In the middle was a large carpet-covered table for underwater cameras and video equipment. Behind that and toward the stern was a fill station for scuba tanks. Forward from the camera table, a set of stairs led to the upper deck, half-covered and half-open to the sun. Toward the front, walkways on the port and starboard sides led to an open bow. The muffled sounds of a generator rumbled from below. The door leading from the galley onto the stern deck opened, and a man dressed in yachting attire, stepped out, followed by two *Intrepid* crewmembers.

"Eric, what're you doing here?" the gentleman asked in a Texas accent with a hint of surprise in his voice. Wisps of gray hair curled out from under a captain's hat perched precariously on his head, and his face, weathered and wrinkled from years in the sun, framed bright brown eyes. Eric was about to answer when Winfrey stepped in between them.

"Sit down," Winfrey ordered Eric and then turned to face the man. "It looks like our business arrangement has come to an end, Augustus Cramer, now that we've found the treasure."

"You found the treasure?" Augustus said, a tone of excitement creeping into his voice.

"This morning," Winfrey replied, handing him a gold doubloon.

"Where'd you find it?" Augustus asked his mouth agape at the coin.

"I found it, or maybe I should say they found it this morning at Pimlico," Winfrey explained.

"Eric, what's going on? Who are these other people?"

"Gus, he made me snitch on my—" Eric started to explain.

"That's enough," Winfrey said, pointing his finger in Eric's face.

"What's the meaning of this?" Gus demanded

incredulously. "You don't give orders on my yacht!"

"Keep your mouth shut, old man, all of you!" Winfrey ordered, removing a pistol that was tucked into his belt; he pulled the slide, cocked the weapon, and turned to his accomplice holding the rifle. "Richard, escort Gus and his men below and lock them in the fore cabins. The rest of you, bring the remainder of the treasure up here. Now MOVE IT!"

They made the final trip to the van and deposited the remaining treasure sacks in a mound on the teak deck. Then Winfrey escorted them through the dining salon and down a flight of steps to a companionway below. They marched toward the bow of the ship, past numerous doors, and entered the front cabin where they found Augustus Cramer locked inside. The cabin was gracefully embellished with ship models, and magnificent marine paintings covering the walls. The floor was lacquered teak covered with a few small oriental carpets. Large portholes let in ample light on both the port and starboard sides. A king-sized bed was in the center against the forward bulkhead, a large bar on the right; a navigation table with drawers built-in was below, surrounded by chairs to the left. Nautical charts covered the top of the table adjacent to a laptop computer that was running a screen saver and flashing the word *Intrepid* across the screen. Once they were all inside, Winfrey closed the door, locked it, and returned to the upper deck.

"You double-crosser, you betrayed us," Grant grumbled and punched Eric in the stomach. Eric doubled over in agony and fell to the floor.

"Now look here! I don't know what you think you're doing, but I'm captain of this yacht and that's my grandson. I'll have none of that, do you understand me?" Gus yelled angrily, grabbing Grant's shirt collar.

"All right, calm down," John said trying to separate Gus from Grant. "We're all locked up together; let's be civil about this."

"And just who the hell are you?" Gus inquired in a condescending tone while loosening his grip on Grant's shirt.

"I'm Dettor, John Dettor," John stated, introducing himself and the others.

"I'm Augustus Cramer, but folks just call me Gus. You obviously already know my grandson. You okay, Eric?" Gus said, helping him to his feet.

"Yeah, I'm fine," he said in a breathless tone, holding his stomach.

"John Dettor. Wait a minute, I know who you are!" Gus paused in thought, scratching his head. "I've read some of your articles."

"Possibly," John said warily.

Gus stared at John for a few moments, and then scanned the room. "Would someone fill me in on what's going on?" he barked.

"I think I can explain," Eric said, stepping forward and nodding first toward Gus. "My grandfather here owns TSL and this yacht. He hired David Winfrey, Dr. Shubert Stein and a few other men to find the treasure after he bought the Hornigold logbook."

"That's right, I did," added Gus. "Winfrey's a tough old bird, but he had a reputation for getting the job done."

"Yeah," John said. "At any cost!"

"I'll admit I didn't agree with all his tactics. And now it would seem he's turned on me . . . on us!" Gus said, and rolled his eyes around the cabin, as if thinking of a way to escape.

"I really was staying at Rockwood to study marine biology this summer," Eric continued. "I had no interest in my grandfather's treasure hunting. Then you guys showed up with the Hornigold logbook that Dr. Stein apparently stashed in your backpack at the airport and…"

"Shubert did what?" Gus said, surprised.

"Apparently, he was trying to smuggle the Hornigold logbook off the island. Winfrey chased him to the airport," Eric explained. "Stein stuffed the logbook into Justin's backpack to try to hide it from Winfrey just before he caught up with him in the airport bathroom."

"Winfrey told me Shubert had left the island!" Gus said.

"I'm afraid he'll never leave the island, at least not alive" John said. "I've some bad news for you. Shubert Stein was murdered. We discovered his body a few days ago floating in the halocline of a blue hole. He'd been shot in the head, tied up and weighted down. I imagine Winfrey thought he would never be seen again."

"What? Good lord!" Gus said. Shocked by the news, he sat down in the chair in front of the navigation station.

"Why didn't you tell us he was murdered, John?" Jeff asked.

"I'm sorry! I was only trying to protect you. You didn't need to know those details. That's why I couldn't allow you all to continue with the treasure hunt anymore," John explained. "I shouldn't have let you talk me into taking you out today. I knew it was becoming way too dangerous."

"So, what's this about my documents and a backpack?" asked Gus.

"Justin found them later that evening when he was unpacking at the field station," Eric added. "Actually, I was about to enter Justin and Jeff's cabin that evening when I overheard their conversation. I listened to them carry on about the treasure and then I decided I better radio you. You weren't around and Winfrey answered instead. I told Winfrey what I had overheard and asked him to relay the message. He told me that Dr. Stein had stolen the documents and that you wanted them back. He asked me to find the logbook and return it to you.

Winfrey said to make it look like islanders broke in, so I did."

"You should have told us, Eric," said Justin.

"Why?"

"Because we trusted you," Justin said, flashing his eyes angrily at Eric.

"I know you weren't aware of it at the time, but you were in the possession of stolen property, stolen from my grandfather who paid a lot of money for it. And then I overheard you and Jeff talk about keeping it for yourselves, or asking around to see if anyone knew about Hornigold," Eric responded.

"So what, I thought it was a joke. I didn't take any of this seriously until the logbook went missing, and then Stilly asked us to meet later that night in his office, including you," Justin said.

"That's right. But I was only invited because no one knew that my grandfather owned TSL and John needed additional divers. So I went along with it because I wanted to know what you were all up too."

"So you played us like a bunch of idiots? Wow, this is unbelievable," Justin said. "And I guess you had spies listening to our conversations too, like the guy the night when we met in Stilly's office! And my sister Laura! I guess you really enjoyed playing her too? I should punch you for that" Justin stepped toward Eric.

"There'll be none of that!" Gus said, moving between Eric and Justin.

"Look, dude!" Eric said sharply. "I wasn't playing your sister. We actually found things in common like scuba diving and became friends. Back at the blue hole, Winfrey asked about Laura and Beth and I said nothing when John told him that they had decided not to come today. I protected them the best I could. Even though things might look a certain way, my loyalties are with my grandfather and you guys, and certainly not with Winfrey. As far as spying, no one was spying on you."

"Except you," Justin interjected.

"The idea of being spied on got started that night we met in Stilly's office. One of Winfrey's men was there to pick up the logbook from me later that evening beside the dive shop. Unfortunately, the idiot ran into a trash can in the dark and you guys chased him off," Eric said.

"Great company you keep, Eric," Justin said. "Look what happened to Dr. Stein!"

"That's enough," Gus said. "Eric had nothing to do with that."

Eric sat quietly in a chair for a long moment before he spoke. "I feel really bad about that. I do wonder if telling Winfrey about the Hornigold documents may have had something to do with his death. I mean at that point, Winfrey knew I had the documents, so he had no more use for Stein and killed him."

"You couldn't have known, Eric," Gus said. "You trusted Winfrey at that moment as one of my employees."

"I know, but I should have contacted the police myself when Stein turned up dead," Eric responded, his voice quiet as a whisper. "I had a feeling that it was him when Beth and Jeff found the body in the blue hole."

"Then why didn't you call the cops?" asked Jeff.

"I tried to reach my grandfather again on the radio to warn him, but Winfrey had informed his companions to intercept all of my calls. I told Winfrey that I was going to the Andros police and tell them what happened. Winfrey said that if I did, I would never see my grandfather alive again. Then he said the same would happen to me if I didn't continue to keep an eye on you, and if you somehow got to the treasure first, I'd better get word to him or else. So I was forced to call and tell him about Beth's discovery and our plans to dive at Pimlico this morning." Eric took a deep breath, glanced at his grandfather then at Jeff, and continued:

"If we had found the treasure and not turned it over

to Winfrey, he would have killed my grandfather!'"

"Good lord, boy!" Gus shuddered. "I had no idea all of this was going on. Winfrey's been lying to me."

"I'm so sorry, Gus, I didn't know what to do," said Eric.

"It's okay, son, you did your best," Gus assured his grandson and paused briefly in thought. "So, John Dettor, please tell me just how you came to be mixed up in all of this? I thought I was the only one hunting for the treasure!"

"The antique dealer in Nassau who sold you the Hornigold documents was an old acquaintance of mine. He sold me a copy of the documents, too. We found out later that we had the only complete set, including pages that were removed from the original he sold you. It didn't really do us a lot of good, other than narrow our search to inland blue holes and speed up the search. Grant and I have been discretely hunting for weeks, diving as many of the blue holes as we could muster. But our time appeared to be running out with your arrival. Islanders were keeping an eye on Winfrey and reported his whereabouts to me, and that's how we'd been able to stay away from him and keep our hunting a secret. Of course that started to unravel as soon as Stein put the documents into Justin's backpack. Then I got the students and Eric involved. We had no idea Eric was informing Winfrey of our whereabouts until Winfrey showed up at the blue hole, took the treasure and us as hostages. But now it makes sense why we ran into Winfrey at the first blue hole instead of him being off the island like the islanders said. If I had been in your situation, Eric, I would've done the same thing to protect someone I loved. So, I don't begrudge you." John turned to Eric, who nodded his thanks.

John concluded, "The rest of the story you know."

Gus slouched down in a chair beside Eric, amazed and bewildered by all that had happened. "Well, I obviously hired the wrong man. I should've hired you," Gus said with a tentative smile. "I'm really sorry. If I'd have known any of this was going to happen, I would've called this treasure hunt off long ago. I'm not like Winfrey. I have a passion for treasure hunting, but I never wanted to see anyone hurt, that's for sure. I just love the excitement of the search…gives me something to get up and look forward to every day," Gus said, his voice taking on a West Texas drawl.

"Well, now we know both sides of the story," John said. "But what can we do about getting out of here and contacting the police?"

"Well," Gus said standing. He walked to the bar and poured himself a drink. It disappeared in one swift gulp. He then offered the bottle of Scotch to whoever wanted a drink, but only John took a gulp from the bottle. "There's no radio down here, hmmm," Gus said to himself, crossing one arm over his chest, perching the elbow of his other arm on top, and rubbing his chin with his free hand.

"Is there any way to open the cabin door? Have you got any guns down here? Weapons? Anything?" John asked, looking around the cabin.

"There's a pistol hidden under the bed, but not much use unless we can get out of here. We could break down the door, but that would just put us into a fight with Winfrey and his cutthroats. There's the intercom to the bridge we can turn on and might catch some conversation, but other than that I can't think of anything useful." Gus toggled the intercom on, but no one was on the bridge. He then retrieved the pistol and tucked it into his belt.

They strategized for a while, trying to come up with any and all ideas that might help them escape, but all suggestions were either not viable or could potentially lead to someone getting hurt or even killed.

Then in the late afternoon voices could be heard

through the yacht intercom as Winfrey climbed the ladder up to the bridge. With the intercom system turned on at the bridge, all conversations could be heard in Gus's cabin below.

"It's Winfrey. He's up on the bridge," Gus said as he walked over to the cabin's intercom remote station and turned the volume up. "Listen!"

"Moon Dog to Sea Devil. Moon Dog to Sea Devil, come in Sea Devil over," Winfrey spoke into the hand-held microphone of the marine radio.

"I wonder who he's trying to reach?" Justin asked.

"Quiet, listen!"

"This is Sea Devil, come in Moon Dog, over."

"Moon Dog, chicken has come home to roost. Meet at rendezvous point at eight PM, over."

"Affirmative. Sea Devil out."

As the group locked in the cabin discussed what Winfrey's message might mean Winfrey peered from the bridge over the plantation grounds for any sign of the Jeep and the crew members.

"Where are those clowns? They're way past due and we need to leave, now," Winfrey said to an accomplice on the bridge. From the stern, the unmistakable sound of the twin diesel engines rumbled to life. "Okay, cast off the lines; we're getting underway. I guess they're going to donate their share of the treasure to us," he said with a smile. "We really don't need them anymore. They've used up their importance to me and are now just extra baggage."

Below, there was further speculation:

"I wonder where he's taking us," Jeff wondered.

"Beats me," Gus responded. "From here on out, with Winfrey at the helm, you have as good of a chance of guessing as I do!"

"And it sounds like those men Winfrey left behind at the blue hole didn't make it back. I hope my sister and Beth are okay," Justin said, concerned.

They felt the yacht motoring along for about three hours, hearing little bits of conversation from the bridge but nothing that suggested a destination or plans. In the west, the sun was setting and night was beginning to close in on the *Intrepid*. Then, over the intercom, they heard Winfrey.

"How long has the radio been on this channel?" Winfrey said.

"I suppose ever since you last used the radio," his associate answered him.

The radio was then heard being tuned past several active channels and some that had nothing but static. Then Winfrey said, "See that the radio is left on this channel."

"Yes, sir," his associate responded.

Several minutes later, a man started to speak on the channel Winfrey set on the radio.

"This is a repeat of an emergency bulletin. Anyone in the area due east of Andros Island, please be on the lookout for a large white motor yacht named *Intrepid*. There are hostages on board and the assailants are armed and dangerous. Do not, and I repeat, do not under any circumstances attempt to apprehend the yacht. If you know the whereabouts of the *Intrepid*, alert the Coast Guard immediately."

Winfrey was yelling from the bridge while the report was repeated. "You leave them behind and then they go out and rat on you!" The group trapped below had a different reaction:

"Does this mean Laura and Beth made it back to the field station?" Justin asked.

"I'm not sure, but it's certainly possible," John said.

"Maybe they did get back and told everything," Jeff offered.

"And if they did—" John let his voice trail off.

About an hour later the sound of droning engines on an airplane washed across the *Intrepid* and passed overhead. The plane made a wide, sweeping turn, circling the yacht and lining up with the wind to set up for a landing in the choppy seas.

"It's a seaplane!" Gus said, straining to see out of the starboard porthole.

"Must be Winfrey's rendezvous," Justin suggested.

"Looks that way," Gus replied. The yacht slowed, the diesels engines were switched off, and they drifted with the current. The red and white plane skimmed across the surface, slowed to taxiing speed, and motored to the stern of the *Intrepid* and out of sight.

"Wonder what he's doing?" Jeff asked.

"I can't see them, but they're probably loading the treasure into the seaplane. Guess he thinks he's going to fly away with it," Gus surmised.

From inside the cabin, they soon heard the engines of the seaplane cough to life again. Moments later, it rumbled away from the yacht, revved its engines and accelerated to take off speed. Through the porthole, they watched as it gained altitude into the late evening sky and disappeared behind a cloud surrounded by the first glimpse of stars.

Back at the stern, the generator rumbled with its incessant noise and choppy waves lapped against the hull of the yacht. Then they heard an outboard motor start that swiftly moved away from the stern.

"What was that, Gus?" Eric asked.

"Sounds like someone took off in the Zodiac," replied Gus, "but I can't see them through the porthole."

The muffled sound of the outboard engine as it sped away was replaced with the deafening noise of an explosion that rocked the drifting yacht, knocking the hostages off their feet. The force of the explosion blew the metal engine room door off its hinges and hurled it down the hallway where it crashed into the far bulkhead outside of the door to the front cabin. The generator died and the lights flickered on and off and then completely out, leaving the *Intrepid* powerless in the approaching Bahamian night. The dim glow of emergency lights flickered on, illuminating the interior of the cabin, reflecting off a mix of oil and seawater that began to ooze under the cabin door.

21

WAITING FOR AN OUTCOME

Back at Rockwood, the mood was somber and tense while the EcoExplorers and field station staff waited impatiently for updated news. Outside, the late afternoon air was still, the ocean dead flat, as if the entire island held its breath in anticipation. After dinner a police officer questioned the girls again at length, but offered no news in return. Soon after the officer left, a car pulled up along the side of the lodge, and a few barking dogs jumped from their shallow scrapes in the loamy soil and ambled over to greet a visitor. The man got out of his vehicle, scratched his head and spied a strange black Jeep that looked like it had barely survived a war. Footsteps along the side of the lodge announced his approach, the screen door creaked open, and he entered.

"Evening," Nelson Horton said, entering the lodge, sounding tired and looking a little haggard. "That must be the Jeep the girls escaped in?" he asked, pointing over his shoulder with his thumb and knowing very well that it was.

"Nelson, it's good to see you," Mike said, standing to shake Nelson's hand. "That's it, if you can imagine."

"Um, who was driving?"

"I was," Beth said.

"Let me know when you'll be driving next!" Nelson said.

"Why?"

"So I can stay off the road and out of your way!" Nelson jested.

"Very funny," Beth said, not amused, standing with her hands on her hips.

"Any news," Mike inquired.

"Well, I do have a few scattered details. Maybe we should go back in Dr. Lounsbury's office to discuss them," Nelson suggested, not knowing how much information he should make available to the others.

"No! That's not fair," Laura complained. "That's my brother and my friends out there. You can't hide the details from us. If you know something, we all deserve to hear it!"

"I don't really know much," Nelson began, tentatively.

"It's all right," Dr. Lounsbury said, understanding his hesitation. "They'll find out sooner or later, might as well tell them now."

"Oh no, are they all right?" Beth asked with a growing startled look. "Is that why you don't want to tell us?"

"Now slow down, I'll tell you what I know, but don't be jumping to any conclusions," Nelson said. He walked over to the bar and took a seat on a stool. "They've found the two men you girls left stranded in the jungle. The Andros police said you left them out there with only their wet suits and scuba gear. They caught them hiking out of the jungle. They were bug-eaten, dehydrated, and demoralized," he said with a chuckle.

"Serves them right," Beth asserted.

"They started talking right away, like guilty boys that can't wait to confess," Nelson explained. "Claimed Mr. Winfrey had double-crossed them and left them stranded without transportation at the blue hole. They were more than willing to squeal on him, thinking he had cut them out of their share of the treasure." Nelson smiled at the girls. "They had no idea you were the ones who'd taken their Jeep and left them behind."

"Anything else, Nelson," Mike asked. "Do you know where they are?"

"They told us where the yacht was moored. It was docked up the north coast at an old sisal plantation. But by the time the police arrived, the yacht was gone. They did find the field station van on the property, so they know they had been there. We have all available personnel out right now looking for the yacht. Don't you worry, we'll find them."

"Thanks, Nelson," Mike said, and stood to leave the lodge, only to stop and look at the students, frowning. "I've got phone calls to make back to the States. Under the circumstances, we had to phone all of your parents to keep them informed of the situation. The phone's been ringing off the hook. Some of your parents are attempting to fly to Andros on the next available flight." He headed towards the door to get back to the numerous phone calls he had been fielding.

"What! My parents are flying here?" Laura asked, surprised.

Mike stopped at the door and looked intently at Laura. "Yes. Your mom and Jeff's dad are attempting to come. They're really concerned."

"Oh no, they're going to kill me," Laura said, her brows knitted with concern.

"Right now, they're more concerned for the wellbeing of your brother and the others." He nodded at Laura and continued: "Your father will call back soon and wants to talk with you. You were busy earlier when he called talking with the police officer."

Mike swung open the door and left the lodge. The others stood around, silent, nervous, not sure what to do. Carmen finally broke the quiet:

"If there's anything I can do, just let me know," she offered.

"That goes for all of us," Stilly added.

"Cookies and brownies are on the table in the dining room," Ooma added.

"I just want them back safely," Laura said, fighting back tears.

"Oh, there's something else that I forgot to mention," Nelson said. "I've heard reports that crews from CNN News and other media outlets are heading for the island."

Mitch walked over to the bar, turned on the television, and selected CNN News. "Hey! You're right, they're talking about us," Mitch yelped with amazement.

"Turn it up!" Laura requested, wiping her tears away. She pulled out a bar stool and sat next to Nelson.

"Currently, a massive air and sea hunt is underway just off the island of Andros, Bahamas," a reporter was saying while a banner across the bottom of the screen proclaimed Breaking News.

"Two men and three teenage boys have been taken hostage. According to Andros police, the kidnapper is a known criminal named David Winfrey from the United States, accompanied by a man who has not yet been identified. They're reported to be armed and extremely dangerous. The teenagers, a staff member from Rockwood Field Station on Andros, and a maritime archaeologist are at this hour believed to be held captive aboard the yacht, *Intrepid*. According to sources here on Andros, the teenagers were members of a student group called the EcoExplorers from Virginia and were participating with others in a hunt for a lost pirate's treasure on Andros. The yacht *Intrepid* is listed as being owned by a U.S. corporation called Treasure Seekers Limited or TSL and its whereabouts are unknown at this time. Again, authorities from the U.S. and Bahamian governments are conducting a massive air and sea hunt for the hostages and the missing yacht. We'll keep you informed of this breaking story as it develops."

The reporter paused for a second and then dove into another news story.

"Wow! How did this story make the news so fast?" Laura wondered. Nelson responded:

"The police were trying to hail the yacht on the marine radio and an APB went out for David Winfrey. Anyone who has access to the marine and police bands could hear the bulletin, including the local press. The local news desk may have gotten wind of the story and called the police station here on Andros. The officials probably thought it best to get maximum news coverage quickly to help locate the missing yacht. Now you've got anyone with two good eyes on the lookout for Winfrey and the *Intrepid*. They don't have a chance of getting away."

"Hey, they're back with more," Molly said, pointing to the TV.

"I'm reporting live from the village of Fresh Creek, on the island of Andros, Bahamas, where a massive air and sea hunt is currently underway," a reporter barked into his microphone. In the background was the police headquarters at Fresh Creek. The reporter quickly restated the situation, and then the camera zoomed out to include a Bahamian officer. "I have here with me the Captain of the Andros police, Captain Peters. Captain, can you tell us what you currently know about the situation?" The reporter pushed his microphone into the officer's face.

"Three teenagers and two adults have been taken hostage aboard the yacht, *Intrepid*," he said in a heavy Bahamian accent. "They left Andros, we believe, around four o'clock this afternoon. Their destination at this time is unknown. I've been in contact with the American Embassy in Nassau, and they immediately contacted the American State Department. I've been assured that every means will be used in the search. In fact, the United States Coast Guard is out right now searching with two helicopters and a Coast Guard cutter is on its way from Miami. We're doing everything in our power to find the fugitives and bring about a favorable conclusion for the hostages."

"With darkness falling soon, will you be able to continue the search?"

"Absolutely," responded Captain Peters. "The Coast Guard will search by both boat and helicopters throughout the night."

"Can you tell us anything about the treasure?"

"The information concerning the treasure is still unclear, but we do have participants in its recovery staying here on Andros. I've personally not had the opportunity to talk with them, but they were at the scene of the kidnapping and were lucky enough to be able to escape unharmed. Two of the men who were allied with the kidnappers were apprehended today near the treasure recovery site and arrested. All the facts and leads we know of at this time are being pursued and hopefully will help us locate the hostages aboard the yacht."

"Thank you, Captain Peters, for your time." The reporter looked directly into the camera, his face conveying the seriousness of the situation. "I'm Douglas Emerson, reporting live from Fresh Creek, Andros Island, Bahamas." The newscaster kept his gaze on the camera until the station broke for a commercial.

"I can't believe they are televising all of these details," Molly said. "At least they are not using their names."

"The police are very careful about disclosing personal details in an ongoing investigation. However, in this situation, I'm sure Officer Peters, as I've already said, wants this news spread around now to aid in their recovery. That way, the chances of finding Winfrey and the yacht are vastly increased," Nelson explained.

"Well, I'd better go and help Mike with the phone calls to parents. With the news reports, I'm sure we're in for a long evening," Molly said, rising from the couch to leave.

"Laura!" Dr. Lounsbury said as he walked into the lodge.

"Yes?"

"Your father is on the phone and wants to speak with you."

Laura followed Dr. Lounsbury to his office and picked up the phone.

"Daddy?" she began tentatively.

"How's my girl doing?" her father, Jim Dulaney, asked.

"Okay, I guess. I'm so sorry dad for getting mixed up in this," Laura said.

"Right now we need to stay upbeat and positive for the return of Justin and the others guys. I just saw the report on TV and we can only hope and pray that they will be safe. Let's stay strong for their sake and for everyone. Your mother is trying to get a flight to Andros and may be here tomorrow," Mr. Dulaney said.

"I love you, daddy!" Laura said, crying.

"I love you too. Mom sends her love. Hang in there; it will all turn out all right."

"Thanks Dad," Laura said, and they both hung up. Molly and Laura walked back over to the lodge just as Mitch was yelling about a news update on the television.

"Look!" Mitch said, turning up the volume. "They have an object on a radar scope. Maybe it's the yacht!"

"Turn it up," Jane yelled.

"I'm reporting from our news helicopter from Nassau, just east of Andros. We have a radar blip on the screen that might be the hijacked yacht *Intrepid*," a reporter was saying through static on the radio. A picture of the reporter was on one side and the other contained a radar screen with a few scattered blips. A circle was drawn over a particular blip as the reporter continued. "All other positions in the area have been hailed by radio and identified. The one the studio tells me they've circled on the map shown on your television screen is still to be searched. The authorities are calling the yacht on all marine band radio frequencies, and they've yet to receive a response. It's becoming too dark to see and we cannot get close enough for a visual because the Bahamian police have put an emergency exclusion zone around the yacht for all except the proper authorities. We will keep you up-to-date as long as we are in the air," the reporter explained as they turned the helicopter around, returning to Nassau. Then CNN broke for a commercial.

"It's got to be them!" Steve said.

"Wish we had a radio so we could listen to the ship to shore conversations," Mitch said, and they debated the issue during the commercial break.

"They're back!" Beth yelled, as the reporter returned moments later with an update.

"A second radar blip merged with the one we believe is the yacht," the reporter explained.

"What does that mean?"

"Hush!"

"Our studio experts informed me that based on the speed of approach, the time the radar blips merged, and then the speed of departure, that we have witnessed something that is consistent with the landing and takeoff of a seaplane," the reporter announced.

"They've been found!" Laura yelled and danced with Beth as they both embraced and cried with tears of joy.

Mike and Molly rushed from Dr. Lounsbury's office and joined the pandemonium in the lodge. The kids explained the recent events, and everyone was excited and upbeat about the news.

"How come no one can call them?" Mitch asked, not cheering, still glued to the television.

"What?" Jane asked, while the noisy exuberance died down.

"I mean if they're been found, then why don't we have contact with the aircraft?" Mitch asked.

"Maybe it's a radio problem," Nelson suggested. "Or the U.S. Coast Guard wouldn't broadcast rescue operations like news reporters."

"Shhh, listen," Beth said as the reporter continued.

"The radar blip we've been tracking, believed to be the hijacked yacht, has disappeared from our radar screen. The second object, thought to be a seaplane, continues on a bearing that would lead it back to the United States. I repeat: the original radar image, thought to be the motor yacht *Intrepid*, has disappeared from the screen. It may be a malfunction, or perhaps the yacht has—" the reporter was cut off and they immediately switched to a commercial.

"What's going on?" Laura asked. "What did they mean the blip disappeared? Why did they break away so fast?"

"Blips don't just disappear unless—" Mitch said with eyes wide open.

"Unless what?" asked Laura with a troubled expression on her face. She turned and looked to Mike.

"Unless what?"

22

THE INTREPID

Flames on the stern of the *Intrepid*, fed from the explosion in the engine room, began to engulf the back deck with thick, acrid smoke. Two crew members, locked in the middle cabin, shouted frantically while bloodying their knuckles as they banged on the cabin door. In Gus' forward cabin, a mixture of salt water and diesel fuel poured through a louvered ventilation panel at the bottom of the teak door and was rapidly gaining in height. The yacht listed to port and the stern sat lower in the water. A dim glow of emergency lighting flickered overhead; groaning sounds came from the stern. Trapped, the boys had panic-shivers of fright coursing up and down their spines. They tasted adrenalin on their tongues as the gravity of their situation electrified their minds.

"What're we going to do?" Eric yelled anxiously as he tested the door to see if he could somehow get it to open. "The water's pouring in, we're going to drown!"

"Gus, where's your pistol?" John asked his mind racing with ideas about how to break out of what would soon become their coffin. "Maybe you can shoot the lock out of the door."

"I'll try," Gus said. He pulled the pistol from his belt. "Everyone stand back!" While the yacht rocked and continued to dip further into the sea, he stood with his legs shoulder wide, aimed the pistol at the door's lock, and fired. A loud blast echoed throughout the cabin. The first shots went wide of the lock and splintered the mahogany wood frame; the smell of gun smoke mixed with the overwhelming stench of diesel fuel. Moving a little closer to the door and taking careful aim, Gus fired a second time. The bullet hit near the keyhole, but the door stayed defiantly in place. His third shot was well placed near the second, but still the door stayed securely closed, blocking their escape.

"Here, let me give that a try," John said, with a note of urgency in his voice.

"I never could hit much with that pistol," Gus said, handing it to John.

Taking careful aim, at near point-blank range, John fired the fourth, fifth, and sixth shot, emptying the revolver. The wood had splintered around the lock, as smoke from the hallway spilled through the splintered openings. He grabbed the knob and began to tug on the door with all his strength. Gritting his teeth, with a white-knuckled grip on the handle, he pulled and pulled. Then he put his leg up against the frame for more leverage and yanked again. The door flew open, throwing him backward into the cabin; he splashed into the water on the floor and came to rest against the corner of the bed. The inrush of water swept them all off their feet and threw them down into the swirling whirlpool. The diesel fuel stung their eyes, making it extremely difficult to see; the dim light overhead flickered on and off, and smoky, noxious fumes flowed into and filled the upper half of the cabin.

"Is everyone all right?" John asked, getting to his feet.

A gash on his forehead trickled a stream of blood down his face. He staggered to keep his footing.

"I'm okay," Jeff yelled, getting to his feet. "How about you, John?" he asked, noticing John's bloody forehead.

"Yeah, I'll live. Let's get out of here," John said urgently. The water in the companionway was now waist-deep. A smoky gloom, illuminated by the emergency lights, hovered like a cloud, and down the hallway, the engine room hissed, as the rising water doused flames but turned to steam on hot metal. Several electrical circuits shorted out and showered sparks like fireworks.

"Everyone up to the bow," Gus yelled. "Life vests are in the forward locker. Move it! Abandon ship!"

Jeff, Justin, Eric and Grant made their way to the upper deck. John quickly unlocked the adjacent cabin door and two grateful *Intrepid* crewmembers rushed out. John and the crewmembers stepped back into the cabin with Gus and found him searching through papers on the navigation station.

"Cap'n! We've got to get out, she's sinking quick, sir!" one crew member said.

"Bill, Rodger," Gus said looking in their direction, "go to the bridge quick and put out a distress call on the VHF. Then help the others and abandon ship! I'll be right behind." Gus then went back to rifling through the papers he was putting into a plastic bag. The men quickly sloshed through the rapidly rising rush of incoming water toward the stern and climbed the ladder leading to the upper deck.

"Gus, come on, we don't have much time," John said in a tone of urgency.

"Here take this dive light," Gus said stuffing a plastic bag filled with documents under his shirt.

"Come on, that stuff is of no use to you if you stay in here and drown," John yelled. "Let's go, now!"

"Okay, we're out of here," Gus said. The emergency lights then shorted out, casting them into darkness with only the faint light that streamed through the cabin portholes from the last light of the day. The water had now risen to chest deep in the cabin. A beam of light cut into the smoke-choked air as John turned on the dive light and pointed it down the flooding passageway. The engine room was completely filled to the ceiling with water and the stern was now well below the surface. The ladder to the upper deck leaned at a steep angle, the yacht slipped deeper into the sea and the top was covered, blocking their escape.

"Come on, hurry, we're going to have to swim our way out," John yelled. They both rushed down the narrow hallway to the point where the water was swirling around their necks.

"You take the light and swim for it. I'll follow," John said.

"No, I'm the captain, you go first," Gus demanded.

"Look, Gus, we don't have time for that nonsense, just move it!"

"This is my yacht and I'm the captain. Now get up that ladder and do it now," Gus ordered.

"Stubborn old fool," John barked. He held his breath and splashed into the diesel-tainted water. He fumbled about in the darkness with his hands and found a rung on the ladder. Pulling himself up, rung by rung, he reached the last one and dragged himself out of the water and into the galley. He gulped down the salty sea air, relieving some of the burning from his lungs. The bow of the yacht had now risen out of the water to the point where the deck was at a forty-five degree angle.

"Where's Gus?" Grant asked when he saw John come out of the water alone.

"He's right behind me!" John replied his voice cracking as he gasped for more air. "Where's everyone else?"

"They're up on the bow." Grant frowned and continued:

"We have a problem. The locker holding the life vests is padlocked!" "Well get back to the others and jump overboard," John replied, his voice more sure as his breathing returned to normal. "I'll wait here for Gus and join you in a minute. Swim as far away from the yacht as possible. Understand?"

Grant nodded and dashed back to the bow, ordering them off the yacht. With the bow suspended out of the water, they jumped eight feet down into the ocean. John stood in the cabin as the water pooled up over his calves—but still no signs of Gus. Cursing to himself, he stepped through the stairway and shined the light down in the rising water to illuminate the way. With time running out, John plunged back into the water and swam back into a trapped air pocket.

"What are you waiting for," John yelled, surfacing right beside Gus.

"Every time I swam for the ladder, I lost my way and had to come back," Gus said. He seemed to be panicked, fatigued. His face ashen gray, he breathed hard, struggling to catch his breath.

"Grab my hand; we'll swim out together," John yelled. Not giving Gus any time to respond, John grabbed him tight by the wrist and pulled him under. With the dive light illuminating their way, John found the ladder, made sure Gus had both hands gripped on it and shouldered him up. John was now blocked until Gus could clear the passage. With his lungs starving for oxygen, he pushed at Gus with all his might, trying to move him along, but the extra exertion was burning up the last of his oxygen. His mind raced, He felt like he was near drowning. Finally, he made it up and out into the galley—but he still clamored for the surface. The water in the galley was well above the center work table, and the door leading to the back deck was nearly submerged. Finally, he burst through the water, his deprived lungs filling with air. Turning to Gus, he shouted:

"Come on, let's get out of here before we're sucked down with the ship" Wading through the water, John and Gus exited the cabin to the starboard side. The sea had swallowed the back deck, a few loose items bobbed on the surface and heavy steam rose from the scorching hot metal surfaces in the engine room.

"Come on, we've got to swim for it," John said.

"No! There're life vests on the bow. Come on," Gus began to climb in that direction.

"Winfrey padlocked the locker," John replied, but Gus was already pulling himself up along the inclined railing.

"Come on Gus!" John yelled. "Are you trying to kill yourself? We have to get off now."

"I can't believe it" Gus screamed and kept moving toward the bow. John caught up to him next to the locker. The bow of the ship was rising further out of the water and tilting at a steeper angle. The galley, now submerged, unleashed an array of pots and pans that banged into one another when the last of the air below billowed to the surface in a frothy spray.

"We have to jump for it; come on, there's no time." John said. Grabbing Gus by the shirt, he dragged him to the railing. He half-pushed Gus and both of them went off the inclined bow of the yacht, splashing into the ocean.

23

THE TONGUE OF THE OCEAN

Gus and John swam away from the sinking yacht as fast as they could move, using up the last of their strength, finally reaching the others that had gathered together in the dark, choppy Atlantic.

To the west the sun had set and the gloomy twilight illuminated the pointed bow of the yacht in its final moment afloat. The water was now above the pilot house windows, and it seemed to pause in that position as if it would sink no further. Then, as the air in the pilothouse bubbled out through open windows, the yacht slipped farther into the abysmal waters of the Tongue of the Ocean and toward a bottom six-thousand feet below. Nearly vertical now, the bow resembled for a moment the top of a small iceberg. Then, with a final exhalation, the yacht disappeared below the surface. Large rings of air continued to escape from the sinking *Intrepid* and boil on the surface. A few plastic bowls that had washed through the galley sprang out of the water.

Overhead, stars began to emerge as darkness closed in on them. Together, the eight survivors stared with awestruck eyes at the calamity that had just disappeared down into the black water below them.

"I can't believe it," Gus said breaking the hypnotic silence that had enveloped them. Watching his yacht go down was like the cruel death of an old friend and the emotional wake that followed.

"Is everyone all right?" Grant asked.

"Fine!" they all agreed in unison. "How's your head, John?"

"Not bad, it'll heal," John replied. "Do we have any flotation devices?"

"The life vests are locked up and all of the life rings have been removed," Grant replied.

"Seems that Winfrey didn't want to leave us any means to survive," Gus surmised. "I don't know what he did in the engine room, but that man nearly killed us all."

"I think that was the idea," John replied, sarcastically.

"Did anyone get the EPIRIB off the yacht?" Gus said, and then realized what he was asking. "Let me guess, Winfrey!"

"We looked for it, Cap'n, but it was gone, along with the flare gun, Zodiac and anything else that we might've used. We got to the bridge, but when we tried the radio all the circuits shorted out," one of his crew members explained.

"I guess the only thing we can do now is wait. I know the Coast Guard is out looking for us right now and I'm sure they'll find us soon," Gus explained.

"Will they search through the night?"

"Absolutely," John quickly said. "You heard the report over the radio from the bridge earlier. I'm sure they have all available personnel out, bearing down on our position."

"I'm getting a little cold," Justin said.

"Save your energy. Does anyone know the survival

float?" Grant asked, remembering his divemaster training.

"What do you mean?" Justin inquired.

"The best way to conserve energy is to put your face down in the water and just rise up when you need to breathe," Grant pointed out. "Or, just float on your back, but either way it's less tiring than treading water."

Time passed slowly. No land was in sight. The stars were out and the night was clear. A waning gibbous moon rose bright-red, reflecting its light across the dark Atlantic water like a jagged dagger. John still had the dive light that he had strapped around his wrist. Swimming anywhere was a waste of time and energy; they just drifted along in the ocean current. Their only real hope of survival was a quick rescue. Thoughts of friends and family and whether or not they would ever see them again crossed their minds. Gus was beginning to tire; everyone else was relaxed and bobbing up and down in the rolling seas, trying to conserve energy. Justin tried the survival float face down, but his mind began to play tricks on him when he started to consider all of the things that could be between him and the bottom of the abyss. Thoughts of sharks, giant squids and other creatures of the deep haunted him. Jeff seemed to be dealing with the same dilemma, because after several minutes face-down, he was floating on his back as well.

"What was that?" Jeff said when something splashed to the surface not far from him. He swam over to it and found a partially inflated BC with scuba tank attached to it that had broken loose from the *Intrepid* and bobbed to the surface.

"What is it?" Justin asked.

"It's a BC. I guess that makes one life vest," Jeff explained.

"Give it to Gus first so he can take a rest," John said.

"No! You young folks use it, I'll be fine," Gus said weakly.

John got the BC from Jeff, pressed the button to inflate it with air, and then disconnected the tank from the BC as it was no longer of any use. The steel tank being negatively buoyant slipped toward a bottom that it would not reach for more than an hour. John then swam over to Gus and gave him the BC, under protest, so that Gus could use it like a floating life ring to rest. The escape from the yacht had taken its toll and he was exhausted, but he was too stubborn to admit it. Then the conversations died down again. They floated along, bobbing like corks, in the Atlantic Ocean current; time seemed to pass by at a snail's pace. Occasionally, other items would surface that had been jettisoned by the sinking *Intrepid*, but nothing of use to the drifting castaways.

An hour later, the quietness was interrupted by the far-off sounds of whirling blades.

"Do you hear that?" John asked.

"Hear what?" Gus asked.

"Sounds like a helicopter to me," John replied, his voice tinged with excitement.

"My hearing is not what it used to be. I don't hear anything," Gus said.

"Hey! I hear it. It's got to be a helicopter," Eric said.

"We're going to be rescued," Justin whooped.

John checked the dive light to make sure that it was still functioning. "If they get close, we can use it as a signal light."

From the distance, the unmistakable chopping of helicopter blades reverberated across the water. Soon the running lights were visible and the sound grew louder. It passed just to the north of them at about five-hundred feet and continued in an easterly direction.

"It's going away," Jeff said.

"Maybe it will come back," Justin said.

"They should have known the last GPS coordinates of the yacht before it sank. We couldn't have drifted that far away," John added.

The helicopter made a banking turn to the south. It flew for a few minutes and banked again towards the west. Dropping lower to the surface, it shined a very bright spot light on the water and began to make a search pattern. After a while it hovered when the crew found the debris field from the *Intrepid*. Swinging to the north they began to follow the drifting debris.

John turned the dive light on and off, pointed toward the helicopter. Soon the search light swung in their direction. The bright light onboard the helicopter illuminated them as they waved their tired arms above their heads, signaling from the water for help. Overhead the helicopter soon came to a hover as the searchlight shone directly down on them. A side door swung open and a Coast Guard rescue diver leaped out, splashing into the ocean, and quickly swam over to the castaways.

"I'm Lieutenant Coleman from the U.S. Coast Guard. What's your situation?" he asked with a voice of authority.

"There are eight of us here in the water. No injuries, but we are getting hypothermic," John replied.

"Okay, we're going to lift each of you into the chopper. I have a harness here. Who's first?" Lt. Coleman asked.

"Start with the boys. I'm the captain, I'll be last," said Gus.

Justin put the harness on and the helicopter moved overhead. A metal cable came down, and the lieutenant attached the D-ring to the harness. He signaled to the chopper, and Justin was hoisted aboard. Jeff soon followed with Eric, John and Grant after him. The two crew members were next, and then Gus, true to the captain's honorable role at sea, was the last onboard. A second coast guardsman onboard the helicopter handed out blankets to the survivors. Then the lieutenant came up, the door closed, and they turned west for Andros.

"Fresh Creek Tower, Coast Guard Rescue two-niner, departing station with eight survivors, heading to Fresh Creek," the helicopter pilot said over the radio.

"Coast Guard Rescue two-niner, Fresh Creek Tower, Roger. cleared to land on heli-pad two; landing is at your own risk. Do you require medical assistance?"

"Tower, Rescue two-niner, negative, EMS not required, cleared to land heli-pad two."

24

FRESH CREEK

Dr. Lounsbury drove a field station van through the dark Androsian night, heading due south toward Fresh Creek. No one knew the implications of the news report regarding the lost radar image and further reports had avoided any speculation. He had grown frustrated trying to call the police by telephone, because the lines were constantly busy. So he decided instead to drive to where they might be able to get some answers: The Royal Bahamas Police station at Fresh Creek and everybody joined him except Stilly.

The mood in the van was tense and conversation was as sparse as the empty highway that was illuminated by the lights from the van. Seeing a sign on the side of the road marking the police station, Dr. Lounsbury slowed, turned onto a paved lane, pulled the van as close as he could to the building and parked. A large crowd was gathered outside, with reporters stalking about like vultures waiting for prey. They walked together towards the police station but found their way blocked by the crowd. To the side of the building, they heard the unmistakable rumble of a helicopter landing at the helipad.

A young newsman, eager for a scoop, recognized Dr. Lounsbury from a circulated photo, and rushed over to them with a cameraman on his heels. "Dr. Lounsbury, how do you feel now that they've all been rescued?" he asked. "I heard David Winfrey might even be among them!"

"Rescued?" Laura asked, with a lump in her throat.

"Yes! Haven't you heard? A coast guard helicopter picked up the survivors from the water, and it's landing now!"

"Are you folks from the Rockwood Field Station?"

"Yes," Dr. Lounsbury said, as a mob of reporters caught on to whom they were and descended upon them.

"Which are the two girls who escaped?" one reporter asked.

"What do you think happened to the treasure?" asked another.

"What did you mean by survivors?" Dr. Lounsbury asked, trying to get answers himself.

More reporters moved in and suddenly overwhelmed the group with questions. Bright lights from various video cameras shone into their eyes as the reporters scrambled for comments. Flashing strobes from digital cameras captured the moment with images that would soon be beamed around the world.

The helicopter hovered for a moment then gently touched down on the helipad, temporarily drowning out the obnoxious reporters. The side door slid open and Laura, with Beth close on her heels, pushed through the crowd to see. A helmeted man got out. Inside the helicopter were Grant, John, Eric, and several unfamiliar men. The girls pushed their way further through the crowd. A policeman raised his arm, signaling them to stop and keeping them from getting closer. Then Laura saw Justin next to Jeff, and with unbridled exuberance pushed past the yelling policeman and out onto the helipad.

"Justin," Laura squealed, meeting her brother under the rotating blades of the coast guard helicopter. She jumped into his arms and gave him a tremendous hug, then kissed him on the cheek. "We were all so worried; we thought we'd lost you. I can't believe you're here."

Beth immediately joined Laura and threw herself into Justin's arms. She began to cry, then turned and hugged Jeff. "Thank god, you're safe," she said, yelling for both to hear.

Carmen and Nicole rushed past the police officer as well, now overwhelmed by hordes of people dashing over to greet the survivors. The blades of the helicopter continued to beat overhead, blowing their hair from the downwash of the rotor blades.

"We thought you were lost with the yacht. That's what they led us to believe with the last news report," Carmen said to Grant, embracing him, teary-eyed.

"We barely got out!" Grant started to explain what happened, but his words were drowned out by the others rushing over to greet them.

Hugs, tears, and a heartfelt reunion ensued in earnest on the helipad. The police were trying to hold back the press. Dr. Lounsbury, Mike, Molly and the rest of the field station staff had managed to push past the police and were shaking hands and giving hugs as the joyful reunion continued. The Androsians behind the police were straining to see, hoping to get a glimpse of the treasure. This was the most excitement that the natives had ever experienced on their quiet island.

"Okay, for your safety, I need everyone to move away from the helicopter," Lieutenant Coleman ordered. "Please, may I have your attention? Please move away from the helicopter."

They reluctantly began to move, and moved slowly,

more interested in their reunion than the shouting lieutenant. The Royal Bahamas police officers had managed to keep the press at bay and created a barrier between them and the walkway leading to the front door of the police station. The boisterous group walked to the door and spilled into the police station. Several officers entered with the castaways and the Rockwood group. Once inside, the door was closed, muffling the numerous and insistent questions from the mob of press anxious for their story.

The front of the police station consisted of a long counter running nearly the length of the room. On each end of the counter, hallways led to offices in the back of the building. Benches hugged the front wall on either side of the door and paintings of the Bahamas graced the walls. Behind the counter an officer stood with a set look on his weathered face.

"Good evening everyone. I'm the officer-in-charge, Robert Peters. Please quiet down, we have questions to ask. First, I want everyone who arrived on the helicopter to the right of the room, and everyone who did not arrive on the helicopter to the left." Officer Peters pointed with his hands to emphasize his directions. The eight wet castaways moved to one side and the dry EcoExplorers from Rockwood moved to the other, Dr. Lounsbury and his staff joining them. Several officers surrounded the castaways. "The customs document I have here lists the owner of the *Intrepid* as Augustus Cramer. Are you present, sir?"

"Yes, sir, I am Augustus Cramer here with my grandson, Eric, and my two crewmembers, Bill and Rodger."

"I radioed the helicopter, as you know, and got your names while you were in flight, but just so I know you were not under some duress, is there a David Winfrey among you?" Officer Peters said.

"No, sir, he is not," Gus said.

"Do you know his whereabouts?"

"We believe he got away in a seaplane with his accomplice and the treasure."

"What happened to the yacht?"

"Winfrey put a bomb in the engine room of the yacht. It blew up and sank. The *Intrepid* is gone. We narrowly escaped."

"Then Mr. Cramer, if you, your grandson and crewmembers will follow the officer, you each need to give a statement," Officer Peters said, and they were led into the back of the building. Peters turned to John. "And your name sir?"

"John Dettor," he replied, and Officer Peter's eyes seemed to bore into him.

"You will follow the officer to the back to give a statement," he said sternly, and John left the room. He looked at the others. "And your names?"

"Grant Campbell."

"Justin Dulaney."

"Jeff Lounden."

"Dr. Lounsbury, do you know who these people are?" Officer Peters asked.

"Yes sir. Grant is employed by the field station; Jeff and Justin are student guests here this week."

"I see. And the three of you will verify the story about the seaplane, the yacht sinking, and Winfrey and his two companions getting away?"

"Yes sir!" they said in unison.

"On the table over there," Officer Peters said, "are blankets, hot coffee and hot chocolate. Please help yourselves. We'll take some to your friends in the back shortly."

The guys helped themselves and returned to stand in front of Officer Peters. For the next hour, Officer Peters questioned Grant, Jeff and Justin about the entire ordeal, from the airport at the beginning of the week all the way up to the sinking of the *Intrepid* and how Winfrey coerced Eric into becoming an informant.

"Simply amazing," Officer Peters said when every question and explanation had been exhausted. "Never in all of my days have I heard a story like that. I'd have to say that if your story was a novel, I'd never believe it! I guess it goes to show that the truth can be stranger than fiction."

"Well, it's all true," Justin said. Grant and Jeff nodded in agreement.

"It does sound a bit unbelievable," Dr. Lounsbury said. "I had a hard time believing it myself when the girls told us the story at the field station, but I know they're telling you the truth."

"Well, then, the only remaining question unanswered is, where David Winfrey and his companions are, and where is the treasure?" Officer Peters said. Unfortunately, no one had the answer. "Everyone is allowed to return to the field station; however, until you have my permission, no one is allowed to leave the island."

Outside, they pushed their way through the crowd of reporters, trying to make it to the van. They got stopped when the reporters corralled them, leaving them with no choice but to answer the multitude of rapid questions. Soon, an officer came out and ordered the reporters away, allowing them to make their way to the van.

The return trip was in direct contrast to their arrival. Conversation filled the van and they all talked over each other, excitedly discussing the events. Arriving at the field station, they tuned into CNN and watched themselves on TV. Ooma and Stilly had stayed behind and prepared sandwiches, soup, cookies, and hot chocolate. They talked long into the night and eventually, exhausted—but comforted knowing that they were all safe—they collapsed into their beds and drifted off to a much-needed rest.

25

AUGUSTUS CRAMER

Early into the next afternoon the lodge at the wind-swept field station was a hive of activity. Mike had canceled the final snorkeling trip and was helping Dr. Lounsbury and Newby replace the boards on the benches in front of the lodge while Molly, Carmen, Nicole and Stilly were busy washing windows. Mitch and Steve were trying to get a finicky computer to download all of their photographs and produce DVD's for sharing, but were mostly glued to CNN for ongoing coverage and updates of yesterday's incidents. Laura and Beth walked to cabin number two where Jeff and Justin, exhausted from their ordeal, still slept soundly.

"Shhh!" Beth whispered when the boards creaked on the steps outside the boys' cabin.

"I wouldn't worry about it too much," Laura said when the distant whirr of a circular saw bit into another board for the bench project, the sound reverberating through the palms. "Justin can sleep though almost anything. Now give it a try!"

"This is so mean!" Beth said holding the field station

conch.

"I know," Laura responded with a smile. "But we leave tomorrow and I know they don't want to sleep the day away."

Beth put the conch up to her lips and blew into the shell. Producing no more than a timid snort, she tried again and managed a grunting bellow that made them laugh. Then she tried again and produced a groaning whine—a cross between an elk and moose—that made them laugh even harder. Finally, between fits of laughter, Beth trumpeted the conch and then heard a dull thump from inside the cabin.

"Mitch! You better run before I get to the door," Justin yelled in a drowsy shout and yanked the cabin door open. His eyes widened when he saw the girls on the steps outside. His straw-colored hair stuck straight up in back from a fitful night on a pillow. "Laura! Beth?"

"Come on, its time you guys got out of bed!" Laura yelped, her smile wide.

"Cute boxers," Beth said, looking at Justin's starfish-patterned shorts.

Justin partially closed the door to shield himself and asked what time it was.

"We had lunch a while ago, so it must be mid-afternoon," Laura explained. "You going to get up?"

"Whatever! I'm sure you'd just come back with the dogs," Justin said and closed the door.

"Don't give us any ideas!" Beth said in a slightly elevated voice to be sure that Justin could hear through the closed cabin door.

Jeff and Justin soon showered, dressed and walked toward the lodge. They spoke with Mike and inspected the project he was working on with Dr. Lounsbury and Newby. Then they walked over next to the battered black Jeep Cherokee that was wrapped with several strands of police tape proclaiming the words, SECURED AREA – DO NOT CROSS, in bold letters.

"Beth explained last night in the van about what happened to the Jeep. But I guess I was so tired, I was not really comprehending what she was saying," Justin said. He walked around the totaled vehicle, shaking his head.

"Seeing is believing!" Jeff said. "Hey! Wonder who that is?"

"I'm sure it's not Winfrey with the treasure!" Justin replied as a taxi pulled up beside the Jeep and a white-haired man stepped out and paid the driver. "Mr. Cramer . . . I mean Captain Cramer—"

"Gus is fine, Justin. How are you doing today?" Augustus Cramer asked and shook the boy's hand while the taxi backed away and drove out the lane.

"Fine! We actually just got out of bed a little while ago. We were pretty exhausted," Justin said. "Where's your grandson, Grant and John?"

"Things in the islands and the Bahamas run on a slower schedule than what we're used to in the states," Gus said in his Texas drawl. "Many people call it island time. Anyway, I got away early this morning and managed some sleep in a motel. Eric, Grant and John were still being questioned when I left. I expect you'll be seeing them before long."

"They're not in trouble, are they?" Justin asked, concern in his tone.

"No! Just a complicated story—and lots of explaining," Gus said.

Mike had walked over to the Jeep with Dr. Lounsbury and Newby. "Who's in trouble?" He glanced at Gus.

"Um . . . no one, I think!" Justin said and then introduced Gus.

"It's nice to meet you, Gus," Mike said and shook his hand. Then Dr. Lounsbury and Newby stepped up and did the same.

"We couldn't help but hear you saying that the police

are still interrogating," Dr. Lounsbury said.

"Yes! With all of the publicity the top officials from Nassau arrived this morning. That seems to be what is slowing things down," Gus explained.

"It's my understanding that you're the owner of Treasure Seekers Limited and responsible for some of this mess," Mike said.

"Well, I guess I am to blame. I hired David Winfrey and Dr. Shubert Stein to assist in finding the treasure. They were both considered to be two of the best in their field, Shubert for research and Winfrey as a treasure hunter. But I had nothing to do with Shubert's murder and it turns out Winfrey's intentions as an employee of TSL from the day he was hired was deceptive." Gus frowned and for a moment seemed lost in thought.

"I expect you'll not be holding Beth responsible for the Jeep?" Mike said.

"Jeep! What Jeep?" Gus said with a dumbfounded expression on his face.

"That Jeep," Mike said, and pointed to the mud-covered wreck.

"Good God! That thing's more crooked than a barrel of snakes! Is that the Jeep I rented?"

"That's the Jeep that Beth and Laura used to get back here from the blue hole where the treasure was found," Mike explained.

"As the islanders say, no worries! My insurance will cover this. But I would like to meet the young filly that drove that vehicle into submission. I wanted to first apologize to you folks and to discuss with you a personal offering," Gus said.

"An offering," Dr. Lounsbury asked.

"Is there somewhere we can sit down and talk," Gus asked.

Inside the lodge Gus was introduced to the rest of the EcoExplorers and field-station staff.

"That's quite a job you did on my Jeep, young lady,"

Gus said, turning to Beth. "I've seen cars in a demolition derby survive better!"

"Um, sorry!" Beth said while her wide eyes darted between Gus and Laura. "I promise to someday pay you back for the damage."

"Now don't you worry about that Jeep. I'll take care of it," Gus explained in a soothing tone.

"Hey! Turn it up," Mitch yelled to Debbie, who was holding the remote control and had muted the volume when Gus arrived. "They're televising a new report."

"The police have impounded a seaplane in Key Largo, Florida, and are holding the pilot for further questioning. According to the owner, the seaplane was chartered earlier that afternoon by David Winfrey with instructions to fly to a specific coordinate off the coast of Andros to pick up two passengers. The pilot told the authorities that when he arrived he was instructed that their services were no longer needed and he returned to Florida. The police searched the seaplane earlier this morning and found no clues to the whereabouts of the fugitives, or the treasure."

"Oh no!" Jane cried out. "He's getting away with the treasure."

Gus thought about it for a moment, remembering back to yesterday's events aboard the *Intrepid*. "That old coot! I bet you he used the seaplane as a decoy, to throw anyone off their trail. We couldn't see what was happening with the plane because it was out of our view, so we just assumed that Winfrey and his colleague left with the plane. Now I know why we heard the outboard motor before the *Intrepid* blew up. He used the seaplane as a decoy and the dinghy to get away under the radar. That man might be ruthless, but he's not stupid...he's crafty as a fox." "You had something you wanted to talk to us about," Dr. Lounsbury mentioned, getting back to their discussion.

"Yes I do," replied Gus. "Mind if I sit? My legs are

still aching from treading water out in the ocean."

"Please do." Dr. Lounsbury said.

Gus sat on a couch and everyone gathered around. He began:

"You all know my grandson, Eric. Well, when he was just nine-years old my son, his father, and my daughter-in-law were killed in a plane crash. It was devastating to me and to Eric. I filled the hole in my heart by raising Eric and later on getting into treasure hunting. And I didn't just get into it, I was obsessed by it. I don't know if Eric told you, but he spent his life after the plane crash either in boarding school, on the yacht, or sometimes on the ranch in Texas. He was always interested in the ocean and wanted to be the next Jacques Cousteau. If you put a gold doubloon and a dive mask in front of him, he would choose the mask every time. So, this summer was perfect for both of us. While I pursued the treasure hunt here on Andros, Eric could stay here and get some experience around scientists. He was having a blast and living the life of the marine biologist that I know he will become one day. This morning, in the police station, we had a long talk. A heart-to-heart, you might say. Seems he felt that I was always pushing him off into boarding schools because I didn't want him around. And he's partially right because he needed to have the best education that I could buy, and I was too busy chasing after lost treasure. Such was my obsession, I didn't focus on him as much as I should've when he was young, and I'm sorry for that. Now for me, the treasure obsession, shall we say, sank with the *Intrepid*! What we've decided to do is to form a foundation he'll run when he graduates from college. That foundation, he suggested, would be named EcoExplorers—"

"Hey, that's our name, I mean Mike's organization's name," Mitch said.

"Well, it would be used with your permission of course," Gus said looking at Mitch, then Mike, "and we would like to have the McNeil's on the board of directors and to help create the organization from the beginning. But, regardless of the name, we would like to use Rockwood Field Station as the inspiration to create a world-wide network of field stations to expand this way of learning in the field for students."

"That sounds really wonderful," Molly said.

"And to start we would like to donate funds to Rockwood for new boats, outboard motors and a new compressor to replace the one damaged by Winfrey. That is, of course, if it's all right with you, Dr. Lounsbury." Gus said.

"Well, you need not feel obligated to us," Dr. Lounsbury said. "But our field station is always in need of operating funds and new equipment."

"There's another news report on CNN," Mitch said, glued to the television.

"We're reporting live from Nassau, Bahamas," a woman announced while a "Breaking News" banner crawled along the bottom of the television screen. "Just about an hour ago, we received a report that the fugitive David Winfrey and his associate were apprehended on the island of New Providence. At this time the police have not released any information about the whereabouts of the treasure."

Everyone in the lodge broke into rounds of cheers.

"I hope they show the treasure soon," Mitch said.

"I must say, despite all the trouble it has caused us, I would like to see Hornigold's treasure one day," Gus said.

"Will you be returning to Texas," Molly asked. "And what about your yacht?"

"Maybe Texas for a while. I've actually been looking at a cattle ranch in Wyoming. I think once I get home, I'll give the real estate agent a call and see if it's still for sale. As far as the yacht, I suppose insurance might cover the loss, but it is now just another shipwreck lost in the depths of the Atlantic," Gus explained. "Oh! I just remembered. Eric sent a message to you."

"What message?" Laura asked.

"He said that some items were taken during a staged break-in and that you would find them in a box beneath his bunk," Gus said.

"My passport and money," Jane said.

"And my necklace," Jeff added.

The rest of the afternoon CNN recapped the previous reports, but offered no additional news concerning the treasure. The guys returned to work outside on the benches. Stilly and Molly led the party washing windows. Gus received a personal tour of the field station with an elated Dr. Lounsbury who was enthusiastically pointing out all of the non-funded yet needed improvements while Gus was tallying up a list of donations. Near dinner time Mitch trumpeted the conch earlier than usual and soon the dining room was filled with the EcoExplorers, staff and Augustus Cramer.

"I asked Mitch to call you to the dining room a bit early this evening," said Dr. Lounsbury. "Stilly's final dinner for our guests is always something memorable, but before we get to that, please take a seat because I have a few announcements." They all took seats, and Dr. Lounsbury continued:

"First, I want to thank Mike and Molly McNeil for their continued support of the field station. It's teachers like them throughout the years who have kept us growing and students learning. Thank you both from all of us!" This drew a round of cheers, applause and clinks on cups. Stilly and Ooma began to put utensils on the buffet table. Dr. Lounsbury waited for things to settle down again, then said:

"Some weeks here at the field station we have a chance to bond with our visiting students more than others. This week, being a smaller group, we've gotten to know each of you quite well. And at the end of those special weeks, we, the staff, like to hand out a few awards. Now if you don't get one, you may be thankful, and if you do, please know that we offer them to you for both appreciation and in the spirit of Rockwood. Now, I knew this week was going to be somewhat out of the ordinary when I woke and saw Beth chasing Jeff past my cabin with a broom," Dr. Lounsbury smiled broadly, and the room erupted in laughter. He continued:

"Beth, the staff and I have chosen you to receive an honorary title and award for your most talented use of this special cleaning apparatus. We have dubbed you Miss Clean Sweep!" Everyone laughed again. Then, timing it perfectly to coincide with the diminishing laughter, Dr. Lounsbury pulled a short handmade broom from a bag. The appearance of the broom brought another round of laughter, and then Dr. Lounsbury revealed the words Miss Clean Sweep carved into the handle. "Please come and accept your award—and we have a certificate." He pulled a sheet of blue paper from a folder. "It states, 'Beth Britton, Miss Clean Sweep, Rockwood Field Station.'" Beth collected the little broom and certificate, bowed to all and took her seat.

"Next we have another award that we've never given before. It is for an individual who has demonstrated his musical talent again and again this week. This award is titled Androsian Conch Trumpeter and goes to Mitch Martin." Dr. Lounsbury paused while cheers filled the room. Mitch came forward to collect the certificate, then Nicole handed him a conch shell of his own.

"Thanks," Mitch said, "but I haven't been able to find one that sounds like the field station conch."

"Give it a try," Carmen said. Mitch tried the conch and it immediately trumpeted a bit louder than the other. He sat back down amongst clapping and cheers while Stilly and Ooma began to cover the buffet table with dinner.

"We've saved the best award for last," said Dr.

Lounsbury. "Ever since the founding of Rockwood, we've had dignitaries, esteemed colleagues, groups of renowned scientists, authors, explorers—even Jacque Cousteau himself visited us—but I'll have to say when considering the history of this field station, that the EcoExplorers win hands down the Most Memorable Guests Award." The room again filled with the sounds of tableware clicking against cups. "So, to honor you, we'll have a framed photograph of the EcoExplorers that will hang in the lodge for all future visitors to see." The EcoExplorers leapt to their feet and clapped. "Let's not forget to get a group picture before you leave tomorrow. Now it looks like Stilly's dinner is ready, so please help yourselves."

Throughout the dinner lively conversations filled the great room in the lodge. Afterwards, Mitch monitored the television with Steve, while Dr. Lounsbury continued discussing his ideas with Gus and Molly led a last walk down the beach with everyone else.

"I can't believe we're going home tomorrow," Beth said as they walked on the beach past the boats: Kontiki, Flat Foot, and Day Tripper. The dogs followed.

"You know, days seem to last forever on this island, but the time ends up passing so fast," Molly said.

"So much has happened this week. I'm not ready yet to go home," Laura said.

"That's why Mike and I've been coming back for years. This place gets in your blood and seems to call you back," Molly said.

"Maybe next year we can all come back," Jeff said.

They walked for about an hour and returned to the lodge just as a flatbed truck was taking away the Jeep. Mitch was yelling in the lodge and they all entered.

"They said they would be back in just a minute with an update on the treasure!" Mitch explained.

The commercial ended and a reporter began to speak. "I'm reporting live from the southern end of New

Providence Island, just south of Nassau. According to the Royal Bahamas Police, David Winfrey has been charged with the murder of Dr. Shubert Stein, eight counts of kidnapping, eight counts of attempted murder, grand larceny, destruction of property, and a list of additional charges too numerous to mention. The police apprehended David Winfrey and a colleague motoring toward the island earlier in this small Zodiac boat," the reporter continued; the camera zoomed out to show the boat and then moved back into a tight shot on the reporter.

"The police were also looking for an 18th century treasure alleged to have belonged once to a Captain Benjamin Hornigold, a pirate that sailed through these waters in the beginning of the eighteenth century. The treasure, discovered on the island of Andros by a group of students under the leadership of the little-known historian, author and adventurer, John Dettor, was immediately taken by David Winfrey as it was being removed from its recovery site on Andros. According to the police, when the fugitives were apprehended, the treasure, reputed to be worth millions of dollars, was not on board and its whereabouts are still unknown. I'm Lisa Cravatti, reporting live, New Providence Island, Bahamas."

"I can't believe it. That pirate Winfrey has hidden the treasure," Gus Cramer said, sitting on a couch in the lodge.

"Well, with all of those charges, I doubt he'll be seeing the treasure anytime soon," Molly said. "And after what he's put all of you through, I hope he spends a lot of time in prison."

"He deserves everything that's coming to him," Justin added from across the room.

"You bet!" Beth said.

"So Hornigold's treasure's lost again," Mitch said, eyes sparkling, and his face grinning. "Maybe next year we can all come back and hunt for the treasure again. I'll be a scuba diver then and we could track Winfrey's route to New Providence and—"

"Mitch!" they all said in unison.

26

FAREWELL TO ROCKWOOD

Prepared for an early morning departure, luggage had been carried from the cabins and stacked out in front of the lodge, while everyone waited inside for the taxis that would soon take them to the airport. Their week at the field station had finally come to an end. Dr. Lounsbury was talking to the EcoExplorers with Carmen, Nicole, and Newby. Stilly came through the kitchen door and asked Jeff, Justin, Beth and Laura to meet him and Ooma back in the kitchen.

"Good morning," said John Dettor, who had walked in through the back kitchen door.

"Morning, John," Beth said greeting him with the others.

"I just wanted to stop in and say goodbye. Despite the way it all turned out, you're all the best bunch of treasure hunters I've ever had the honor of associating with."

"Thanks, John," Beth said, giving him a hug.

"At least Winfrey didn't get away with the treasure," Jeff said.

"True, it's still hidden somewhere in the Bahamas, and one day I'm sure it'll turn up," John replied, and smiled at Jeff.

They said their goodbyes and then went back into the lodge to gather with the others. A knock sounded, and Dr. Lounsbury walked over and opened the lodge door.

"Officer Peters! Good morning, sir. Please come in."

"I believe you were instructed that none of you can leave the island until you have my permission," Officer Peters said. "And it looks like, with all this luggage stacked outside, that you're ready to depart."

"Officer Peters!" Dr. Lounsbury began. "Surely after what everyone has been through this week you don't plan on making them stay and miss their flight?"

"Actually, no, I came to escort you to the airport to make sure you leave the island," Officer Peters said with a grin. "But there is one condition before you leave."

"What's that?" asked Laura.

"You must all promise me that you will not return next year for another treasure hunt, ghost hunt, monster hunt or any other kind of hunt beyond hunting for seashells on our beautiful seashores."

Beth smiled and gave Laura a whimsical look. "I think we can manage that," she said.

Beep...beep...beep.

"Well, the taxis are here," Dr. Lounsbury said. "I've enjoyed having all of you here this week, and it's a week we'll never forget!" he said.

They all said their goodbyes with lots of hugs between staff and EcoExplorers. Jeff walked back into the dining room for another bagel before they departed while the others walked out to the taxis.

"Thanks for everything, Stilly," John was saying in the kitchen.

"It's been quite a week. You certainly livened things up around here," Stilly said with raised eyebrows.

"Well, it didn't turn out as I wished, but it's been a

real adventure. I'll see you around, my old friend."

"It's been so good to see you again after all of these years too, my good friend, Ross Rockwood," Stilly said.

Jeff, standing just outside the kitchen door, overheard the conversation and scratched his head. Then a wave of recognition washed over his face. "I can't believe it, we've been had," Jeff thought to himself.

"Hey Jeff, come on, you're about to be left behind," Justin yelled from outside.

"Be right there," Jeff yelled back.

Jeff walked out of the dining room into the lounge, paused and looked closely at a vintage black and white photograph of a young Ross Rockwood standing next to a much younger Stilly in front of the lodge. It was the same photograph the little girl had pointed to in Stilly's story told around the beach fire earlier in the week. For the first time, Jeff recognized something in the picture that he had never noticed before. A smile spread over his face, and he left the lodge to join the others.

In the taxi Jeff, Laura, Beth, and Justin rode back to the airport with Basky.

"You folks have made quite a stir on this island this week," Basky began.

"You can say that again!" Justin said.

"Hey Basky, I've got a question for you?" Jeff said.

"I don't know where your treasure be, if that's what you want," Basky joked.

"When I was leaving the dining room, I overheard Stilly saying goodbye to John Dettor. But instead, the man we know as John Dettor, Stilly called Ross Rockwood!"

"Oh come on, Jeff, enough of your jokes already," Beth said and rolled her eyes in disgust.

"Well, there's a picture in the lodge of Ross Rockwood together with Stilly back when they built the lodge and the resemblance, despite the years, is uncanny," Jeff explained.

"You spent all that time with him this week. Didn't he tell you?"

"Tell us what?"

"John Dettor, well, he's not really John Dettor. That's his pen name. He's Ross Rockwood! The man who built and named the field station," Basky revealed.

"What? No way," Laura said.

"Actually it now makes sense. Remember when we asked him about meeting Ross, he changed the subject," Justin said.

"No, what he said was that he probably knew him better than anyone," Jeff said, remembering the conversation.

"I can't believe it!" Justin said.

"Does everyone on the island know?"

"Just Stilly and me and maybe a few others. Me and Stilly are cousins, you know." Basky scratched his face full of powder-white whiskers, lost in thought for a moment. "Well, I suppose Ross wanted it that way. I tell you what. You best keep his secrets…you folk understand."

"Cross my heart," Beth said.

After the drive up the Queen's Highway, the EcoExplorers arrived at the airport with Big Blue rumbling behind. They all got out and said goodbye to Basky.

"Photo-op!" Jeff yelled.

"Yeah, let's get a group picture," Laura suggested.

They all lined up near Big Blue, handing numerous cameras to Dr. Lounsbury.

"Come on, Officer Peters, join us," Jeff said, as the man appeared from behind the old truck.

"Actually, let me take the picture,' Peters smiled. "You know mug shots are my specialty!"

The band of friends finally walked together towards the entrance of the airport. A distant voice called out from behind. It was Eric.

"Laura," he hollered. "Wait, I need to talk to you."

Laura stopped and waited as the rest of the group, except Beth, continued on.

"I'll wait for you over by the wall," Beth said, smiling.

"Laura," Eric said again, slightly out of breath. "I was afraid that I was going to miss you. I stopped by the field station, but you had already left."

"Okay, you're here, what is it?" she asked, arms crossed below a solemn face.

"I just wanted to say goodbye to you in person."

"Whatever," Laura replied indignantly. "I've got to go. They're waiting for me." She began to walk away.

"Please, give me a minute," Eric said sincerely. "I don't want you to leave feeling this way about me. I know you're angry and I'm sorry. I never meant to hurt you. And I want you to know that I really do care about you. That part wasn't an act. Can I write? There's a lot more explaining that I need to do."

"You have my email address. Write if you like."

"I'll miss you," he said, stepped over and hugged her, then kissed her cheek. "Goodbye, Laura."

Eric turned and walked away without saying another word.

Laura caught up with Beth and they headed together towards the plane on the tarmac.

"You okay?" Beth asked.

"Never better," Laura answered through a thin smile. "Let's go home."

Over on the other side of the rocky wall, separating the tarmac from the shady tree-covered square was the incoming group of high school students, just arriving for their week-long adventure.

"Check out the wild clothes and braided hair on those girls," Beth and Laura overheard a couple of girls commenting about them as they passed by.

Laura looked at Beth and smiled. "I couldn't imagine leaving here dressed any other way than in our batik outfits, it just wouldn't be fitting." They were both envious of the adventure the incoming students were about to have on Andros while staying at Rockwood.

"Okay, let's load the luggage into the plane. The captain said he's about ready to depart," Mike announced, then turned to Dr. Lounsbury. "Thank you for a wonderful week. I'm sure it's one that we'll both never forget."

"You can be sure of that," Dr. Lounsbury said. He shook Mike's hand and embraced Molly. "I'll see you both next year. Can't wait to see what your EcoExplorers will do to liven up the place next time."

"I think we'll make sure that they stick to the program," Mike said, and turned to leave.

Dr. Lounsbury waved goodbye, then walked over, wearing a big smile, to greet the newly arrived students.

Newby backed Big Blue toward a jet.

27

BEACH FIRE

Later that evening, back at the field station, the next group of students had settled in, eaten dinner and was gathered around the beach fire waiting for Stilly's stories. The fire reflected a warm orange glow on the faces of the new arrivals and little streams of sputtering sparks flew up into the starry night sky. The resident dogs curled up near the warmth, getting attention from whoever would pet them.

"I want to hear about the Chickcharnies," one girl said.

"No, I want to hear about the Lusca Monster," a young man insisted.

"Let's hear ghost stories first," another suggested.

"Humph," Stilly grunted, sitting on top of a log stool, as he sipped from his steaming cup of coffee. On his lap slept a very young puppy with markings similar to Loona. "Those all be good stories. And I'll get to each one of them in time. But first, let me tell you 'bout the Legend of Hornigold's Treasure."

ECOFACTS

A glossary of terms with definitions throughout the novel that describe the flora, fauna and geology of the story location as well as the people, places and things that relate to the location's history, traditions and folklore. EcoFacts for "The Legend of Hornigold's Treasure" can be found in alphabetical order on our website at **www.EcoExplorers.com**. EcoFacts are linked directly to web-based encyclopedias for precise definitions, articles and visual images for each term. Enjoy!

AUTHORS

Allen B. Graves

Growing up in Virginia, the pastoral hills of Albemarle County sparked an inner yearning for adventure in me. Playgrounds like the Shenandoah National Park, the Blue Ridge Mountains and the Chesapeake Bay added to my adventurous side. I heard that whisper all explorers must hear from the gentle wind, or the surf on the beach, which is the call to see over the next mountain range, across the horizon on the ocean and around the next bend in the road. My appreciation for nature, animals, wilderness, and the incredible bio diversity of planet Earth, also sparked a creative passion for photography and writing.

Yearning for adventure led me to scuba diving in the early 1990's and over the next decade my Scuba travels took me back to the Bahamas many times and also to the Galapagos Islands, Honduras, Turks & Caicos, Bahamas, Mexico, Netherlands Antilles, and the Florida Keys.

C. Joseph Elder

High adventure is my choice for the books that I read, the movies that I watch and the world in which I live.

Though not quite as adventurous as my favorite characters, I have traveled to many faraway places and have had my own list of great adventures. I've searched and found rare antiques: some of my finds are on display in museums in England and in the United States. As a scuba diver, I have dived in foreign waters and very unique places. I've even had the opportunity to work on underwater archaeology projects on historic shipwrecks off the coast of England. In fact, the idea for the EcoExplorers was developed with Allen as we returned from a trip wreck diving. We also dove the walls at Andros and the blue holes that appear in this novel.

As a profession, I own Skipjack Nautical Wares & Marine Gallery with my wife Alison, located on the waterfront in our adopted hometown of historic Portsmouth, Virginia.

40952328R00183

Made in the USA
Middletown, DE
27 February 2017